Z-BURBIA 2
PARKWAY TO HELL

JAKE BIBLE

Foreword

Welcome back to the world of Z-Burbia!

Totally stoked you decided to join Jace and his family, and the others from Whispering Pines, in their never ending battle to stay alive in a zombie infested Asheville, NC. Speaking of Asheville, I have to say that my fellow citizens of the Cesspool of Sin have taken to this series like zombies to brains. Who knew a city filled with artists, intellectuals, hippies, rebels, misfits, and freaks would love zombies so much?

Well, I had a hunch since I put a little something for everyone in the novel.

Which brings me to my favorite review of Z-Burbia on Amazon:

"Z-Burbia" (The title) originally made me chuckle. Although, this play on words did not meet my humorous expectations! This book takes you places that are believable and frightening. This novel has the right marriage of suspense and thrill to keep readers on the edge of their seats. I recommend this book to the serious as well as the novice Zombie enthusiast."

This review nailed Z-Burbia on the head! I wanted it to be funny, but not jokey. There had to be horror and thrills and suspense to make it work as a true zombie novel. To get a review like that tells me I was on the right path. Sweet!

So now to Z-Burbia 2: Parkway To Hell.

I get to include some of the surrounding area in this one. There is so much great material to mine for story ideas that I can keep the Z-Burbia series going for a long time. I hope you join me on each leg of this journey of horror, satire, suspense, and thrills. There's a lot more to come!

Cheers,
Jake

CHAPTER ONE

"Your guess is as good as mine," James *'Don't call me Jimmy'* Stuart says, as he lowers the binoculars and looks over at Weapons Sergeant Sammy "John" Baptiste. "But I don't think they're part of Vance's group."

"No, they aren't," John replies, moving his eye from the scope of his M110 sniper rifle. He looks over at Stuart and frowns. "Those aren't crooks. That's not crime, that's business."

"Business?" Stuart asks, looking into the binoculars again. "What business could they possibly be in then?"

John returns his eye to the scope and they both study the building across the street and above the ruined golf course. The Grove Park Inn. From the early 1900s right up to Z-Day, the GPI was the place for the affluent to stay when vacationing in Asheville, NC. Everyone from F. Scott Fitzgerald to President Barak Obama stayed at the GPI. Artists, actors, diplomats, masters of industry, all called it a temporary home at one point or another. Now the five story stone, brick, and wood luxury inn, is home to a different element, an unknown element.

Z-Day hit Asheville the same day as it hit the rest of the world. No one knows what caused it. A virus was ruled out because of the simultaneous occurrences of the undead rising from graves, beds, morgues, and battlefields. Some said it was a comet that came too close to the Earth's atmosphere; others said it was God's wrath on the wicked.

Whatever caused it, the result was the same: the dead rose and were hungry. Hungry for the flesh of the living. The apocalypse was on; and the Blue Ridge Mountains of Western North Carolina couldn't escape it. Civilization broke down as the living dead multiplied exponentially. A bite meant sickness, death, and then undeath. And those that died of "natural" causes rose as well. Soon the undead outnumbered the living. The world as everyone knew it ended and a post-Z world hunkered down and hid in the shadows.

The undead, or Zs, could hear, could smell, and could see the living. Movement and sound attracted them; the smell of flesh drove them into a frenzy. It was a shambling, slow-moving frenzy, but get enough of the Zs in one place and a herd would form, surrounding any living that were unlucky enough to be caught.

Survivor pockets emerged, some good, some not so good. The Farm, Whispering Pines, Critter's Holler, were just a few of the good pockets; places that humanity set up to survive in. Most of Asheville was uninhabited (by the living, at least) except for isolated individuals and groups of cannies. Cannibals. Everyone has to eat sometime.

Stuart watches the men and women that patrol the back balconies and massive porch of the Grove Park Inn and tries to figure out what category they fit in: good or bad. They all sport various automatic rifles. Not standard military issue and not just hanging out at the local Wal-Mart. Highly customizable, Stuart counts no less than six different types being carried by the armor-clad men and women, mostly versions of the Ares Defense Shrike, though.

"Mercs then?" Stuart asks.

"No," John replies, "too uniform. Look at the gear. Except for the weapons, they all have the same gear. Same body armor. Shit, man, they even have the same boots on."

"Private contractors then?"

"That's my guess," John says. "You say they were there when you were running from Vance and his goons?"

"Affirmative," Stuart says. "Patrolling the Inn just like now. I only had a minute to observe them, but didn't think too much of it. I figured they were with Vance."

"But they obviously aren't. Which isn't good."

"Because if they could hold the Grove Park against Vance and his people, then they are not something we want to tangle with," Stuart says.

"Oh, I'd love to tangle with them," John says, "but not before we have more intel. They stink of private contractors."

"Blackwater then?"

"Who fucking knows? I don't really care who they are, just who has hired them."

"Maybe they're on their own. Not hired out to anyone. If I ran a private military company, I'd want all of my resources and assets for myself. Screw the clients. Z-Day changed commerce like that forever."

"Unless someone has enough resources to make a job worth it," John says, "and that scares me."

"Yeah, me too."

"We better get back to Whispering Pines and check in," John says, slowly scooting back from the rhododendron bushes they are hidden in. "Captain Leeds and Long Pork will be back soon."

"Maybe," Stuart nods, "if they figured out what was wrong at the gas transfer station."

***

Gas stinks, man.

Or to be more specific: natural gas. Did you know they add that dead meat smell to it? That way if there's a leak way out in the middle of nowhere, they can spot it by the circling buzzards overhead. Kinda cool.

Know what's not cool? The natural gas infrastructure I am currently staring at. I haven't a clue what I'm looking for, I just know that the flow of gas has stopped and we need it to rebuild Whispering Pines. Not a single person has refrained from reminding me that my idea to blow the fuck out of Whispering Pines two months ago, was probably what caused the gas transfer station to shut down. Some failsafe kicked in and the lines went dead. It was the last vestige of civilization post-Z. Shit may have sucked with everything else, but at least we could count on the gas to flow and the water to be hot. Oh, and the gas furnaces to run during those super cold nights.

3

Yes, we might have been a little spoiled in Whispering Pines when it comes to apocalypse amenities. But we aren't spoiled now. There's barely a single dwelling left in the entire subdivision. Crews are there sorting debris into useable and non-useable piles. In between the Z attacks, that is. Quite a bit of the fortifications surrounding the neighborhood were damaged, which means stray Zs are coming in all the time.

I'm being blamed for that too. Fuckers.

"Thoughts, Stanford?" Captain Leeds asks me, as we stand on a small hill overlooking the transfer station.

I'm very grateful he doesn't call me Long Pork like everyone else. I picked up the unfortunate nickname from a canny girl I rescued. Elsbeth. Badass. You do not piss Elsbeth off. She called me Long Pork first and everyone else joined in. Really kinda sucks. You know why? Because long pork is a euphemism for human meat. It's what's for canny dinner! Long pork: the other white meat. And black meat. And yellow meat, brown meat, red meat. My actual name is Jason Stanford, but I prefer Jace.

"Oh, I have lots of thoughts, Captain," I say, looking at the pipes and equipment before me. "But none useful. I don't know shit about natural gas lines."

"Critter?" Leeds asks, turning to the older, lanky, wiry man next to us. "Any experience?"

"None, I'm afraid," Critter says as he unceremoniously scratches his nuts. "Long Pork done fucked this shit up. We're gonna need an expert on this one."

"Don't happen to have one back at your holler, do you?" Leeds asks. "Maybe one of your gambling customers or inebriates?"

"I don't call them customers," Critter says. "I prefer suckers. No need to mince words during the apocalypse."

"Fair enough," Leeds smiles. "Would one of those suckers know about natural gas?"

"Possibly," Critter shrugs, studying the station, "but I wouldn't know who. Maybe we should get inside and see if there is some switch we can hit. Could be simple as that."

"I wish," I say. "Nothing's ever as simple as that."

"Usually is for me," Critter smiles. "But then I avoid all the hard shit. Narrows down my options, right quick."

"That's one way to go through life," Leeds smirks.

Captain Walt Leeds is the commanding officer for ODA Cobra, a US Army Special Forces team out of Fort Bragg that was on a training exercise when Z-Day hit. They stayed alive and hidden during the entire apocalypse, until they met up with me. Two of Leeds men, Weapons Sergeant Danny "Stick" Kim, and Engineer Sergeant Dale "Cob" Corning, were killed helping save my ass in Whispering Pines. That is my fault. I take full responsibility for that. I will for the rest of my life.

"Boys," Critter says, turning to a group of men standing off to the side. "How's about you go down there and take care of those Zs? Get that gate open and we'll be down shortly."

The men, many of them looking like they could eat nails and like it, don't even blink at the order Critter gives them. If they did, they wouldn't last long. Not around Critter. He's a good guy, don't get me wrong, but he wasn't exactly Mr. Morals before Z-Day. Now? Let's just say he doesn't have the time or patience for anyone that wants to waste his time or patience.

We watch as the men walk down the grassy hill towards the swarm of Zs that surround the transfer station. Did I mention the dead meat smell? Yeah, that's not so good when the world is overrun by flesh-hungry undead. Since there's no movement or sound inside the fence, the Zs don't get all worked up. The smell just attracts them to the station and then they stand there, staring between the chain links, waiting.

Despite each of them having pistols holstered to their belts, the men use only melee weapons: crowbars, lengths of pipe, baseball bats, and machetes. I have my own baseball bat I have dubbed The Bitch. It used to be Elsbeth's, but she gave it to me after I lost mine. We thought The Bitch was lost, but we found it in the rubble of Whispering Pines, its wood scorched a little, but still deadly as hell with the steel spikes driven through the end.

The men spread out, dividing up the swarm of Zs. It doesn't take long for the things to realize fresh meat is behind them. One turns, then another, and finally all of them do, their rotting bodies stutter stepping their way towards the men. These aren't fast Zs like in the later zombie movies pre-Z. These are the shambling kind. Slow and easy to pick off; they don't get dangerous until there's a bunch of them, or if you let your guard down and one sneaks up on you.

That's not a problem for Critter's men. These guys are pros. They've been killing Zs since Z-Day and they are damn fucking good at it. I watch as one of the men goes down on a knee, acting like he's wounded. The entire swarm goes for him, seeing easy prey. Systematically, the others start to pick apart the swarm, smashing and piercing skulls in a deliberate pattern that divides the swarm into smaller, more manageable groups. Group by group the men whittle down the numbers until there are only a couple left, their teeth gnashing at the men closing on them.

I swear I almost see fear in those Z eyes, but that's just the grey rot that clouds them. Zs are dead; there's nothing there that knows fear, or happiness, or love, or loss. They are empty, flesh-eating monsters. Putting them down is a mercy; after all, they were human once.

"Clear," one of the men calls out.

I look around immediately, worried the sound of his voice will bring more Zs, but after a few moments, it's obvious we are alone in the area. For now.

"What the fuck?" another man says as he gets to the chain link gate. "This shit's locked!"

"Now that's curious," Critter says as we walk down the hill, "who'd go and do a stupid thing like that?"

"That's a very good question," Leeds says, "I'd like an answer to it."

"Maybe Vance locked it up before he died," I say.

"You mean before you jammed a pick axe up in his skull?" Critter laughs. "Take credit when it's due, boy. Don't be ashamed of your accomplishments. They're about all we have in this damn apocalypse."

"Yeah, you've said that before," I reply. "But I'm not proud of it. Killing Zs is one thing, but killing people? Even people that deserve it? That's a little harder to stomach."

"It should be," Leeds says. "Taking a life is not a casual affair."

Critter shrugs. "You two can hug it out later. How's about we get inside this fence and see what we can see? Boys?"

One of the men produces a bolt cutter and slices right through the chain, sending the padlock falling to the pavement. They shove the gate open and we walk up to the concrete building that houses the controls for the transfer station. Windows rim the top of the walls in order to let some natural light inside, but other than that, it's solid concrete with a steel door. Critter tries the handle, but it's locked.

"Dammit, this shit is getting old," Critter says. "Who's got the bumps?"

One of the men steps forward with a ring of keys and a hammer. I tried actually learning their names once, but Critter frowned on that. He said he wanted his guys to be detached from the rest of us in case he had to kill us all. I'm about 75% sure he was kidding. The guy inserts a key then gives it a bump with the hammer as he turns it. After three tries, he's able to get the door unlocked.

Unfortunately, he's the first in line as Zs burst from the building, coming at us hard. The man falls to the ground, his throat opened by the jagged teeth of a Z wearing a Postal Service uniform. He screams and shoves the monster away, but it takes half of his neck with it, flaps of skin hanging from its teeth. Blood spurts and sprays everywhere, sending the rest of the Zs into a frenzy. We'll have more on us soon; Zs can smell fresh blood a mile away.

"Fuck!" Critter yells as he decapitates a Z with his machete. The body falls one way, the head the other, its teeth still gnashing. Critter kicks the head aside; he'll get to it later.

Leeds holds a collapsible steel baton with the end sharpened. He flicks it hard and it extends and locks into place. He dodges around one Z, then jams the business end of the baton through the eye of another. The thing stops moving and falls when Leeds pulls the baton free. He instantly spins about and dispatches the Z that he'd dodged. He drops to one knee and lets another Z tumble over him, coming up hard and flipping the thing ass over teakettle.

I've always liked that saying. I need to ask my wife, Stella, where the saying comes from. She's a teacher and would probably know.

"Jace!" Critter yells as three Zs come at me. "Get your head out of your ass!"

I sometimes space off. Even when Zs are trying to eat me. It's a side effect of my way of thinking. I tend to get lost in my head, thoughts swirling everywhere.

But, I get it together and slam The Bitch into the skull of one Z, while I plant my foot against the belly of another. And my foot slips into its abdomen. The smell makes me gag and I struggle not to vomit when I pull my foot free. Rotted intestines are wrapped around my ankle. I pull The Bitch from the first Z and swing it around into the skull of Gutsy the Stinky Zombie. Half of his head caves in and he falls in a heap.

The third Z grabs my Bitch arm and is about to take a nice little chomp at it when her left eye explodes, spraying goo all over my face. I wipe the black blood away and flick it off my hand.

"Thanks," I say to Leeds as he pulls his baton out of the thing's skull.

"No problem," he nods, turning back to the rest of the Zs.

And there's a fuck ton of them. The building must have been jam-packed. Someone really wanted to keep us out. Or keep everyone out. But my gut tells me this is about our group of folks.

My gut also tells me to duck, so I do, letting the reaching Z arms swipe above me. I come up and bury The Bitch's spikes into the soft part under a Z's chin. Well, that doesn't narrow it down since most parts of a Z are soft; you know, because of the rotting flesh and all. But, the softer the better! I pull up and rip the thing's jaw right off, and then bring The Bitch down hard on top of its skull.

Fingers grab at my arm and I shake them off, putting The Bitch into the face of the offender. Another Z down, only about twenty to go. Fuck me. Critter's guys are doing well, but as I look past the chain link fence, I can see we have company.

"More Zs," I announce, "I count another fifteen at least, coming down the hill."

"I see a dozen coming up from below," Leeds says, pointing with his baton before he pierces two Z skulls at once. The Z heads knock together; the sound reminds me of coconuts.

"Eight over there," one of Critter's guys says.

"Fuck," I mutter as I take down two more Zs. "In the building and get secure? Or fight our way out and come back later?"

"I'll leave the strategy to soldier boy," Critter says. "What you feelin', Captain?"

"Jace and I will get inside and hunker down," Leeds says. "Try to see if we can figure out what's going on with the gas. You and your men split into two teams. One draws the Zs off, while the other hoofs it to Whispering Pines for reinforcements. How's that sound?"

"Sounds like a fine plan," Critter says. "Let's take a few more out before we make our move. Less Zs to see y'all go in there."

We do just that and kill half the Zs in the station before Leeds and I duck into the building and slam the door. There's enough light for us to see, but Leeds pulls out a flashlight and cranks the handle, bringing the bulb to life. He shines it around and we both cover our nose from the stench. The place is coated with Z gunk. It's all over the banks of instruments and the couple of rolling chairs that are pushed into the corners.

"God," Leeds says, "they must have been packed in here shoulder to shoulder."

"I'm guessing they were lured in by that," I say, pointing to the nearly picked clean bones strewn around the room.

The space is maybe twenty feet by twenty feet. An efficient concrete building designed to keep the transfer station controls secure and out of the elements. Not exactly built for comfort. I roll one of the chairs against the wall and stand up on it. I can just peek out of the window and see Critter splitting his group in two. One group heads off towards Whispering Pines, while the other starts jumping and shouting, drawing the Zs after them and away from us. I can see that Critter has stayed with the diversion group. Guy may be self-serving at times, but he's got balls.

"Are they gone?" Leeds asks, watching me carefully. Which is the only way the man watches anything: carefully. He isn't one to leave things to chance. If there is one thing I have learned in the past two months, it's that Captain Walt Leeds likes to be informed. He doesn't rush into decisions.

"They are now," I say, "well, except for a few stragglers, but that was to be expected."

"Then we better keep it down," Leeds says, motioning for me to get off the chair, "and stay out of sight. They see motion in here, then they'll wander over to investigate. That'll just bring more."

"Yep," I smile as I step onto the soiled concrete. "Not my first Z rodeo."

"Of course not," Leeds smiles, "I'm just used to giving orders."

"I'm married, so I'm used to taking them," I laugh then look at him seriously. "Don't tell Stella I said that. Please."

"Wouldn't think of it, Jace," he says then starts to look at the control panels. "We should probably make the best use of our time and figure this out. Cob would have been able to make sense of this stuff. He was the team engineer."

"Yeah, sorry," I frown.

"For what?" Leeds asks, looking at me. "You aren't still blaming yourself for Cob and Stick, are you? If you are, then knock it off right now, Stanford. They were soldiers and they died fighting. No better honor."

"Well, there are a few better honors I can think of than saving some spoiled suburbanite's ass. Especially since I got y'all into that fight in the first place."

Leeds waves me off. "We were going to have to get into the fight eventually." He takes a deep breath and turns away from the controls to face me. "Listen, Jace. Vance was a psycho, pure and simple. He was a corrupt banker that likened himself the Appalachian Al Capone. And that was pre-Z. Post-Z? He thought he was a Roman emperor. And just as sick and twisted. My team was already coming across more and more of his followers every time we ventured close to Asheville. Your situation may have chosen the time for us, but it was our fight."

"Yeah, but-"

"No buts. None. Don't disgrace the memories of my men by looking for excuses. They helped stop a dangerous man that was going to kill many of your friends. In this day and age, we can't afford to lose a single life."

"Which is my point," I counter, "we couldn't afford to lose Stick and Cob."

"Fair enough," Leeds nods, "point taken. And rejected. They died doing what they love and what they were born to do. They were soldiers, just like me. At some point, we die horrible, bloody deaths. That's our nature."

"So I'm guessing you don't have plans to retire in Boca and play golf until the next apocalypse then?"

He grins. "No, don't think so."

"Well, then we better crack the code to this shit," I say, putting my hands on the control bank. Then pulling my hands away and wiping them on my jeans. Z yuck. Ugh.

The control bank is made up of dials, knobs, levers, and other doodads that look completely random. Labels and names are faded or covered in gunk. I gingerly wipe off as much Z yuck as I can, hoping a little clarity will occur. It doesn't. Just looks like a bunch of dials, knobs, levers, and other doodads.

"What? Is this the 1950's?" I ask. "Looks like the set to a bad scifi movie."

"USB ports are over here," Leeds says. "Instead of yanking the whole unit out, they just upgraded with a computer interface."

"Good thing the place is solar powered," I say, "or we'd really be fucked. Now, I can just plug my computer in and…oh, wait, I don't have one. Never mind. We are really fucked."

"For a man of intelligence, you can be very stupid sometimes," Leeds says pointing to a shelf across the room. "You think they only had PhDs working this station? Not likely."

"Manuals?" I ask.

"Manuals," Leeds nods. "We better get to reading before we lose the light."

"Lose the light?" I glance up at the windows. "You don't think they'll be back to get us before dark?"

"Not without a vehicle," he answers, "which will make too much noise and put us back in the same position we were in before. We'll spend our time and resources fighting Zs instead of fixing this station. No, they'll be back in the morning."

"Wish I had my blankie."

He grabs a binder from the shelf and tosses it to me. "Cuddle up with this. It should warm the cockles of your heart."

"Captain, I'm gonna need you to buy me dinner first, if there's gonna be any cockles warming." Leeds doesn't laugh. "Okay, fine, not my best joke."

"Less joking and more reading."

"Roger," I say as I plop into one of the chairs and crack open the binder. "More reading. Got it."

It doesn't take me long to realize the manual isn't going to tell me much without some context. I look up at the shelf and see a binder marked, "Reference." Handy. I take it down and open it. This is what I need. It's filled with basic definitions and procedures. All I need to do is study this manual and I'll have at least a key to understanding the rest.

I sigh and settle in to get the job done. After a few minutes, I look up and see Leeds watching me.

"What?" I ask.

"You just remind me of my nephew," Leeds says. "He had a brain like yours. What do you call it?"

"I call my brain Steve," I say.

"No, smart ass, what do you call it that you do?"

"I'm a generalist," I shrug. "I have a knack for understanding pretty much any subject with just a little research. I tend to master skills quickly and then move on. Not everything sticks, but the majority does."

"What doesn't stick?"

"I can't wrap a present worth a shit," I say. "I have tried and tried. I take my time, I'm careful as hell, but they always look like a four year old did it. Can't figure it out."

"But this isn't a problem?" he asks, indicating the control banks.

"I don't know yet," I say, tapping the reference manual in my hands, "I'll let you know."

"You do that."

"Are you finding anything?" I ask.

"Nothing I can understand," Leeds says. "I have found names for the individual controls, but nothing about what they do."

"Can I see that?" I ask. He hands me his manual. I look it over and then roll my chair up to the control bank. I set both manuals down, side by side. "Can I keep this one?"

"You can keep them all if you think it will help."

"Between these two, I should be able to get us up to speed." I look up at the windows. "I wonder if we can cover those. I'm gonna need light soon, but I don't want it to bring the Zs."

"Yeah, I know," Leeds sighs. "I have an idea."

I have an idea too, but don't want to say it. It's not fun. As Leeds gets up and starts to gather up the Z yuck, I see he has the same idea. I go back to the manuals while he busies himself with coating the windows with gunk. Soon the room is cast in a hazy, reddish glow. Leeds finishes and walks to the door, flicking the light switch next to it.

"Will that work?" he asks.

"It'll work perfectly," I say, "but, will it attract Zs is the real question?"

"We'll find out once the sun goes down," Leeds says. He rolls a chair to the door and leans back against it, his head turned so his ear is right on the steel. "You do your brain thing and I'll do my soldier thing. If I hear them coming, I'll turn out the lights until they wander off."

"And if they don't wander off?"

"Then study hall is over and we wait it out in the dark," Leeds says. "I'd recommend sleeping, but I doubt either one of us will if we have Zs knocking to get in."

"Then let's hope they don't knock," I say, focusing harder on the manuals.

"One can only hope," Leeds replies.

At least a couple hours go by before I make my first breakthrough. I spin around and look at the control banks against the wall behind me.

"Find something?" Leeds asks. His eyes are closed so I'd figured he'd gone to sleep.

"I don't know yet," I say, studying the control panels. "I think so."

I trace the panels with my fingers, looking at the manuals, and then at the panels; back and forth, back and forth.

"I didn't cause the shut down," I say. "That's a relief. Maybe Brenda will shut the fuck up about it."

"Not likely," Leeds says as he gets up from the chair and leans over me to look at the panels.

Brenda Kelly is the HOA Board Chairperson. Yes, despite the fact that Whispering Pines pretty much burned to the ground, there is still a Home Owners' Association. And that's not the surprising part! Brenda colluded with Vance, to what extent none of us knows, but she still colluded with him and it resulted in the deaths of my friends and neighbors.

Yet, the HOA voted her back in as Chairperson of the Board! Why? Because they are frightened sheep and because she undermined any faith in me by leveraging the fact that I blew up Whispering Pines. Sure, I did it to help everyone and to try to stop Vance and his crazies. Problem was that I was in a semi-coma for a few days while she was busy rallying her troops. One vote later and she's still in charge of Whispering Pines, and I'm out here, my hands sticky with Z yuck, while I try to figure out how to make things better for everyone. Unlike Brenda Kelly, the fat twat.

Not that I want the Chairperson job. Fuck no to that! Thankless job and one that is filled with bullshit. Some folks are made for bureaucracy. I am not one of those folks. I like to think around red tape, not create more just for the fuck of it.

"Jace? Hello, Stanford. You in there?"

"What? Sorry," I smile, "just mentally hating Brenda, that's all."

"Hate on your own time," Leeds says. "Tell me why you don't think the gas shut down was your fault."

I point at a diagram in one of the manuals then at the control panels. "Each of these panels controls a sub-region of Asheville, see?"

He looks the panels over and then shakes his head. "No, what am I looking for?"

"See this one? West. This one? East. There's north, south, downtown, etc. You can shut down specific regions without shutting the whole station down."

"Makes sense," he nods. "So what did you find?"

"Look at these panels," I say, pointing to all but one. They are dark, not a blinking light. The last one isn't dark, but has quite a few active lights. "They've been switched off. Not tripped because of any failsafe, but switched off." I flip through the reference manual. "According to this, the failsafe is local. Whispering Pines did get shut off automatically, but probably at the main pipe down the road from the development, not from here."

"That still sounds like it was your fault," Leeds says. "Not judging, just observing."

"Yeah, yeah, you're right, but it can be fixed at Whispering Pines. As soon as it's safe to turn the gas back on, we can do it locally. We don't need to come here."

"What's that one?" he asks, pointing to the active control panel. "Where does it go?"

"North Asheville," I reply, "and if I'm right, that includes us, unless we're on the west line. I'm not sure. Doesn't really matter for right now. What does matter, is that someone intentionally turned every region off except for this one."

"So it was Vance then," Leeds says. "What was he up to?"

"No, I don't think it was Vance," I reply. "Remember, his mansion is down in Biltmore. He may have set up shop in North Asheville, but the crazy fucker had his undead family still in the south part of town. Why would he shut off a resource to there? I'm sure he would still need it for something."

"New player?"

"Maybe," I shrug, "I haven't got a fucking clue. I'm focusing on this right now."

"Keep studying," he says and sits back down, "you've done great so far. Keep at it."

"Great pep talk," I smile as I get up and grab all of the binders, spreading them out before me.

Leeds closes his eyes and smiles. "I'm a born leader. Just comes naturally."

I notice the fluorescent lights flickering slightly above and look over my shoulder. It's dark outside. Fingers crossed, I can work it all out before we have to turn the lights off.

"We'll have company soon," Leeds says.

"How do you know?" I ask, looking over at him. His eyes are still closed.

He taps his ears. "I can hear them out there. Not many, but enough. How are you doing?"

"I think I have a few things figured out," I say. "How much time do I have?"

"An hour, maybe longer," Leeds says. "What have you figured out?"

"I'm pretty sure I can switch these panels on and get the gas flowing to the entire town again," I say.

"Do we want to do that?" he asks.

"Can't hurt," I say.

He opens one eye and locks it on me. "We're talking about natural gas, Stanford. It can hurt quite a bit."

15

"Right. My bad," I say. "But that's what failsafes are for. If there is anything wrong with the lines, then they'll shut down locally."

"That's quite an assumption," Leeds says. "Maybe they were all shut down for a reason. Maybe it was Vance and despite his mansion in Biltmore, he cut the gas on purpose."

"My gut says no to that," I answer, "I can't say why, just that it doesn't feel right. Doesn't seem like Vance's style."

"You killed the man, Jace," Leeds says. "You didn't hang out and read each others' diaries. You have no clue what his style was or what he was thinking."

"What are you? The devil's advocate? I'm floundering here at best. I could use a confidence boost, not a smack down."

Leeds sighs and leans forward, his forearms resting on his knees. He fixes me with that Captain's glare of his. "My job is to protect lives, not coddle intellectual egos. Your job is to be smart, not coddle your own ego. If I do my job and you do your job, then shit will get better. If either of us fail, then shit will get shittier. How's that for a confidence boost?"

"Perfect," I say, giving him a thumbs up. "I feel like I can do anything now."

"Good," Leeds says. He cocks his head and then shakes it. "More Zs. The windows aren't clouded enough. And they can probably hear us. Time to get silent. You have maybe twenty minutes before we go dark and really hunker down."

I don't even answer, just get back to studying. Five minutes, ten minutes, twenty minutes go by and I'm even more sure that Vance didn't shut the gas off. But who did?

"I want to turn it all on," I say finally, "before we sit here in the dark for the rest of the night."

Leeds studies me for a very long minute. "You're sure about this?"

"No," I answer honestly, "I'm never sure about anything, yet everyone still asks me to figure it out. We're going to have to take a risk."

"And why turn them all on?"

That's a good question. Why do it? Why not leave them off since the line that (probably) feeds Whispering Pines is already on?

16

"Because I can," I say. "And because there could be other survivors huddled in their basements way over in East Asheville that need this gas to get through the next few days. If it isn't already too late."

"It's the apocalypse, Jace," Leeds says. "If they can't figure out how to survive without natural gas, then they aren't going to last long no matter what we do."

"Just give me a shot, will ya?" I ask. "I won't blow us up."

"Right."

"Seriously," I say, showing him a diagram and the paragraph below it, "the transfer station has backflow regulators. If something goes wrong, this place is perfectly safe. We'd have to pry open a pipe and drop a match inside to do any damage here."

Another long minute of the Leeds stare.

"Captain?" I ask. Now I can hear the Zs outside. Their moans are getting louder. I don't know how many are out there, but enough to hear our voices. We have to decide now.

"Fine," Leeds says, "do it."

"Cool," I smile. "Wish me luck."

"No," Leeds says, "luck better not have anything to do with this."

I nod and look at the manuals, then at the control panels. Slowly, carefully, I start to flick switches. I systematically go from one panel to the next, turning them on until the entire control bank is blinking and flickering.

"There," I smile, wiping my hands together, "Asheville has gas again."

"Good," Leeds says. He reaches over and turns the overhead lights off, plunging us into a darkness lit only by the control bank. "Now get some sleep and rest that brain. We'll have some killing to do in the morning, I'm sure."

I try to get comfortable in the rolling chair, but it just isn't working. I contemplate lying on the floor, but the amount of Z yuck discourages that thought. It's going to be a long night.

Then the explosions start. Quite a few of them. Way off across town towards the east.

"Long Pork," Leeds snarls.

Dammit.

CHAPTER TWO

"On your left," Julio calls out as he pivots to the side and jams a spear through the eye socket of a Z staggering towards him. He twists the spear about and tosses the Z onto an ever-increasing pile of corpses filling the entrance to Whispering Pines.

Julio is a short Hispanic man, the parts of his torso that show from under the black tank top he wears is covered in dark black and blue tattoos. They run all the way up his arms and up his neck. His head is shaved except for a thin, short Mohawk. On his belt, strapped to his right leg, is a nasty looking short sword. But the spear is more appropriate for the Z clearing job at hand.

The person he's talking to, Elsbeth, doesn't pause to answer, just spins and slices the head off the Z with one of two curved long blades she holds. She kicks the head and the falling body towards the pile, but isn't as precise as Julio. She is a tall, young woman, intensely beautiful. Her hair is cut short and tucked under a Hello Kitty trucker's cap. The sleeveless t-shirt she wears shows off her muscled arms, and she moves about with the grace of a cat. A very deadly cat.

"Are you even going to try to hit the pile?" Julio asks as he spears another Z and disposes of it on the pile.

Elsbeth shrugs as she ducks under the outstretched arms of a Z and comes up with a blade through its chin, piercing the skull. The thing's jaws clamp shut and it grows still as she pulls the blade free and kicks the Z over. It misses the pile by several feet. Elsbeth looks over her shoulder at Julio and smiles. The condition of her

18

teeth is all that mars her beauty, but being raised a cannibal didn't lend itself to a lifestyle of proper oral care.

"I kill them," Elsbeth grins, "let the others clean up."

"Except we will be the ones cleaning them up since half the camp went back to the Farm today," Julio says. "We're short teamed until the new crew shows up in two days."

"Why do we have to do all the work?" Elsbeth asks, a small whine in her voice. Most wouldn't notice, but Julio has been fighting Zs with her, shoulder to shoulder for two months straight. He notices.

"Because we do it right," Julio says. "Better us than some of those lazy asses we're doing this for. We'd just have to come back and finish the job anyway."

"I don't like the lazy asses," Elsbeth says, both blades lashing out, separating Z heads from Z bodies. She makes a small effort to push the bodies and heads towards the pile. "They should work harder. Not us. Them. Poop snotty fart faces."

"You've been hanging out with the kids too much," Julio laughs as he spears a Z in the gut, then turns it to block two that are coming at him from the left. Elsbeth moves in and takes the heads of all three. Julio yanks his spear free and stabs each decapitated head through the skull, ending their gnashing thrashing. Even separated from their bodies, the Zs still try to chomp some human flesh. Only way to stop them is to kill the brain. Such is the way in the zombie apocalypse.

"So?" Elsbeth asks. "The kids are fun."

"Not as fun as me," Julio grins, his eyes looking Elsbeth up and down. He loves how the sweat soaks her t-shirt between her boobs and across her belly.

"No," she grins back, "not as fun as you. We'll have fun tonight, right? You fell asleep last night."

"I was tired, El," Julio says. "We spent the whole day killing Zs. A man needs his rest."

"A girl needs her fun," Elsbeth counters. "No sleeping tonight."

"You're so cruel," Julio laughs, "but I think I can handle it."

"Promise."

"I promise. No sleeping tonight."

Elsbeth moves away from the Whispering Pines entrance and takes out one, two, three, four, five Zs before retreating. Julio joins her, dropping three. They stand there for a second, looking at all the Z corpses that litter that part of State Highway 251. The sun is setting and the French Broad River that is across the highway, about twenty yards from the entrance, starts to reflect the sky's orange and red glow.

"Pretty," Elsbeth says.

"I can't believe you decided to turn down Special Forces training to be part of this crew," Julio says. "You're crazy."

"Crazy for you," Elsbeth says, grabbing his ass. "Mmmmm. And Platt yells a lot. I don't like the yelling."

"How about some screaming?" he asks, giving her a wink. "I know you like to scream."

Julio takes her up in his arms and kisses her hard. Her hands squeeze his ass harder, making him jump. She presses against him and lifts one leg up over his hip. Their mouths are jammed together, hungry with passion.

"Jesus," John says as he and Stuart come walking around the bend in the road. "Can't you wait until you're in your tent?"

"And have cleaned up," Stuart adds, "you two are covered in Z."

Elsbeth pulls away from Julio and smiles at the two men. "He's not falling asleep tonight. I'll be on him for hours."

Julio shakes his head and takes her hand, pulling her towards the new gate that stands open at the Whispering Pines entrance. It isn't as big or secure as the original gate, but it keeps the Zs out for the most part. Enough for those inside to get a good night's sleep with only a couple of sentries on duty.

"You are one lucky bastard," John says to Julio as he follows them inside, shutting the gate once Stuart is in. He and Stuart place reinforced bars across the gate, securing it for the night.

"It's not luck," Elsbeth says. "He has to work hard for me. No lazy ass gets in my pants. Nope, nope, nope."

"Yeah, how about we eat a little, and then clean up the Zs?" Julio asks. "You two up to lend a hand?"

"Sure," Stuart says. "Let us stow our gear and grab a bite too."

"I gotta shit something wicked," John says. "Been holding it for the last mile."

"Ooh, me too," Elsbeth says. "I'll come shit with you. We can talk about your day."

"Still working on that personal space thing, eh?" John laughs.

"I don't need any," Elsbeth shrugs. "Not my problem if others do." She looks at Stuart. "Except for Stuart. He has to have space or he's a grumpy bear. Grumpy bear Stuart is not fun."

"You can say that again," John says.

"Hey, lay off," Stuart says. "I can be fun."

"Yes, you're a barrel of laughs," Julio says. He winks at Elsbeth. "Have fun taking that shit. Wash your hands before we eat."

"Right," Elsbeth nods, "wash my hands. You'll remind me, right, John?"

"You can count on it," John says, smiling and offering his arm. She looks at it and frowns. He drops it and shakes his head. "Right. Off to the shitter we go."

Julio and Stuart watch them walk away, and then Julio turns to Stuart, his face serious.

"What did you find?" He asks as they walk up the hill towards the small, temporary camp set up while Whispering Pines is being rebuilt and put back together. All about them are burned out houses and scorched yards, from when Edward Vance and his people lay siege to the development.

"Nothing conclusive," Stuart says. "We don't know if the people are part of Vance's crew or not. Our guess is no, but we can't know for certain."

"Why no?" Julio asks as he tosses his spear onto the ground and grabs a ladle from a large water barrel. He takes a drink and hands it to Stuart who does the same.

"For one thing, they are pros," Stuart says. "Weapons and gear point to a private military company. I've seen my share over the years. They look the part."

"Why the Grove Park Inn?" Julio asks as he takes a seat on a large log set next to a small campfire.

Other men and women are busy cooking their evening meals at other campfires spread out across the subdivision. It would be more efficient to all cook together, but for security and safety, it's better if the rebuild crew keeps to smaller, separate groups. That

21

way, the whole team can't get boxed in if the Zs get through the perimeter of the development.

The back of Phase One of Whispering Pines butts up against a fifty-foot limestone cliff. At the top of the cliff is a long, wide meadow. The meadow is filled with row after row of steel fenced razor wire interspersed between long and various ditches. There was a deck built into the cliff at the top so that sentries could watch twenty-four hours a day for Zs. But that was destroyed in the battle with Vance. It is one of the first rebuild priorities.

Part of Phase One and all of Phase Two, which is up on the second plateau of the development, is surrounded on two sides by a 100-yard deep ravine of huge rocks and boulders. Gotta love natural erosion. The ravine sides are covered in steel fencing and razor wire also. If the Zs make it into the ravine, they never make it up the sides. Or that was the theory before all the damage. Now sentries keep watch on all fronts to make sure stragglers don't shamble through and eat the rebuild team in the night.

"I don't know why the Grove Park," Stuart answers, "but something, or someone, important is in there. Otherwise, there wouldn't be such a show of force."

"Big Daddy won't like this," Julio says.

"Big Daddy doesn't like anything that upsets the balance of things and his plans," Stuart says. "But that's life in the dead city."

Hollis "Big Daddy" Fitzpatrick is the head of the Farm. A huge parcel of land over in Leicester, about thirty miles west, the Farm is where the residents of Whispering Pines have been holing up while their homes are rebuilt. A devout man, Big Daddy believes Z-Day happened for a reason, and he aims to make sure that reason is for good and not evil as some would have it. His brother, Critter, is pretty ambivalent about the good versus evil part, but agrees with Big Daddy that a rebuilt Whispering Pines, and Asheville as a whole, is how they'll all survive.

"Was that a joke, Stuart?" Julio smiles as he places a pot of chopped vegetables and water into the campfire.

"I hope not," Stuart says, "that would ruin my reputation as a grumpy bear."

"Can't have that."

"No, we can't."

Stuart sits with his back against the log and stretches his arms above his head. A retired Marine Gunnery Sergeant, Stuart is in his mid-fifties, but stronger and more capable than most of the twenty year olds back at the Farm. He rolls his head around on his neck, letting the vertebrae crack and pop. There is a chill in the late autumn air and Stuart looks up at the darkening sky above them.

"Jace and the rest aren't back yet then?" he asks.

"Not yet," Julio says, "but didn't really expect them to be. Fixing that transfer station, if they can, could take a couple of days."

"John'll head over and check on them tomorrow," Stuart says. "He won't have to go all the way, just find a vantage point and scope them out to make sure everything is all good."

"Good," Julio says. "He may be a pain in the ass, but we can't lose that brain of his. Guy is fucking smart."

"That he is," Stuart says.

"Long Pork?" Elsbeth asks as she walks up with John and plops down next to Julio, pushing him with her hip, making him scoot his ass down the log. "You've heard from Long Pork?"

"No, no," Stuart says. "We were just talking about-"

"Runners!" a shout goes up down by the gate.

"Son of a bitch," Julio swears. "How many times do we have to tell them not to shout? It'll bring more Zs."

They all get up and make their way quickly to the gate. They are joined by a few of the others on the rebuild crew. One of the sentries pulls open the gate and several of Critter's men hurry in. Once they've caught their breath, Stuart gets the story of what happened at the transfer station out of them.

"We have to go help," Elsbeth insists. "I won't have Zs eating Long Pork."

"I don't think anyone should eat long pork," Julio jokes, then clams up as he sees the serious look on Elsbeth's face. "Sorry. Chill, girl. We'll go help Long Pork and Captain Leeds."

"Not tonight," Stuart says as the last rays of sunlight fade over the hills across the French Broad River. "It'll have to be a job for the morning."

"We can't leave them there!" Elsbeth cries. "No! Not leaving Long Pork!"

She starts for the gate, but Julio and John grab her arms, both ready to get smacked around. Stuart stands right in front of her, his face just an inch from hers.

"You may be able to make it there in the dark, but it's too dangerous for everyone else," Stuart says. "And I'm not letting you go by yourself. End of discussion. We leave at dawn and we'll double time it until we get to the transfer station."

"It's a couple hours at a hard jog," John says.

"Tell us about it," one of Critter's men says as he sits slumped against the gate, his body drenched in sweat and his chest still heaving from the exertion.

"Tomorrow," Stuart says.

"Dawn?" Elsbeth asks. "When the sun comes up?"

"As soon as we can see enough to take a piss," Stuart says.

"I can piss in the dark," Elsbeth counters.

"You know what I mean."

Elsbeth stares at him for a moment then nods. "Dawn."

"Dawn," Stuart agrees.

"Let's get you guys some food," Julio says, "and some rest. We'll be up early it looks like."

The camp buzzes with the news, despite the threat of danger to their friends. More than enough volunteer to go, and Stuart actually has to refuse some so there are still folks working on Whispering Pines. There's some grumbling, but everyone has learned not to argue much with Stuart.

It's fully dark by the time Elsbeth and Julio crawl into their tent for some much needed sleep. Although, as Elsbeth strips down and crawls on top of Julio, sleep is the furthest thing from her mind. They are going at it hot and heavy when the explosions start.

They scramble from their tent, Julio struggling to pull on a pair of jeans, while Elsbeth just stands there naked. The light from the campfire plays across her skin, casting shadows against the multitude of burns and scars that cover almost every inch of her; gifts from her dead father.

"Jesus," Stuart says as he sees Elsbeth, "put some underwear on at least."

She ignores him as they all stare towards the east and the glowing light of fire.

"What the hell do you think that is?" John asks appearing from the shadows like the sniper he is.

"Fuck if I know," Julio says.

"Long Pork," Elsbeth nods as if that decides it.

They all look at her and then at each other. Stuart rubs his face.

"She's probably right," he says. "What the fuck do you think he did now?"

"Looks like he got the gas on," Julio says, "and found out maybe why it was off in the first place."

"Great," Stuart says.

"We gonna go now?" Elsbeth asks. "Go check on that and Long Pork?"

"Jace is the opposite direction from those explosions," Stuart says. "And right now, every Z in Asheville is shambling towards those sounds. That'll make things clearer tomorrow when we go to the transfer station, at least."

"If the transfer station is still there," Julio says. "He could have blown that up too." Elsbeth gives him a look of death. "What? I'm just saying what everyone else is thinking."

"Tomorrow," Stuart states. "Everyone get some sleep. Double watch tonight. Those explosions are gonna stir up the Zs. We could see more activity around the perimeters."

There's a general grumble at the news of the extra watch, but everyone heads off to their tents or duties, leaving Stuart by himself.

"Dammit, Jace," he whispers, "what did you do now?"

***

I just sit here, exhausted, as I watch the dawn start to light up the windows. The explosions kept going for most of the night. Whatever I did, I fucked shit up big time.

"You get any sleep?" Leeds asks me.

"Nope. You?" I ask, standing up from the chair and stretching.

"Not a bit," Leeds replies.

"Sorry," I say. "I thought I had it figured out."

"Oh, you had it figured out," Leeds says. "You just hadn't thought it through."

"You could have stopped me," I counter.

"Let's not get into it again," Leeds says. "The explosions drew away the Zs. I don't hear any out there. We should be clear."

"After you," I say, motioning to the door.

"Gee, thanks," Leeds says, "Long Pork."

"Are you really gonna start calling me that?" I ask as he slowly opens the door. A quick peek and he nods at me, stepping outside into the crisp, morning air.

"You redeem yourself and I'll go back to calling you Stanford," Leeds says, taking deep breaths of the fresh air. It'll take us both a while to get the smell of the Z yuck out of our nose.

"No Jace?"

"You're gonna have to really redeem yourself to get to that name," Leeds says. "Until then, it's Long Pork."

"Great," I say, "thanks."

We both stare at the pillars of smoke off in the east.

"Not good," Leeds says. "Ready for a trip?"

"A trip? What?" I ask. "Shouldn't we get back to Whispering Pines and meet up with the others?"

"That'll take time we may not have," Leeds says. "We need to reconnoiter the explosions and gather intel on the situation. We have to know what was damaged and how bad it is. If there's a blaze out of control, then we'll hustle back to Whispering Pines and warn the others."

"Just the two of us? Not liking the sound of that."

"I know you can handle yourself," Leeds says, "and I'm no slouch in the field. We'll move fast and stay quiet. We should get there by this afternoon at the latest."

"What about the others? They'll be looking for us?"

Leeds pulls his knife and kneels down, making what look like random marks on the concrete. "John'll know what to do when he sees this. To anyone else, it'll just be more marks in the ground."

"We'll be out of food and water by the time we get there," I say, trying to find any excuse not to go. I really hate field trips into the Z infested unknown.

"Listen, if you want to stay here or go back to Whispering Pines, then do it," Leeds says as he starts walking. "But I'm going that way. Do your thing or join me, Long Pork. Your decision.

You're not one of my men, so I can't force you, or order you to come."

I hurry to catch up. "No, of course not. You'll just shame me into it."

"Your shame is your problem, not mine," Leeds smiles. "But glad you're coming. It'll give us a chance to talk."

"We had all night to talk," I say.

"Yes, but I wanted to pound your face in last night," Leeds says. "The fresh air has cleared my head. Now we can talk."

"It's a wonder what getting away from the stench of rot will do for one's disposition."

We walk for a while without talking, though. Our eyes and ears are busy searching for approaching Zs, as we wind our way along Riverside Dr and the French Broad River, heading towards what was called the River Arts District pre-Z. Old industrial buildings that had been refurbished and turned into art studios, cafes, and lofts. We could cut up through Asheville and probably get to the smoke faster, but that would mean cutting through downtown. Between the Zs and the cannies, not the best idea. So we stick to Riverside.

We're just past an old BBQ restaurant called 12 Bones when we see our first group of Zs. I'm actually surprised we didn't come across more sooner. Maybe Leeds was right and the explosions drew them towards the east, which is the direction we are headed, so we'll catch up eventually. Joy.

The Zs are hunkered down, feeding, and don't even notice us come up on them. By the time they do, they only get a few hisses out before Leeds and I take them down. Only four, so not too hard.

We look at the remains of the unlucky victim they were snacking on.

"Canny?" Leeds asks.

"Not sure," I say, nudging the corpses with the toe of my boot.

It's a woman, we can see that, and she's dressed in nasty looking rags, but something sticks out that troubles me. Her boots. Not nasty like her clothes, but almost new, steel-toed work boots.

Leeds notices them too and crouches down, getting a closer look. He lifts up her foot and checks the sole, then lets it fall back to the ground.

"Not a canny," I say.

"No," Leeds says.

Her torso is pretty much ripped apart and her head is attached by a tendon or two and nothing more. Leeds doesn't let this stop him as he pushes up her sleeves to examine her arms. He sighs and gets to his feet.

"TF," he says. "She has the bar code tattooed on the inside of her arm."

"TF? What the fuck is TF?"

"Tersch-Foster," he answers, "Private military contractors."

"Mercenaries?" I ask.

"No, no, they are legit," Leeds says. "Well, that's debatable in some circles. They tackled the civilian jobs we couldn't tackle."

"So black ops for hire?"

"Close enough," Leeds says, looking around.

"You think she's on her own?" I ask, having my own look. Every rustle of a bush, every creak of a tree branch has me twitching. I thought looking out for Zs was stressful, not even close to looking out for highly trained, very deadly people. People are the worst, man.

"She's on a mission, that's for sure," Leeds says. "Her boots are off market Danners. You have to have a behind the scenes contract to get those. And they are pretty new."

"Are you saying a company is still making military boots?" I laugh.

"No, don't be dense," Leeds says. "I'm saying she had access to a fresh supply. I doubt she's just carrying them around with her."

"So ratty clothes to blend in, look like a survivor, but new boots to keep her alive? And somewhere is a supply of boots? Is that what you're saying?"

"Oh, I'm sure there's a supply of more than just boots," Leeds says. He walks a few feet away and kneels down, coming up with a small, black piece of plastic. He sighs deeply as he puts it in his ear. The normal frown on his face turns to a seriously troubled frown. He pulls out the plastic and tosses it towards the river. "Time to jog."

"What? Why?"

"That com earpiece was active," he replies as he starts jogging down the road. I catch up to him quickly, but don't know exactly how long I'll be able to keep the pace.

"Active? Earpiece? What the fuck, Captain?"

"Whoever was on the other end was trying to get her to answer," Leeds says. "That was state of the art. They'll track it to her location, which means they'll track it to us if we don't put some pavement between her body and our bodies."

"Fucking great," I say. "Just what we need: tourists."

"Maybe these are the people Stuart and John were going to look in on," Leeds says. "The ones at the Grove Park?"

"Could be," I say. "I never saw their boots as we were fleeing Vance that day. Too busy shouting and pissing my pants."

"At least you can admit it," Leeds smiles. He hasn't even broken a sweat yet. While I'm starting to cramp up in my side. "You gonna make it, Long Pork?"

"Probably not," I huff, "but at least I'll die miserable."

"Good man."

I think I make it a mile before I want to collapse. I'd toss my pack, since the weight of it is not helping, but it holds the last of my water and the little food I have. Plus some needed med supplies. Not that I expect to live much longer if we keep up this pace. I really should be in better shape, and I was at one point, but I took quite a beating when I fought Vance a couple months ago. I'm still not 100%. But I don't say a word, I just keep pushing, trying to keep pace with Leeds. Never let 'em see ya sweat, right? Isn't that how the old commercial went? Or was it never let them see you cry like a baby because your guts are on fire and you're going to puke any second? Tomayto, tomahto.

"Here," Leeds says, and turns to a stand of trees off to our left. I follow and barely manage to keep my feet under me. While he looks like he could do this all day. Fucker.

We get through the trees and head to one of the dozens of concrete buildings covering the area. Old railroad buildings. Leeds stops and holds up his hand. I stop and gulp air. He looks way more professional than I do, but I haven't puked yet, so points for me.

"In there," he says, pointing to one of the buildings.

29

He jogs (more jogging!) over to the building and forces the door open, waving me inside. We are in quickly and he has the door closed when I hear it: a vehicle.

"You hear that?" I ask.

"Shhhh," he warns.

It sounds like a truck and I hear the crunch of gravel as it drives past. It's not out on the road, but driving next to the buildings. Did it see us? Does it know where we're hiding? Fuck. Now instead of feeling like I'm gonna puke, I feel like I'm gonna shit my pants. My guts are messed up.

We wait until the sound of the truck is long gone. It's probably twenty minutes before Leeds opens the door and peers outside.

"Clear," he says. I follow him outside and we stick close to the buildings as we continue our course.

"Can we just walk?" I ask. He gives me a look. "What? I'm fucking dying, man."

"We just took a break we couldn't afford to," Leeds says. "We need to make up that time."

"How much time will we lose if you have to fucking carry me?" I ask. I'm serious.

He shakes his head. "Fast walk," he says, "like really fast. Can you handle that?"

"I'm all for a brisk hike," I reply. "Just no more jogging. I beg of you, Captain. Please, sir, no more."

"Stop being a melodramatic pussy," he says, but smiles in spite of himself.

Brisk hike, my ass. He pretty much pushes us back to a slow jog. If my arms have to bend and pump to keep going, then we are neither walking nor hiking, we're fucking jogging. Fucker.

Another mile and we're facing the overpass that lets Riverside cross over the rows of railroad tracks that make up the main depot area in Asheville. We cross the tracks and head under the overpass, our eyes on the shadows, looking for Zs and people. Have I mentioned how much people have made the apocalypse suck? I can handle Zs, they're easy. You see a Z and you know what it wants; you know where you stand. People? Who fucking knows?

We follow the tracks until we get to Biltmore Ave. If we turn left we can make our way into downtown; turn right, and it becomes Hendersonville Rd and the former sprawl of South Asheville. Or what's left of it. But ahead is Swannanoa River Rd. This will take us further east and towards the smoke.

We stand in the shadows of an old gas station and listen. Neither of us wants to cross the street without knowing for sure we're alone. It's at least thirty yards of open space before we can get to cover. Swannanoa River Rd has plenty of trees and we can even duck down into the ravine the small river flows through, but until we get there, we are sitting ducks.

I look over my shoulder, back towards the tracks and can see the entrance to the Biltmore Estate just past them. Was that movement? I could swear I saw something. I tap Leeds's shoulder and he follows my line of sight, raising his eyebrows. I shrug. We watch for a few minutes, but see nothing. I shake my head in apology and he nods.

When Z-Day hit, the Biltmore locked its gates and as far as I know, no one has gone onto the estate to check it out. Even Critter just shakes his head when anyone brings it up, and he and his people have "scavenged" every inch of the area. I don't fault him for staying away, really. It was a Sunday when Z-Day hit. That's a pretty busy day for the estate. My guess? There were at least a few thousand tourists on the property when it all went to hell.

They can keep those gates closed, thank you.

Leeds takes off first and runs in a crouch across the street. He gets to the side of an old Wendy's restaurant and flattens himself against the wall. We wait. After a few minutes, he waves me over. I run/crouch the same way, but highly doubt I look as good doing it. I get to him and my heart is pounding a mile a minute. We both wait and listen.

Nothing.

"Let's go," he says and we walk around the Wendy's and onto Swannanoa River Rd.

And run right into a small horde of Zs. And I'm actually surprised. I'm so focused on watching out for paramilitary types, that I almost forget that I live in the zombie apocalypse. Hello! Flesh eating undead walking about! Duh!

"I count fifteen," Leeds says, not bothering to keep quiet since the Zs spotted us instantly. "You go right, I'll go left. Take down what you can and I'll finish up the rest."

Basically, he's telling me to flail like I do and he'll rescue my ass when I get outnumbered and surrounded. Confidence boost!

But fuck it, I have The Bitch and I know how to use her. Leeds can keep his condescension and cram it up his-

"Jace!" Leeds yells as five come at me. "Batter up!"

Damn skippy.

I raise The Bitch and take my shot. The closest Z gets a caved in skull for her effort. Putrid brains splatter all over the Zs next to her and they hiss and snarl at me.

"What? You got a problem, mother fuckers?" I yell, taking down Z number two with an upswing to its head, ripping the entire front of its skull off. I'm a little stunned as I watch its brain slide right out the front and splat on the pavement.

However, the Zs aren't stunned. Takes a lot to impress a Z, let me tell you. Three Zs converge on me and I swing out, knocking one back, but letting the other two in. A hard kick to the knee drops one and an elbow to the temple drops the other. They aren't finished, by any stretch of the imagination, but they're delayed enough so I can crush the forehead of the first one.

Its head makes a loud pop and it crumples. I jump over the corpse and turn, putting my momentum into my swing. The timing is perfect and I watch the kneecapped Z's head spin away, tumbling through the air like a bloody volleyball. Wilson, come back!

The last Z grabs me by the legs and I go down hard. My head slams into the asphalt and I see stars a poppin' before my eyes. The thing crawls up me, its fingers trying to push through the denim of my jeans to get at my tasty, tasty legs. I go to smash it, but The Bitch is out of my grasp and out of my reach. I stretch for it, but it's no use.

"Fuck you!" I yell as I pound my fist into the top of the Zs skull, over and over.

I hear the crunching of bones and when the pain explodes in my hand, I realize it's not just the Z's skull that's breaking. Fuck. This sucks. You know, just once, I'd like to get through a fight without getting injured. Is that too much to ask?

The Z flies off me as Leeds kicks it in the ribs, sending it rolling across the pavement. He raises his sharpened baton and plunges it into the Z's eye socket, stilling the abomination instantly. He pulls it out, flicks off the goo, then collapses it and offers me a hand. I start to reach with my right one, but it's on fire.

"What happened?" Leeds asks.

"Thought I could beat it off me," I say then laugh. "Ha. Beat it off."

"Seriously?" Leeds frowns. He pulls me up by my left hand, then takes my right carefully. "Let me look. Could just be a sprain."

He presses the bones of my hand together and I nearly scream. Only years of living with the threat of Zs keeps me from crying out.

"Nope, not a sprain," he says. "Sorry."

Leeds opens his pack and pulls out a med kit. He finds a bandage and then looks me in the eye.

"This is going to hurt like a mother fucker," he warns me. "Just grit down and take it. You'll feel better once I get it wrapped. The bones won't shift and grind together."

"Good. Grinding bones is bad. Unless you're making bread. And a giant. I guess only giants make bread by grinding bones. Why would they do that? Is bone meal a traditional- MOTHER FUCKER!"

I fail on the quiet part that time. Jesus F-ing Christ, that shit fucking hurts. Cold sweat breaks out all over my body and I start to shiver. Leeds purses his lips.

"Suck it up, Long Pork," he chides. "You broke your fucking hand, that's all. You didn't get shot or stabbed. Keep the shock in check, will you please?"

"Sorry," I say. "Not trying to puss out or anything."

"There. Done," he says.

He walks over and grabs The Bitch, handing it to me. I take it with my left hand and test the weight. I am hopelessly right handed, so this injury is going to suck. My batting average is gonna go way down.

"You going to be able to use that?" he asks, nodding towards The Bitch.

"Let's hope so," I say. "Come on. We need to get to the smoke before it gets dark. I'm not feeling too secure with only one hand. I want to make sure we are locked down tight tonight."

"I'm sure we'll find a place we can hole up in," Leeds says.

We start out, keeping to the riverside of Swannanoa River Rd. My hand throbs and I'd give anything for some ibuprofen. Or morphine. Shit, I'd take some moonshine right about now. But that would slow me down. I'm already slower than Leeds and with an injured hand, I'm really just dead weight. What's the point of me even being here? Why the hell did I agree to come investigate this shit? What the fuck is wrong with me?

"You want to go for a swim?" Leeds asks, just as I start to step off the road and almost fall down the embankment to the river below. "Get out of your head, Long Pork."

"Come on, Captain," I say. "Can you knock it off with the Long Pork crap? I get it, I fucked up. I shouldn't have turned anything on until I understood the system fully. My bad. Just one more fuck up to add to the Jason Stanford list of fuck ups."

"Self-pity doesn't become you," Leeds scolds. "Accept your mistake and move on. Keep dwelling in the past and you won't see the present."

"Like the river to my right," I reply.

"Exactly."

"Fine. No more self-pity if you stop calling me Long Pork. I really hate that nickname."

"Even when Elsbeth calls you that?"

"She can't help it. It's just her way. But it does suck that my kids call me that now."

"What about Stella?"

"She pretends to hate it, but I caught her smiling once when the kids were really laying it on thick."

"It is funny," Leeds smiles, "sorry, but it is."

"Bite me."

"No thanks. Long pork isn't to my taste."

"Ha ha, you are so fucking fun--- Oh…"

"Weapons on the ground," the man says. "Packs too."

He's muscled, tall, wide, dressed in black body armor. Did I mention the muscles? Fuck. I guess he'd have to be muscled to carry the very large rifle in his hands. Doesn't look like an AR-15, but something more specialized.

"I'm sorry," the man says, "was I not clear on what you are to do right this fucking second?"

34

The barrel of the large rifle points at me, at a spot just below my belly. Not liking that.

"Weapons and packs down," Leeds says, moving slowly and complying. I follow suit. "And you are? Didn't catch your name?"

"Don't need to," the man says. He nods at our gear and suddenly two men step past us, pick up our gear, and join the first man. All wear black body armor. Nice, new, body armor. "Follow us."

He turns and starts to walk away, the two other men right behind. I actually think about laughing and just turning and running, but Leeds can sense this and grabs my arm, nodding over his shoulder. I look back and see two more men and a woman. Black body armor, big guns.

"Who are you?" I ask. "What the fuck is this?"

"Shut up," the first man says. "Too many zeds around. Stay quiet and you can live to ask questions later."

"You know, I'd rather we went the other direction," I say. "I really should be getting home. The wife will worry. You know what I mean?"

"That is not shutting up," the man says as he spins on his heel and stomps towards me. I back up, but hit a wall of body armor behind me.

Leeds gets in front of me, blocking the man, who looks the captain up and down, and then smiles.

"Fort Bragg?" he asks. Leeds doesn't answer. "Did my time there. Wasn't to my liking. I moved on." Leeds stays quiet. "Fine. Whatever. Your civvie pal here isn't going to make it for dinner. And both of you will be coming with us. Is there going to be a problem?"

"That's up to you, mercenary trash," Leeds says, a smile spreading across his face.

The man is twitching with violence. Calling anyone trash would piss them off, but he seems way too angry for that. Is calling someone a mercenary a bad thing?

"Call me a merc again and we will have a problem," the man says. "I solve problems. One way or another."

"Hey, I solve problems too," I say. "Is your go to solution, duct tape? It always works for me. That and super glue. If you can't fix it with duct tape or super glue, then it doesn't deserve to be fixed. Am I right? Huh?"

I smile and look around at the others. They do not smile back. Wasn't expecting them to, but a guy's gotta try.

"We won't have a problem as long as you understand your place, cowboy," Leeds says.

"Oh, I know my place, *Captain*," Cowboy says. "I'm paid very well to know it. Move."

Leeds nods and starts walking. I follow quickly.

"You said you get paid," I say. "Paid with what? I really hope you aren't taking cash. Not sure if you know, but the whole country has kinda gone poopy. That cash isn't worth much except to wipe your ass. Although I wouldn't recommend that. It scratches the hell out of you. Like really scratches. I couldn't sit for like-"

"Jace?" Leeds asks.

"Yes?"

"Please be quiet so you do not get us shot."

"Oh, sorry. I was doing my jabbering thing to distract them, thinking you have a plan to get us away from Kevlar and the Gang."

One of the guys behind me snorts. Score!

"I do not have a plan, Jace. We will follow these private contractors until they deliver us to whomever hired them." Leeds clears his throat. "May I ask if you were looking for us specifically, or did you just stumble on us and are playing it by ear? Just want to know what we are walking into."

"What you are walking into is a whole lot of shut the fuck up," Cowboy says. "Last warning. Don't test me."

"Noted," Leeds says, glancing at me. "Understood, Jace?"

"Got it," I nod. "Whole lot of shut the fuck up. Commencing now."

Hey, he's calling me Jace again! That's a plus. Of course, he's probably doing that so that the last thing someone calls me before I die isn't Long Pork. Either way, I do appreciate the effort.

Now, I wonder where the fuck we are headed? And do they have some ibuprofen? Because my hand hurts like a motherfucker.

CHAPTER THREE

The frown on Stella's face is more from exasperation than anger. She's getting tired of having to track the two teenagers down and get them back on task. Her son, Charlie, is sixteen, and he should know that by now, when he's asked to do something, he needs to do it without being asked again. Even if a cute girl distracts him.

And that's the problem there, the cute girl. Jennifer Patel. Dark and very attractive, she has Charlie wrapped around her finger. Stella doesn't think she's toying with him. No, Stella can tell that Jennifer sincerely likes Charlie. But, having been a teenage girl once herself, Stella knows that Jennifer is testing Charlie, seeing how much he'll do for her before he either stops, or they get in trouble.

Stella doesn't want to know where the line is drawn in Jennifer's mind. Social morals and boundaries are a thing of the past for the generation growing up in the apocalypse. Survival is key, and that tends to push some common sense out the window.

Which is why she isn't too surprised to find Jennifer and Charlie in a shed behind the main barn, half dressed.

"Oh, shit! Mom! What are you doing?" Charlie yells.

"Saving you from a big mistake, young man," Stella replies as she pulls her son out of the shed. "We've had this talk, Charlie. We've had it more than a couple of times. You are too young, do you hear me? Too young to be playing with fire like this."

She spins around, leaving Charlie struggling to get his shirt on, and walks up to Jennifer, as she is busy doing the same. Stella's finger gets right up in Jennifer's nose and the girl freezes.

37

"And you, young miss," Stella snaps, "you will stay away from my son. I don't care how much you like him. Neither of you have any understanding of the consequences of your actions."

"We have protection," Jennifer says quietly.

This takes Stella aback and she furrows her brow. "You...what? Excuse me?"

"We have condoms," Jennifer says, "and that gel stuff. I don't want to get pregnant, Mrs. Stanford. I don't want children."

"Not now, at least," Charlie smiles.

"Not ever," Jennifer says, pulling her shirt over her head. "Who would? The world is dead, Mrs. Stanford. I can't bring a baby into this world."

"Seriously?" Charlie asks. "Like not ever? What about when we're older?"

"We won't live that long," Jennifer says. She pushes past Stella and Charlie. "You're an idiot if you think we will. Even on the Farm."

The two Stanfords stand there and watch her go until she's turned the corner and around the massive farmhouse, that is the center of the Farm.

"Well that sucked," Charlie says finally. "I didn't think she never wants kids."

"You shouldn't be thinking about that at all, Charlie," Stella says. "You have to be careful and focused. You need to use your big head, not your little one."

"Mom!" Charlie groans. "Come on, that's just gross. Don't ever say that again."

"I'm going to have to talk to her father," Stella says. "I would want him to talk to me if it was reversed."

"Where do you think Jenny got the condoms from?" Charlie says. "He already knows. His words to me were that if I got her pregnant, he'd gut me in the night and leave me outside the fences for the Zs."

"Oh, my god!" Stella exclaims. "How dare he say that to my son!"

"It's his daughter," Charlie shrugs. "I'm sure dad would gut anyone that got Greta pregnant."

"Take that back this instant, Charles Stanford!" Stella snarls. "Don't' ever say such a thing!"

"You don't think dad would?"

"Oh, I know he would," Stella replies. "I meant about your sister getting pregnant. She's only thirteen and just started getting her period. We do not need that bad karma in our family."

"Jesus, Mom," Charlie frowns. "I do not need to hear that. Yuck."

"Oh, grow up."

"I was trying to before you burst in and ruined my coming of age moment."

Stella and Charlie look at each other; the intensity is broken as they both crack up laughing. Stella wraps him in her arms and kisses his head over and over.

"I love you," she says.

"Love you too," he replies. "So we can keep this from dad?"

"Not a fucking chance, kid," Stella says. "Your father and I haven't made it this long by lying to each other. Expect a long talk with him when he gets back."

"When is that?" Charlie asks. "Isn't he supposed to be back tomorrow?"

"Maybe," Stella says, "depends on how much work he has to do at Whispering Pines to get the gas lines up and working. But you know your dad, he'll figure out the fastest, most efficient way to do it."

"Great," Charlie says as they start to walk towards the farmhouse. "I'll just be stressing over this until he gets here. Awesome."

"Oh, don't worry," Stella smiles. "You'll have plenty of work to keep you busy and your mind off of it."

"Double awesome." Charlie starts to climb the porch that stretches across the entire front of the farmhouse then stops. "What's that smoke?"

Stella shields her eyes and looks off in the distance. She heard something last night just after going to bed, but thought it was thunder. You never know in the mountains when a freak storm will turn up. She didn't think a thing about it this morning.

"I don't know," she says.

"Explosions last night," a deep voice says from the farmhouse doorway. Big Daddy Fitzpatrick. A huge man of a man. Farmer through and through. "I think that husband of yours may have gotten the gas back on. But I'm afraid the results aren't what he was looking for."

"Should we send a team to check it out?" Stella asks.

"I'll see if my Sweetie Mel will want to go," Big Daddy replies. "Not that I'm too worried. There's Stuart, Julio, Leeds, and the rest to watch out for your man and that brain of his. Don't you worry none."

"But you'll send Melissa?" Stella asks.

"I'll see if her and her scavengers want to go rendezvous with the Whispering Pines teams," Big Daddy says. "If she wants. Maybe I'll have her take a couple of her brothers along. I love my boys, but they need to get outside the fence some. And not just to Critter's to gamble and drink. Which they think I don't know about."

"Thanks, Hollis," Stella says.

He looks down at her and smiles. "Of course, ma'am. We're all in this together. The Lord didn't put me here to ignore the wishes of a well meaning lady such as yourself. I see the signs and I follow."

***

"They're going towards the explosions?" Julio asks, his eyes scanning the skyline and the columns of black smoke. "Why would they do that? Why not just come back to Whispering Pines?"

"Because the captain likes to have answers," John says, his sniper rifle resting in the crook of his arm as he studies the scratches in the concrete Leeds left for him. "And he probably wants to march Long Pork around a bit."

"Why would he march Long Pork?" Elsbeth asks. "That's not nice."

"Exactly," John says. "Captain Leeds isn't a violent man by nature. He likes the slow torture instead. You should see the man conduct an interrogation. Fucking brilliant."

"So what now?" Julio asks, looking to Stuart. "We follow?"

"We can't all go," Stuart says. He looks about at Critter's men that came along. "Any idea where your boss went?"

"He took off running to draw away the Zs," one of them answers. "That's the last we saw him."

"So we have Jace and Leeds out there and Critter too," Stuart says. "How many men went with Critter?"

"Three?" the man replies.

"Counting's not your strength, is it?" John jokes. The man just glares at him. "Gunnery Sergeant Stuart? What's the call?"

"Is he in charge?" Julio asks.

"No, but he's got more training and experience in his pinky than you do in that whole inked body of yours," John replies. "I'd like his opinion. And so do you since you just asked him for it three seconds ago."

"I know. Just fucking with you, soldier."

"Okay, boys, put 'em away, will ya?" Stuart laughs.

"Put what away?" Elsbeth asks. "What do they have out? I don't see anything."

"Kinda my point," Stuart says. "As much as I'd like to go off on another adventure in Z land, I'm needed at Whispering Pines. We'll be constructing the stairs and deck to the cliff the next couple of days. That's going to require some serious supervision."

"I'll go with Elsbeth," Julio says. "We'll find them."

"As much as I hate to split you two love birds up, I think I need you with me Julio," Stuart says. "The folks that came from the Farm listen to you. I can't run up against egos while trying to stay on schedule." Stuart looks at Elsbeth, John, and Critter's guys. "You can track them down; make sure they didn't get into any more trouble."

"I'm good at pulling Long Pork out of trouble," Elsbeth nods. "I do it all the time."

"We know," Stuart says. "You cool with that then, Sergeant Baptiste?"

"You got it, gunny," John says. "I'll keep everyone on task and in line."

"We don't take orders from soldiers," one of Critter's men says. "Critter was clear on that. They ain't in charge of us."

"No, they ain't," Stuart says, mocking the man's accent. "But if you want to stay alive, then you best listen to John here. He isn't carrying that rifle around because it compliments his eyes. Got me?"

41

The men start to protest, but Elsbeth steps forward, facing off with them. They shut up quickly. As much as they may not want to follow John's orders, they also don't want to piss off the deadly ex-canny girl. They all look away, shuffling their feet, finding interesting new dirt under their fingernails, watching an imaginary bird fly by.

"Well, that's settled then," Stuart says, looking to Julio. "Ready to get back?"

Julio doesn't look ready. He knows Elsbeth can take care of herself, he even saw her in action back before she joined with the Whispering Pines folks, but their new found affection for each other pulls at him. In the apocalypse, you don't get many chances at happiness and Julio doesn't want to lose this chance.

"Be safe," he tells her.

"Ain't no place safe," Elsbeth says. Everyone has to admit to themselves that she's right.

"I have her six," John says, "and she has mine. We'll be cool."

"Good," Stuart says as he claps John on the shoulder. "We'll see you back at Whispering Pines when you find them."

"Right," John says and looks to Critter's men. "Let's cover some ground, people."

They all mutter about not taking orders from a soldier, but quickly step in line.

***

He left his men to hide and wait for him so he could move faster and not be detected. He loves his guys, but they aren't always the most stealthy or intelligent. When he saw the truck, he knew caution was the key to survival this day.

He's tracked the truck for the better part of the day, wondering what all the decked out wannabe soldiers with their fancy gear want. They just seemed to be driving around in circles. For a minute or two, he wondered if they were looking for him. Sure seemed like they were looking for someone.

So, when Critter sees them march up to the truck and force Jace and Leeds inside, he isn't surprised at all. There was bound to be fallout from the gas explosions. Critter doesn't know what part the wannabes play, but he knows it isn't good. No one needs that much firepower and body armor if they are just taking down Zs. They're geared up for human interaction.

The truck, a long black four-door diesel with a covered bed, pulls down the road, heading towards the smoke. Critter isn't surprised by that either. He'd been hearing whispers through the grapevine that someone was setting up shop in town and making some strange repairs at strategic places in Asheville. If his sense of direction is right, and it is rarely wrong, the smoke is coming from East Asheville right around the former VA hospital.

"What the hell is over there?" Critter wonders. He'd cleaned out the VA a while back. There wasn't a single supply left on any of the shelves.

He waits until the truck is long out of sight and then works his way along the ridge above Swannanoa River Rd. He puzzles over the smoke every time he comes around a bend and gets sight of it again.

Then it hits him.

He knows what's over there. And the value it offers with the right planning. He'd even used it himself a few times when other routes weren't available.

Critter picks up his pace, knowing exactly where the truck is headed.

***

The Zs are thick, but the truck doesn't slow down; we just mow right through them.

"That's gonna be hell on your suspension," I say. Leeds, sitting next to me in the backseat, hands zip tied, just sighs. I tried to be quiet, I really did, but it's hard.

"Well, I know we aren't going to see Tersch," Leeds says to Cowboy who is sitting in the passenger's seat in front of him. "He died two years before Z-Day. Don't tell me I will have the opportunity to meet Mr. Foster. Quite an honor since no one has ever met the man."

"And no one will," Cowboy grins. The driver nods and smiles.

"Am I missing something?" Leeds asks. "You two obviously have information that makes my statement amusing."

"Does he amuse you, is that it? Is he a clown to you, eh?" I say.

"Jace?"

"Sorry, I'll shut up," I reply. "Carry on."

"I'm going to let you figure it out when we get there," Cowboy says. "It should be eye opening."

"And where exactly is 'there'?" Leeds asks. "Must be important if we are wading through this swarm of Zs."

Rotted hands and decayed faces push up against the side windows of the truck. I have to feel sorry for the guys in the bed. Sure, they have a canvas cover around them, but that's not much protection when dealing with Z numbers like this. I haven't seen this many Zs this packed together in a long time.

Actually, I'm not sure I've ever seen this many Zs. Well, not true. Vance had thousands jammed into the empty Beaver Lake. This is like that. A ton of Zs with no fleshless elbowroom.

"Right," Cowboy says, his finger to his ear. He must have one of those com earpieces. Keeping the tech real in the apocalypse. Cowboy turns to the driver and points up ahead. "Stop here. They'll clear a path for us."

The truck slows and stops and we wait and watch. I stare out the windshield at the mass of Zs that have encircled us. Whatever momentum we were able to keep before is gone forever. There is no way we'll get moving again with all the weight of those Zs pressing in on the truck. Why is it that I always seem to end up in a truck surrounded by Zs? Just two months ago, I was in a dump truck, not looking my best, and thought I was going to die there.

But, I don't think I'm going to die here, at least not by the Zs. A rumbling starts to shake the truck, and then we all see it coming from a street off to the left: a massive earthmover. You know, one of those gigantic construction trucks that are like ten stories tall and shit. Okay, maybe not ten stories, but the thing is at least two stories high with a huge blade in front like for a snow plow. Which is exactly what it is when I see it work, but for Zs, not snow. The earthmover just pushes the Zs aside, clearing a wide path for our truck.

Our driver doesn't waste any time and puts the truck in gear, hurrying into the cleared space before it fills up again. There is still a wall of Zs ahead of us, but the earth mover slowly turns, leading us down the road, clearing the way perfectly.

"I don't think that is just for the Zs, is it?" Leeds asks.

"Not my place to say," Cowboy replies. "I'm security, not construction."

"So you were hired to protect the construction crew?"

Cowboy grins at Leeds. I don't like that grin. There is nothing happy about it.

"You'll get your answers," Cowboy says. "Just not from me. Sit back, sit tight, shut the fuck up."

"Captain, that advice you always give me? Yeah, you might want to take it," I say. "You know, regarding the shutting the fuck up."

"First smart thing you've said all day," Cowboy says as he turns back around and faces the windshield.

That's the last words any of us say while riding in the truck. I just sit back and watch the earthmover plow Zs out of the way. They go tumbling and rolling everywhere; Z guts splatter up on our windshield now and then when a particularly juicy one gets under the earthmover's tires. Our driver seems to like it and laughs every time he has to spray the windshield and hit the wipers. Messed up. I clutch my wounded hand to my chest and just wait it out.

It's only a few more minutes before the earthmover pulls aside, driving up over a lawn and nearly crushing the front of a brick house, and we speed past, through a barricade that is held open by more private contractors. Black body armor, baseball caps, black sunglasses, and heavily armed.

I turn to speak to Leeds, but he is intently studying our surroundings. I'm not going to disturb him, so I do the same. We are about a hundred yards from the on ramp to the Blue Ridge Parkway and that is where all the activity is centered. It looks like the staging area for a massive construction site, or would have, if it wasn't for the smoke and scorched machinery. I'm guessing that's my fault.

Several tents are set up across the street from the main parkway entrance and that's where the driver pulls us up to. Five more PCs come walking out, rifles at the ready, centered around a woman dressed similarly, but obviously not one of the men. I don't mean that because she has boobs, I mean that because it's pretty apparent by the body language around her that she is in charge.

"Don't move," Cowboy says as he hops out and walks up to her.

She looks at him for a second and then looks over at us. The windows are tinted, so I know she can't see into the truck, but when she takes off her sunglasses, I swear her ice blue eyes can see into my soul. You'd think by now I'd get tired of saying I have met the Devil, but in the zombie apocalypse, it is surprising how many Devils come out to play.

Her eyes study the truck and then she nods and steps over to the back passenger door; my door. It opens quickly and she takes me in with those eyes. It's a split second that lasts forever, then she looks past me and fixes her gaze on Leeds.

"Captain," she nods.

"Ms. Foster," Leeds nods back.

"Ms. Foster?" I say. "This is the Foster in Tersch and Foster?"

"I am," Foster replies. "Not the founding member. That was my father."

Every single PC hangs his head for a moment and then looks back up. Jesus Christ, it's a mercenary cult! But then, aren't all military groups in a way? That's why I quit Cub Scouts in third grade. Creeped me out.

"I see we owe you an apology for some damage we've done," Leeds says.

"I think this guy here owes the apology," Foster says, looking at me, waiting.

"Oh, right, yeah, sorry about that," I say. "I was trying to figure out why the gas had been shut off."

"So you decided to turn it back on? Thinking back on it, does that sound like a good idea?"

"Not so much," I say to her, trying to smile. I think my lips get halfway up and stop. I can tell by the way she is looking at me that she thinks I'm having some sort of fit. I give up on the smile. "Any chance y'all can give us a ride back to my place? I know my people are probably worried."

"Jason Stanford," she says. "General bullshitter and expert in nothing. Defacto head of the Whispering Pines subdivision."

"That would be Brenda Kelly, actually," I say, "she's head of the HOA Board."

"Yes, she is," Foster says. "But that doesn't mean shit. Just that she's in charge of the cowards in your bunch. I know what you did to Vance. Impressive. Needlessly destructive, but impressive."

"Had some help," I say, hooking a thumb at Leeds. "And I hope you don't mind me asking how you know so much about me?"

She doesn't answer, just steps aside. "Let's walk. After you, Mr. Stanford."

"He prefers to be called Long Pork," Leeds says.

Oh, no he didn't!

"Long Pork? Jesus, really?" Foster asks. "What the fuck is wrong with you people?"

I get out of the truck and follow as two PCs begin to walk over to a large pile of debris. Looking over my shoulder, I see Leeds right behind me and Foster behind him. I've seen him move and know she's easily within grabbing distance, but by the way, she carries herself that also means Leeds is within her grabbing distance. Leeds glances at the debris pile and I follow his gaze. Then stop.

"Problem, Mr. Stanford?" Foster asks.

"Are those people? Pull them out of there, for fuck's sake!" I cry.

"Too late for that," Foster says, walking past us and to the squirming bodies pinned beneath the pile of concrete and steel. "They turned a few minutes ago. I was saving them for you."

She unholsters a pistol and holds it out to me grip first. I look at it, a Beretta 9mm, and look at her.

"Take it," she says, "finish the job."

"You take us captive and then hand me a pistol?" I ask. "Are you high?"

"What are you going to do, Mr. Stanford? Shoot your way free? You aim that 9 at anything other than those zeds and your head will be mist. Poof. I'm not too worried."

"Do it, Jace," Leeds says.

"Jesus," I say as I start to take the 9 with my bandaged right hand and wince.

"Hurt yourself?" Foster asks.

"I always do," I say as I take it with my left hand and walk up to the pile.

The Zs all hiss at me, their broken bodies straining against the debris, trying to get at me. Being brand spanking new, several of them actually manage to shift some concrete; they're always strongest just after turning. I count eight Zs. Maybe there are more in the pile, but I can't see them.

I don't hoo and haw. No need to waste time. It's not like I haven't had to put down Zs before. The 9 feels weird in my left hand, but I steady it and take aim. Then fire.

I fucking miss.

The second shot doesn't and I walk from one Z to the other, take careful aim, and fire. All eight are dead in less than a minute. I eject the magazine and hand the empty pistol back to Foster.

"Afraid I'll use one of the remaining cartridges on you?" she smiles.

"Just thought I'd slow you down," I say. I watch her slap the magazine back into the pistol and rack the slide in a blink. "Or not."

She raises the pistol and aims at my forehead. I don't even have time to think before shit gets crazy. There's a cry behind me, a few grunts, some slamming and scuffling, then Leeds is next to me, a pistol in his hand pointed at Foster's forehead.

She doesn't even glance over at him; her eyes are fixed on me.

"How's this going to go?" Leeds asks.

"I don't know, Captain," she says, "you tell me."

"I'd prefer if it went easy. No one else needs to get hurt," Leeds says. "Sorry about your men there, but shit happens these days."

"Those weren't my men," Foster says. "Those were just some poor suckers that signed on with my employer. Simple labor here to do a job. They probably have families or loved ones. I don't know, I don't care."

"So back to my original question: how is this going to go?"

Foster just watches me. She is doing this weird thing with her mouth, like she's sucking her teeth. I can see her running her tongue up under her lip. What the fuck? People are weird.

"Would you like to meet my employer?" she finally asks. "Could be a good thing for you and yours."

It takes me a second to realize she's asking me, not Leeds.

"Oh, uh, sure," I say, "beats getting shot in the face."

"It does, doesn't it?" she smiles. Why is it whenever military folks smile, it gives me the creeps?

"Is your employer here," Leeds asks, the 9 steady in his hand, never wavering.

"Oh, hell no," Foster laughs. "He leaves the sweating to the slaves."

"Slaves?" Leeds asks.

Foster shrugs and then the 9 is gone. I blink and it's in the holster on her belt.

"Captain? If you please?" she says.

Leeds lowers the pistol and PCs converge on him, but Foster holds up her hand. They stop instantly. She holds out her palm and Leeds places the 9 in it without a word.

"Let's take my car," Foster says, "I'll drive." She looks over at one of the PCs and the woman hurries off. "You'll like my car. Custom made for this job."

In a minute, everyone parts as a rigged out four door Jeep Wrangler comes pulling up. I would have thought a hard top would be more practical, but this Wrangler has the soft top down. Probably makes firing the fifty caliber on top a little easier. On the front bumpers are two miniguns, you know the ones that look like small Gatling guns with the rotating barrels? Yeah, those. I can see ammunition belts feeding under the hood.

But the cool thing (yes, I said cool), is that the entire Jeep is ringed with blades. They look like blades from a sawmill, which they probably are, that have been welded onto the frame just at waist level. I can see the front has a reinforced grill with heavy bars and spikes. The back has the ubiquitous spare tire, but also a wide panel of steel. I can't quite tell what that does.

"Hop in, boys," Foster says as she gets into the driver's seat. "Mr. Stanford, you can ride up front with me. The Captain can ride bitch in the back."

I get in and so does Leeds. He's instantly sandwiched between two men that must weigh eight hundred pounds between them. Food shortage hasn't been an issue for these boys. Damn they are

49

huge. Foster barely waits for the doors to close before she's pulling away. Cowboy gives her a nod and she nods back, as she runs up onto the curb and skirts around a ton of machinery.

"The crew was busy retrofitting some generators for natural gas when you flipped the switch," Foster says. "A few minutes before or a few minutes after, and it would have all been good. But your timing was perfect. The guys working on the retrofit were vaporized. Those zeds you put down were standing fifty feet away."

She looks over at me, and I give her a weak smile.

"You like blowing shit up, don't you Mr. Stanford?"

"I don't set out to do it," I say. "Just seems to happen around me."

"Just seems to happen," she says as she barrels towards a swarm of Zs. "Interesting way to put it."

We get closer and closer to the Zs, but she takes a right just before we hit the swarm. We speed down a hill, take a hard curve, and then speed back up another hill, zigzagging our way through the Haw Creek area of Asheville. I haven't been in this area since before Z-Day. Dozens and dozens of Zs are wandering about in front yards and fields as we zip along the winding road.

"Where are we headed?" I shout over the wind that is whipping past us.

"FOB," she says.

"Oh," I nod, "what does that mean?"

"Forward operating base," Leeds says from behind me. "I have a feeling where that is."

"Do you?" Foster asks as she looks at him in the rear view mirror. My stomach clenches as she keeps looking at him while taking a hairpin turn. "Enlighten me, Captain?"

"You're the folks at the Grove Park Inn," Leeds says.

"That's you guys?" I say. "I really thought that was Vance's people."

"That slimy fuck?" Foster laughs, looking back at the road. "My employer wouldn't let him anywhere near the place. That guy was batshit fucking nuts." She shrugs. "But he had his uses. Guy knew how to round up zeds, that's for sure. My job has gotten a lot harder since you killed him."

"He kinda forced me to," I say.

"Oh, I'm sure he did," Foster says. "I don't doubt that one bit. Still, makes my job harder."

"And what is your job?" Leeds asks.

"Keep the party rolling," Foster says. "Whatever it takes."

Leeds nods, obviously understanding what that means. I, on the other hand, am in the dark as usual.

We pull off the road and head up a steep, switchback of a gravel road.

"Wait," I say. "How are we getting to the Grove Park from here? Haw Creek doesn't connect. There's a mountain in the way."

"You call these mountains?" Foster laughs. "Please. Try spending a winter in the Wakhan Corridor. Then you'll understand what mountains are."

Out of the corner of my eye, I see Leeds stiffen. It's subtle, and most wouldn't notice, but I do. So does Foster. How? I have no idea.

"You putting the pieces together, Captain?" Foster asks.

"That was quite a mess," Leeds says, "took some serious clean up. The Chinese weren't happy."

"Shit gets messy in the field," Foster says. "You of all people should know that."

We keep climbing and climbing as the gravel road turns to dirt then becomes more of an idea of a road than an actual road. Like a wide trail. Then that is gone. I do see tire tracks in the mud and grass that we bump over, so I know this isn't the first time Foster has gone this way.

Then we hit a crest and look out over all of North Asheville. The view is incredible, and sad. There is so much destruction evident from up here. I'm blown away at how much of the city is just gone; rubble on the ground. Sure, I've scouted a lot of it, but seeing it from up here is another thing. The scope of it is breathtaking.

"Asheville hasn't fared so well," Foster says, "but better than a lot of places. It was called the Paris of the South, right?"

"Yeah, it was," I reply.

"It should just be called the Paris of the World, now," she says, "considering what Paris looks like."

"You've seen Paris?" I ask, turning to her. "Post-Z Paris?"

"Yes, Mr. Stanford," she says as she cranks the wheel and follows a ridgeline that is barely as wide as the Jeep. "I've also seen Berlin, New York, Los Angles, Toronto, Sao Paulo, Cape Town, Beijing, and quite a few other places."

"How?" I ask. "By ship?"

Foster furrows her brow. "You do realize zeds can't fly, right, Mr. Stanford? And just because the dead walk the earth, doesn't mean airplanes stopped working?"

"Right. Yeah."

Yes, I feel stupid.

Down the other side of the mountain we go. Foster turns off the trail and I swear we are going to plunge to our deaths, but the Jeep stays upright as we merge onto a lower trail. Winding, winding, winding down we go. Good thing I don't get motion sick. Then we come out into a backyard behind some mansion and I know where we are.

"Town Mountain Road," I say. "I guess you found a short cut."

"Yep," she says, "lot less zeds up here."

We get out onto the road and weave past massive houses that would have gone for millions pre-Z. Now they stand empty. Well, except for that one with the Zs banging on the huge picture window that looks out over Asheville. Guess that dinner party didn't go as planned.

Instead of going down Town Mountain, and into Asheville, Foster goes higher up. I've taken this route before, back when half of Merrimon Ave, the main artery into North Asheville, was under construction and I wanted to avoid the traffic pile up. Soon we are at Webb Cove Road with the Blue Ridge Parkway off to our right.

And there are people working on the parkway. What the fuck?

"I would have just taken the parkway to here, but you kinda blew up the on ramp," Foster says. "Or enough of it that we will be a good two weeks behind."

I hear Leeds snort behind me and look over my shoulder. He just shakes his head.

"Something on your mind, Captain? If so, please share," Foster says, "I'd love to hear it."

"Where'd you start?" Leeds asks.

"Right here," Foster says. "Asheville is blessed with more access points to the Blue Ridge Parkway than any other city. Seemed like the natural place to begin."

"So BOP is in Charlottesville then?"

"There abouts," Foster says, "but I'll leave that for my employer to explain."

"BOP? Charlottesville?" I ask. "What's going on?"

"I'll leave that for her employer to explain," Leeds says.

We weave down Webb Cove Road and then connect to the smaller roads that eventually guide us right into the Grove Park Inn. We have to work through more than a few checkpoints, but no one even glances at Foster. They just raise the gates and let us through. When we pull up to the front entrance, there is a man dressed in jeans and a plaid work shirt standing there, waiting for us.

We hop out of the Jeep, flanked by the muscle men, and he walks up to us.

"Foster," the man says, "are these the people giving us the troubles?"

Foster looks at me. "This one was the issue," she says. "Mr. Stanford was playing with toys he shouldn't have been."

"Mr. Stanford, you have cost me a good amount of resources and labor," the man says. "Maybe we'll figure out a way you can pay that back."

"And why would I do that?" I ask.

"Jace," Leeds warns. I look at him and he shakes his head. "Not the time. Just listen."

"And you are...?" the man asks Leeds.

"Captain Walt Leeds, US Army Special Forces Team Cobra, sir," Leeds says, giving the man a salute. "At your service, Mr. President."

"Mr. President?" I ask, my jaw dropping. "What the fuck are you talking about? This isn't the President of the United States."

"I am now," the man says. He holds out his hand. "Anthony Mondello, former Secretary of Homeland Security."

I look at Leeds, then at Foster. They just stare back at me.

"You people have got to be shitting me," I say.

CHAPTER FOUR

The Fitzpatrick siblings crouch low, letting the convoy of trucks and Humvees pass on the road. They wait until the sound of the engines is a distant rumble, and then come out from their cover, the large, farm-bred men looking to their smaller sister for guidance.

"They're going to the Farm," Blanchard "Buzz" Fitzpatrick says, his eyes narrowed and huge muscled arms quivering with adrenaline. The twins, Jonah "Pup" Fitzpatrick and Jeremiah "Porky" Fitzpatrick, nod in agreement.

"I know," Melissa Fitzpatrick replies, her eyes cast towards the Farm and the vehicles. "Go back?"

"Daddy and everyone else will be there," Pup says. "They can handle them."

"Did you get a good look?" Buzz asks Melissa.

"Not really," Melissa says. "But they looked military. Pretty sure I saw some rifles and maybe Kevlar vests."

"So back, or on to Asheville?" Buzz asks. "We need to decide now."

"Shit, shit, shit," Melissa whispers. "I don't know. We'll be way behind them. They take the Farm and we'll be walking into a shit storm."

"We could be the deciding factor," Porky says. "We may be the numbers Daddy needs to beat these people."

"Assuming they're going to fight," Melissa says. "Maybe they ain't."

"You believe that?" Buzz asks. "With them guns they had?"

"No," Melissa answers, "just a thought, though."

"I say we go back and help," Pup says. "That's what Daddy would want."

"Yeah," Melissa frowns. "True."

"So back then?" Buzz asks.

"Against my better judgment," Melissa says. "Back."

***

"Right there," John says, pointing ahead to a thick covering of pine trees, "they need to work on their hiding skills."

"Yes they do," Elsbeth agrees as she points above them, "and work on their not getting found skills. That's Critter and they don't even know it."

By the time the men have their guns up and pointed at John and Elsbeth, it is already too late. John just shakes his head and laughs as he walks up to the men.

"Boys, you may be good out in your holler, but your city stealth leads something to be desired," he says. "We could smell your cigarettes a couple blocks back."

"And I told you not to smoke while I was gone," Critter says from behind them. "Fucking morons. Half pay and rations for all y'all."

"Aw, come on, Critter!" one of the men complains. "You said to wait here and that's what we done. We waited. Can't blame us for smoking."

"I can and I do, dipshit," Critter says, smacking the man upside the head. "Because it was the smoke that got ya caught."

"Good to see you, Critter," John says, holding out his hand.

"You too, sniper boy," Critter says, shaking John's hand. "And you as well, miss."

"Miss what?" Elsbeth asks. "I didn't miss anything."

Critter just laughs. "No, cain't say you miss much at all." He hooks a thumb back over his shoulder. "If you're looking for the captain and Long Pork, then you missed them, though. Looks like some private soldiers have them all trussed up. I followed as far as I could, but the Zs are thick over east. I did see a Jeep head up Haw Creek road. Not sure where it was going."

"Private soldiers? You mean PCs?" John asks. "Black body armor?"

"Yep," Critter nods. "And all kinds of gear. They's got guns I only seen in magazines."

"What're PCs?" Elsbeth asks.

"Private contractors," John says. "I think I know where they're going. But it'll be a hike."

"You seen 'em before?" Critter asks.

"I have," John says. "Stuart and I did some recon yesterday. They're part of the group holed up in the Grove Park."

"Grove Park?" one of Critter's men asks. "That means we have to get through downtown. It's gonna be dark soon. No way, man. No fucking way."

"Scared little boy," Elsbeth says, then turns and walks off towards downtown Asheville.

"She said it," John smiles and follows.

"Grow a pair, will ya?" Critter snarls at the man. "The rest of ya better too. Long Pork and Captain Leeds need our help."

"What's in it for us?" one of the other men asks.

"You get to keep your tiny nuts," Critter says. "You lookin' for more, are ya?"

"No, sir," the man replies quietly.

"Didn't think so," Critter glares. "Now get to steppin', boys. That girl is gonna out hike y'all."

***

Stella and I would bring the kids to the Grove Park Inn every Christmas to see the gingerbread house competition winners. It was a big thing pre-Z; Food Network did a special each year and the winners would be on Good Morning America. There were some seriously cool gingerbread houses. And some seriously bad ones.

The best thing was the people watching. We'd take a walk around, see the houses, then grab refreshments and park it in the lobby to watch all the families that only venture out of their hollers once a year. It was quite the eye opening anthropological study. More than a few of those family trees didn't have many branches, if any at all. It was snobby of us, but damn it was entertaining.

So, as we walk into the lobby, I can't help but think of those times. A wave of pre-Z nostalgia washes over me as I realize we're only a month or so away from Christmas. Not that we really celebrate it. Kinda loses its charm when you see an undead Santa Claus eating his elves. Yeah. I saw that.

But I can almost smell the pine and the spiced cider, as we are led towards a long table set up by the rows of back windows that look out on the Grove Park's former golf course and the mountains beyond. It is a gorgeous view, even now post-Z. The undead can't take the views from us, dammit!

"Thirsty?" Mondello asks. "Hungry?"

"I could go for a latte," I say. "Maybe some biscotti? The biscotti here is to die for."

"Is it?" Mondello says. "I don't believe there's any left, but I can have someone look."

"He's joking, Mr. President," Leeds says. "He does that a lot. A lot."

"Actually I wasn't joking," I say. "I do like those biscotti. And the lattes here weren't half bad if you got the right person to make them."

"Take a seat, Mr. Stanford," Mondello says, gesturing to a chair at the long table. I glance at the table and the piles of paperwork and maps strewn across it haphazardly. "I'm a tad unorganized at the moment. Your little accident threw me off and I have had to come up with a new plan while we regroup."

"Bummer," I say, taking a seat. Leeds sits next to me, but Foster remains standing just behind Mondello. "You know, I have a reputation for problem solving. Maybe I can take a look at your plans? Give you some pointers?"

"Some pointers?" Mondello asks, looking back at Foster. "Is he for real?"

"Painfully so, sir," Foster says.

"Listen, Mr. Stanford," he says, taking a seat. "Do you know who I am?"

"Apparently you are the President of the United States," I say. "But I don't remember the inauguration parade. Personally I don't think it counts unless you have a parade."

"Oh, it counts," Mondello says. "It's just hard to spread the word nowadays."

"Tell me about it," I say.

"Before becoming Secretary of Homeland Security, I was the CEO of one of the largest construction businesses in the world," Mondello says, "which means, I don't need you to give me any pointers. I have come across situations you can't even think of. The problems you have caused are inconveniences, not roadblocks. I'll work them out, get the new plans to my crews, and we'll be back in business in the next three days."

"What business is that, Mr. President?" Leeds asks.

"Don't call him that," I say. I don't know why, but it really pisses me off that this guy thinks he's president of a government that doesn't exist. "That's all pre-Z. Different world now, different rules."

"Different world for you, maybe, Mr. Stanford," Mondello smiles as he leans back in his chair. "But for those of us that have been part of the larger world picture, this is just another chapter in this country's storied history."

"So when are elections?" I ask. "I didn't get the flyer in the mail. And I'm pretty sure my voter registration card was lost. You're not one of those voter ID nuts, are you? I don't even think I have a driver's license to show."

"Jace...," Leeds warns.

"No, Captain, don't 'Jace' me," I say. I can feel my blood getting hot and I have a choice to make, back off or keep going. My mouth makes the decision for me. "Listen, I'm sorry I fucked your plans up, Mr. Mondello, but I'm not buying this POTUS bullshit. I've been fighting for my family's lives and mine for years now, without help from the US government. I've done things that no self-respecting human being should ever have to do. I've seen things, memories of which I keep locked up in my brain so I don't curl up into a fetal position all day. And during all of this, there hasn't been one single hint that a government existed. Not. One. Hint."

I stand up and look at Leeds.

"Let's go. I'm done with this shit. I have a family to get home to."

"Sit down, Mr. Stanford," Mondello says quietly.

"No, I don't think so," I say. "If you are the President, as you say, then you believe in the rule of law. Are you going to shoot me if I don't sit down? Are you going to try me for sedition and hang me from the balcony out there? I don't think so."

"Jace, sit down," Leeds says, his hand clamping onto my arm.

I shake him off and start to walk away. "Fuck this," I shout. "I'm tired and hungry and worried about my family and friends. I want to get home and make sure they're okay. I want them to know I'm okay. That's my fucking worldview, Mr. Mondello. And that's all I want it to be. So go fuck yourself and your play government. I don't know what you are doing and I don't care as long as you leave me out of it."

"You'd like to see your family again, Mr. Stanford?" Mondello asks, a sly grin on his face. "That will be arranged."

"Fuck, Jace," Leeds says, getting to his feet. "You wouldn't listen."

Foster moves quickly, so do her guys, and Leeds and I are surrounded.

"Captain, last time I checked, you were still a member of the US Armed Forces, am I correct?" Mondello asks.

"Yes, sir, Mr. President," Leeds says.

"Then you have a choice to make, don't you?" Mondello says, pointing at me. "Do your job or join your friend."

"What the fuck does that mean?" I ask. "Do his job? What the fuck job is that?"

"Whatever the fuck I say," Mondello replies. "As Commander-in-Chief, it is his sworn duty to obey my orders. And my orders right now are to shut you the fuck up. With extreme prejudice."

"Extreme prejudice? Wasn't that a movie back in the '80's? Pretty sure it had Nick Nolte and Rip Torn in it," I reply. "I think it sucked."

"I have no idea what you are babbling about," Mondello says, turning away. "Foster, make sure Mr. Stanford is comfortable until end of shift. He'll be tonight's entertainment. I'm sure the crews and your people will enjoy the distraction."

"Mr. Stanford, if you will follow me," Foster says, her eyes on Leeds and not me. "Will this be a problem, Captain?"

Leeds takes a breath and looks over at me, shaking his head. "No, it won't be a problem."

"Good," Foster smiles. "Because you may or may not be surprised to know I have heard of your team. If half the stories are true, then I'd rather not have to deal with any shit from you."

"The stories are true," Leeds nods, "but you misunderstand."

"Excuse me?" Foster asks, stopping. Her eyes dart to her people. "Misunderstand what?"

"By what I mean when I say there won't be a problem," Leeds replies, and then smiles. And his smile is the creepiest of the day. And it has been a day of creepy smiles, believe me.

Mondello turns back to us just as Leeds makes his move. Oh, I get it! There's no problem because Leeds has decided to help me! Good for him! You know, I've always liked-

The next thought is knocked from my head by a very big fist to the back of my skull, as I watch Leeds duck under a swing from one of the muscle guys and come up with a jab to the throat. I fall to the floor hard, my head bouncing off the wood. And it's nice wood. Gorgeous floor. Maybe Stella and I should put hardwood floors in our house when we rebuild Whispering Pines. We always wanted hardwood floors, but just never got around to replacing the carp-

OW! FUCK!

Being kicked in the ribs sucks. OW! "Fucking stop!" I shout. Or think I do. The kicks take my breath away. So I probably just say, "Oooofy oof."

I try to curl up into a fetal position, but someone has my legs and they're dragging me across the gorgeous wood floor, while someone else keeps kicking me in the ribs and gut. Mother fuckers. Nice technique, though. I'll give them that.

And I puke.

It was expected, what with all the kicking.

"Jesus," the kicker says, "this is tonight's entertainment? Gonna be a short show."

I can hear men grunt in pain and I know Leeds is doing better than I am. I hear a man's cry cut short then a gunshot. Two more.

"Get up," Leeds says, suddenly standing over me. I look up and he has a pistol in each hand, covering the room. He taps me with his toe. "Get up, Jace. Now."

Painfully, I get to my feet, clutching my ribs and gut. My side, where I was shot by Vance's Desert Eagle a couple months ago, is on fire and I know Dr. McCormick is gonna be pissed if I reinjured myself. Not that I expect to live long enough for her to find out. The bajillion guns pointed at us will take care of that.

"Captain, put the weapons down," Mondello orders, "you can still salvage this."

"I don't think I can, sir," Leeds says, "because I have to agree with Stanford here. I don't think it counts if there isn't a parade."

I can't help but laugh at that. It's kinda cool when a Special Forces captain is standing there, a pistol in each hand, and uses your joke to make a point.

"Leeds," Foster warns, "I can take you out right now. I don't want to, though. ODA Cobra has quite a reputation. You and your men can do some good. We have room for you here. Put down the guns and we'll talk. No tricks, just soldier to soldier."

"Don't kid yourself, Ms. Foster," Leeds says. "I'm the only soldier in this room. You're just a bunch of mercenaries hired by a puppet."

"Oooh, wrong thing to say," Foster replies. "We don't like being called mercenaries. That's a four letter word in our business."

"It's an eleven letter word, to be exact," I state. "I wonder if it can be played in Scrabble? You'd have to connect it to another word, but I'm not sure what word that would-"

"Dear God, Jace," Leeds says.

"Sorry."

"What's the call, sir?" Foster asks.

"I'd rather they didn't die," Mondello says. "Can you take them down without killing them?"

"Consider it done," Foster says.

"Not without losing a few of your own," Leeds says. "Jace, slowly back to the door."

I do, but my progress is stopped quickly. I turn around and come face to chest with possibly the largest man I've ever seen. The fucker must be seven feet tall and almost as wide across.

"Oh, hey there," I say.

"Jace?" Leeds asks.

"I hit a mountain, Captain," I reply. "I have a feeling it may hit back."

Leeds risks a look over his shoulder. That's all that Foster needs. I hear a snap and then a crackling as Leeds falls to the ground, his body shaking uncontrollably, the pistols sliding across the floor. Two wires protrude from his chest and the smell of burning hair fills the lobby.

"Pick his ass up," Foster orders.

I think she's talking about Leeds, but turns out it's me as the mountain wraps an arm around my waist and lifts me up like I used to do to the kids when they were little. I'd fight, but have you ever tried to fight a mountain? Doesn't work.

"And drag that treasonous fucker with us. That's the second time today he's gotten a bead on me," Foster says. She gets right up in my face. "You're going to take a nap and when you wake up, you'll put on a show. Time to see what life amongst the zeds has taught you."

"It has taught me that dental hygiene is still appropriate," I reply. "Did you brush your teeth today? Because that's quite the stink mouth you've got going-"

The pistol butt to my head ends that conversation as I plummet into unconsciousness.

What brings me out is the soul piercing agony in my right hand.

"MOTHER FUCK!" I scream as I open my eyes. "HOLY FUCKER DICK SUCKING CUNT LICKER!"

"Damn," Foster says from a few feet away, "that's quite a mouth and I've been around the military my whole life."

A man is wrapping my right hand with a thick bandage. It hurts like hell, but in seconds, it's secured and basically immobile. The pain subsides a little and I raise the wrapped hand to my eyes, and then look at Foster

"Uh, thanks?" I say.

"Don't thank me yet," Foster smiles, "eat your dinner first."

A tray of food is on a side table next to the cot I'm lying on. We are in a small room, one of the guest rooms in the Grove Park Inn, but all the furniture has been cleared out to make room for cots. There are eight cots in total, but only two are occupied: one by me, and one by a still unconscious Leeds.

"He gonna get dinner too?" I ask.

"Later," Foster smiles. "Maybe. Depends."

"Depends on what?" I ask. The smell of the food, whatever it is, makes my stomach growl.

"Depends on how you perform tonight," Foster says. "Eat up. You'll need your strength." She walks to the door, but stops and nods at Leeds. "Watch him. It'll be time soon."

The four PCs in the room all nod. The man that wrapped my hand packs up supplies into a small pack and follows Foster out the door, leaving Leeds and me alone with the heavily armed guards.

I lean over, grab the plate of food, and sniff it. Chicken. With some bean mush and maybe what used to be greens. Maybe. Could be moldy bread.

"This isn't poisoned or drugged, is it?" I ask. The PCs don't answer, they just stare at Leeds. "Um, I'm awake and talking. Pretty sure I'm way more interesting than him."

Nothing.

"Fine, whatever," I say, pulling up my legs and steadying the plate against my knees with my wrapped hand. I pick up the plastic fork in my left and start to eat. "Hey...not...bad."

It is pretty bad. I lied. The shit tastes like, well, shit. God, are they feeding me shit? Is this some kind of private contractor joke? Feed the prisoner shit. I look around for video cameras to see if maybe they are watching me. Ha, ha, the fool ate shit, ha, ha.

However, there aren't any cameras, not that I can see, just four PCs watching the captain closely. I finish the food, despite my urge to vomit, since I need the nourishment. Something you learn during the apocalypse, is not to be too picky about what you eat and when. Sure, suburban living in Whispering Pines made things a little better, but you still didn't waste food there. Brown spots on the produce? You eat it. Chicken is stringy and flavorless? Eat. It.

As soon as I set the plate down, two of the men converge on me.

"Get up," one says, "time to go."

"Can I use the potty first?" I ask. "I'm pretty regular. Food goes in and shit comes out. That's just the way my bowels work. Although, considering what I just ate, I'd change that to shit goes in and shittier shit goes out."

The man points to the bathroom door. "Fast." I nod and walk into the bathroom. I try to shut the door, but a large hand stops it. "Door stays open."

"Right," I say. "That way I can't crawl down the drain or anything." I tap my temple. "Good thinking."

I do my business, which isn't easy with only one hand, and walk back into the room.

"Time to go," the man says again.

"Yep, got that," I say, looking at Leeds. "What about the captain?"

"Not time yet," the man says, "he'll be down soon."

We leave the room and skip the elevator, going straight for the service stairs. There are armed men at each floor and I smile at them as we pass. They don't smile back. Would it kill them if they did? I mean, really, come on, I'm smiling and I'm pretty sure I'm being taken to my death. They've got the guns! Be happy about it, for suck's sake!

"Stop daydreaming and move," the man says as he shoves me through a door and out into a service corridor. I can hear a low sound, like a beat, steady, and pounding.

"What is that?" I ask. No one answers. "Is that music?"

The sound gets louder and I can feel a vibration in my feet. What the fuck?

The mystery is revealed as I'm led outside and am instantly blinded by several sets of unbelievably bright work lights. You know the kind that light up constructions sites? Yeah, a bunch of those fuckers. Shielding my eyes with my bandaged hand, I'm shoved forward. The door behind me slams closed and I can hear the lock click.

It takes my eyes a minute to adjust and when I do, I realize I am in deep shit.

"Mr. Stanford, how are you tonight?" Mondello's voice calls from above me, barely heard above the noise. I try to find him, but can't see past the lights.

What I can see, is that I'm in a cleared out section of the grounds behind the Grove Park. A large circle of gravel has been set down and ringing that is a six-foot tall chain link fence. Steel supports brace the fence all around and I can sort of make out what look like bleachers beyond that. Which is where the sound is coming from.

Hundreds of people are seated and all clapping and stamping their feet.

I'm in a mother fucking fight cage. Or arena. Or whatever. Doesn't matter. I'm the gladiator and the plebs want a show. I wonder what Caesar wants?

"I've had better nights, I can tell you that," I say to Mondello. "You really need to speak to your cook. That meal did a number on my guts. I'm ten seconds from a serious shart mishap."

"Sorry to hear that," Mondello laughs. "You live and I'll make sure you get something better to eat."

"If I live?" I shout. "Jesus fuck, people! Will you knock it off with the We Are The Champions bit! I get it; you're excited to see a fight! Good for you!"

The clapping and stomping lessens considerably.

"You can really bring down a mood, Mr. Stanford," Mondello says.

"Oh, just call me Long Pork," I reply. "All my friends do, so my enemies might as well also."

"I'm not your enemy, Mr. Stanford," Mondello replies, "I'm your President."

A cheer goes up amongst the crowd.

"Do we really have to go through all that again?" I ask. "I have a feeling my time is short and I'd rather not waste it on politics."

"Well said," Mondello agrees, "then let's get this started."

"Get what started?" I ask. Then I see. "Oh…"

Part of the chain link parts and three Zs are shoved inside with me. The men that do the shoving hurry to close the chain link, jumping back when the Zs lunge towards them. The men start smiling and laughing, pointing at me. Great.

I quickly take in my surroundings. The earlier cursory observation turns into serious study. I have the following resources at my disposal: gravel, a chain link fence, a bladder that is now full of piss, even though I just went to the bathroom, and a healthy dose of pure terror. Only a couple of those things can help.

I pick up a handful of gravel, really wishing I had two hands to use. The Zs come right for me, no hesitation, and very little slow shambling. I can see they are pretty fresh; must have just turned today. Again, great.

I scramble to my right, tossing the gravel at the Zs, which does exactly zip to slow them down, but it makes me feel like I'm at least participating in my own death. Do your part before you die a horrible, screaming death, should be the official slogan of the apocalypse. There could be t-shirts and shit.

One of the Zs is faster than the others are and gets to me before I can dodge out of the way. Its hands grasp for me, but I knock them away, spinning around the thing and elbowing it in the back, sending it into the fence. Now, here's the problem with chain link fencing: it's got bounce.

So I send the Z into the fence and it just ricochets right off and back at me. We collide and fall to the ground in a pile of living and undead limbs. The monster's jaws snap at my face, but I shove it away, my fingers digging into its cheeks for purchase. It snarls at me as I roll over, pinning it down. I'm about to rip the fucking thing's face right off when Z fingers grab me from behind.

Oh, right, there're two more of the mother fuckers.

I jump back, using my momentum to send the Zs tumbling. I'm lucky and keep my balance, but not for long as a Z hand grips my ankle and pulls. I'm down on my face, gravel digging into my forehead, when I hear a thump. There, just a few feet away, is The Bitch.

"Thought you might like that," Mondello calls out. "Ms. Foster says her man, Jameson, took it off you."

Jameson? Does he mean Cowboy? Who cares, I have The Bitch back!

Now I just have to get to it before I die.

I flail, thrash, and manage to get the Z off me. Rolling over and over, I get close to The Bitch, but not close enough. My hand is inches from it when two Zs are on me. I just start punching and kicking. I connect with a Z and its head rocks back as I get my knees up under it and shove as hard as possible with my legs. The thing flies off me and I slam my elbow into the temple of the second Z. I hear a snap and the Z's head twists to the side, its neck broken. It falls on me and I'm pinned under undead weight. Of course, since I haven't destroyed the brain, the thing's jaws are still working, but at least the body isn't responding.

Barely managing to get the fucking thing off me, I roll once more and I have The Bitch! Then I don't, as I'm tackled by a Z, its teeth gnashing at my face as zombie spittle drips onto my cheek. Fucking gross, man! I slam my good hand against its head over and over and over, but the fucker won't die. Its teeth snag my shirt and I nearly freak out, as I feel it start to bite through the cotton and into my arm.

Adrenaline seriously kicks in and I let out a guttural scream, as I wrap the Z in my arms and roll. Now I'm on top, mother fucker! Despite the intense agony, I grab the Zs head with both hands and twist, breaking its neck and severing the spinal column. It looks up at me with its dead, grey eyes and hisses. Fuck that shit. I get to my feet and stomp the fucker until its skull is in pieces and zombie brains coat the gravel.

I walk over to the other Z and finish it off.

Now, where's the third one? Oh, here it comes.

I duck my shoulder and let the Z run right into me, then I stand up straight, sending the thing flipping over my back. It hits the gravel hard and roars with rage. Oh, did I make the Z angry? Poor widdle Z. Without hesitation, I turn its face into pulp, wiping my boot on the gravel as Z brain drips from the sole.

I walk over and pick up The Bitch, loving the familiar feel, even if it is in my left hand.

"Didn't even need it!" I shout. "How do you like that, asshole?"

The crowd is cheering and hollering at me; I guess I put on a nice show. It was only three Zs, after all. Sure, it got a little hairy, but I've faced worse. They'd have loved me with two working hands. What the fuck am I thinking? This shit is crazy! I really gotta find a way out of here…

"Did I pass the test?" I shout in the direction I think Mondello is. Hard to say with the lights blinding me.

"Test, Mr. Stanford? This isn't a test," Mondello replies. Still can't see the fucker. "This is a show. These people work hard all day long and deserve some entertainment. You've done a fine job so far."

"But there's more, right?" I ask. "The evening is still young and all that. The show must go on. Is that it? Haven't you heard the saying 'leave them wanting more'? I don't mind postponing the rest until tomorrow night. You should see me when I'm rested. I'll do this again and then you can let me and Leeds go. How's that sound? Two nights for the price of one."

"No, no, I don't think so, Mr. Stanford," Mondello laughs. "This is a one night engagement. You should feel honored; you get to perform in front of the President of the United States. Not many get that privilege."

"Oh, I'm not sure I call this privilege," I reply. "So what happens now? You keep sending Zs at me until I die, and then it's Leeds turn?"

"Why wait?" Mondello says. "I think Captain Leeds should have a turn now."

Good. Some backup. I could use it. Maybe while we fight the Zs together we can come up with some plan to get us the fuck out of this shitty situation. Come on, it can't end like this. Not fighting Zs like post-apocalyptic gladiators. I always thought I'd die in a blaze of glory, sacrificing myself to save my family. That's the way to go out, not this shit.

The chain link rattles and Leeds is shoved into the arena with me.

"What? He doesn't get a weapon?" I shout. "Afraid he'll use it against you once we're done killing all the Zs you throw at us?"

"You want him to have a weapon, Mr. Stanford?" Mondello asks.

"Uh, yeah, that's what I just said."

"Fine, he can have a weapon," Mondello says. "How does that sound, folks? Should we give Captain Leeds a weapon?" The crowd erupts into laughter. What the fuck are they laughing at? Is it some inside joke that I'm missing? "Sounds like they want Captain Leeds to have a weapon too, Mr. Stanford."

A large pipe is tossed into the arena, just feet from Leeds.

"Thanks. It's appreciated," I yell then look at Leeds. "Grab that, Captain. You're going to need it."

I grip The Bitch and wait for the next round of Zs. And wait. I look over at Leeds and see he's hanging his head and hasn't even moved an inch towards the pipe.

"Dude, grab that shit and get ready," I call to him.

Pain erupts in my right shoulder and I look down to see a crossbow bolt protruding from me. I pull it out and toss it onto the gravel. The wound isn't deep and the bolt wasn't barbed, but it still hurts.

"What the fuck, Mondello? Didn't think I was wounded enough?" I yell at him.

"Oh, I just needed to motivate Captain Leeds," Mondello says. "They can get so confused when they are fresh. That bit of humanity that still lingers in the synapses."

"What the hell are you…talking…about…?" I say then look closely at Leeds.

His head *was* hanging down, but as soon as the crossbow bolt hits the gravel, it snaps up. His grey eyes lock onto the bolt then he starts to sniff the air. I look at the stain of blood on my shoulder then back at Leeds. His grey eyes are on me.

His dead, grey eyes.

"No, no, no," I whisper. "Please no. Why? Why him?" I begin to shake, a fury like I've never felt before growing in me.

"YOU FUCKS!" I scream. "YOU CRAZY FUCKS! NOT HIM! HE WAS THE GOOD GUY!" My chest hitches as I struggle to get control of myself. "He was my friend…"

And my friend is hungry. For me.

Leeds sprints towards me. He doesn't shamble or shuffle, but sprints. I guess that's what happens when a trained soldier is freshly turned. His body hasn't had a chance to atrophy and rigor mortis hasn't damaged the muscles yet.

The Bitch feels like a ten-ton weight in my hand as I watch Leeds close the distance between us. Mondello, and the crowd are laughing their asses off. I hear the pure joy in their voices, knowing the joke is on me. Ha, ha, ha, mother fuckers. I get out of this and you're all going to die.

I get set and swing out with The Bitch, but Leeds dodges it easily and skids to a stop in the gravel, just feet from me. He watches me hungrily, but he doesn't attack. Somewhere up in that undead brain, he's actually making connections. I've never seen a Z act like this before. Sure, I've been around fresh ones, but there was never any significant cognitive function. Not this way.

I make a mental note to remember that trained killers like Leeds make for really scary Zs.

A low growling comes from Leeds throat and he begins to circle around me, his eyes darting from me to The Bitch. The mother fucker is stalking me! And watching my weapon while doing it. Jesus H. Pooping Christ.

I hoist The Bitch above my head one handed, turning myself to the side so I present a smaller target. Uh, did that just make Leeds smile? Is that a smile on a fucking Z's face? Just when I thought the whole creepy military smile couldn't get creepier, it does. Fucking A.

"Come on, Captain," I say. "Come at me. Let's get this done."

And he does. In a burst of speed, he closes the distance between us. I barely have time to bring The Bitch down. It only grazes him across the back as he tackles me about the waist, sending us both flying through the air, and then skidding across the gravel. I can feel rocks rip through my shirt and into my back.

The smell of blood makes Leeds crazy, but in a good way. He seems to lose control and just starts thrashing on me. I slam my fist into his jaw again and again, giving me time to get a knee under him. I lift and get some space between us. He roars and spits, his hands clawing at me, his jaws chomping on air over my face. I try to shove him off with my leg, but his fingers grip my shirt and he pulls himself down closer. It's a battle of wills as I am barely able to keep him at bay with my leg.

Fuck it.

I start boxing his head with both hands, screaming each time my right hand smashes into him. Leeds tries to shake it off, but I keep at it, knocking that Z brain of his around, sending it bouncing back and forth against the inside of his skull. It doesn't quell his Z rage, but it does disorient him enough that he loses focus. I shove hard with my leg and he tumbles off me.

Rolling, rolling, rolling, I put space between us. And The Bitch. Which sucks. Dammit.

I get to my feet just as he does, and I start to run. I mean fuck it, why not? Around and around in circles we go, me running for my life, him running for a meal. The crowd begins to boo at the lack of action. And I thought this was North Carolina? The home of NASCAR? Don't these fuckers like watching people go around and around and around, over and over and over? It's the Apocalypse 500, y'all!

The running in circles is making me dizzy, or that could be blood loss from my shoulder, and I stumble just enough for Leeds to catch up to me. His hands grab my shoulders and he brings me down like a mother fucking undead lion does to a gazelle. I don't really want to be the gazelle in this scenario. Not that there's *any* scenario where I'd want to be the gazelle.

I use our momentum and tuck my shoulder, sending us into a rolling dive. Leeds ends up on his back, under me, but his head is close enough that I feel the air tickle my ear hairs, as his jaws chomp closed. I slam my elbow into his face and shove myself to my feet, screaming again as I put all my weight on my broken hand.

Holding my hand to my chest, I book ass to The Bitch, scooping it up just as Leeds gets up and comes at me. I don't stop, I don't think, I just swing. And connect. I feel the spikes dig into the soft flesh of his cheek and I pull back, shredding his face.

The crowd goes, "Ooooooooooooohhhhhh!" then erupts into cheers. Guess they liked that. Fuckers.

Leeds hisses at me, but that's all he gets to do as I swing again, shredding the other cheek. Then again, ripping the top of his scalp off. He staggers back, regroups, and lunges for me. But I've got him figured out. The Bitch connects solidly with the top of his head and he stops in his tracks. His grey eyes find mine and for a split second, I think I see the real Leeds. Then he falls to his knees, The Bitch still embedded in his skull; he grunts and crumples to his side.

Leeds is dead. Totally dead.

The crowd is stamping their feet and slapping their hands together. I can just see them past the lights and their faces are filled with bloodlust and violence. And I get it. I understand what this is all about. Mondello keeps them wanting death, craving to see it played out night after night. That way when they experience it during the day, whether by accident or possibly on purpose, they are desensitized; it means nothing.

No wonder the Romans lasted as long as they did. Not a bad strategy.

While not a bad strategy, it is an evil one. I bend down and yank The Bitch from Leeds's skull. It makes a cracking noise as bone splinters under his scalp. I'll remember that sound the rest of my life.

"That all you got, asshole?" I yell as I walk to the center of the arena, spinning around, looking as many people in the eye as I can. "Some pitiful Zs and an old soldier? You think that's what will take me down? Do you, motherfucker? DO YOU?"

The crowd quiets down, all waiting for Mondello's response.

"Well done, Mr. Stanford," he says and I can hear his mocking golf clap. "I honestly didn't think you'd take him. I've watched freshly turned soldiers decimate entire groups of people; they are something to see. But you handled Leeds like a pro. I have underestimated you, and I apologize for that."

The crowd is now silent. Pretty sure they've never heard the cocksucker apologize before.

"I don't accept your apology," I say.

"Nor would I expect you to," Mondello responds, "but, out of respect for your performance tonight, I will agree to your previous request."

"You're letting me go?" I ask. "Great. It was fun. Seriously. We'll do it again sometime."

"Okay, okay," Mondello laughs, "maybe not your full request. But I will let you live, and get a good night's rest, before I put you back in there tomorrow night. How does that sound?"

The crowd begins to chant my name, "Loooong Pooooork! Looooong Poooork!"

Awesome…

"And what happens tomorrow night?" I yell over the crowd.

"That, Mr. Stanford, is entirely up to you," Mondello replies, his voice barely audible over the chanting.

CHAPTER FIVE

They try to use only melee weapons, knowing stealth and silence are the best way to get through downtown, but as the Zs keep coming, they have to switch to firearms, which mean noise, and more Zs.

"I'm out!" one of Critter's men shouts, the slide on his pistol locking back, just before his arm is flayed open by Z teeth. "AAAAAAAAAAA!"

He falls under one then two, three, four Zs, his screams mixing with the hisses and groans of the undead that surround the group.

Elsbeth dances, like a deadly dervish made of anger and sharp steel, cutting down Z after Z that gets in her path. A blade in each hand, she slices off heads, splitting them in two before they touch the ground. She shoves a blade deep into the guts of a Z and yanks up, dissecting the thing up the middle, right through its chest, neck, and skull. Without hesitating, she turns about and pierces the ocular cavity of a Z that is reaching for her.

"I need ammo!" another of Critter's men yells. He slams the empty pistol into the face of a Z, hoping to kill it, but instead, killing himself as the Zs teeth shred the flesh off one of his fingers. He pushes the thing away and pulls the hand to his chest. "I been kilt!"

Critter doesn't waiver one bit and puts a bullet in the man's brain. The body drops to the ground and he kicks it with his foot, sending it rolling down the sidewalk towards more Zs. They jump on the still warm body and begin to rip the flesh off it with their teeth and hands, jamming as much meat into their undead mouth as can fit. Most don't bother to chew, just swallow the bites whole, going in for more.

"Here," John calls out from a side alley, as he kicks in the back door to one of the many businesses that once populated the vibrant downtown of Asheville, North Carolina. "Come on!"

Critter doesn't wait and sprints his way to John. He slaps John on the shoulder and ducks inside, turning to say, "Lay down some fire and get her out of there!"

John takes aim with his rifle, and despite the darkness, takes out six Zs before Elsbeth gets the hint and runs towards him. Critter's men follow, but only two make it, the others getting a few feet before being cut off by swarming Zs. John doesn't bother to look back as they scream and plead for help, he just hurries the two men inside and slams the door shut.

Critter is already there with furniture to barricade the door. He hands it to John and they both secure the entrance before turning and heading up the narrow stairway behind them.

"Where's Elsbeth?" John asks, but doesn't wonder for long as a body falls from a floor above, banging and smashing against the railing on its way down. "Oh."

"Clear up here now," Elsbeth says, peeking over and waving at them.

"Jesus that girl is strange," Critter says as they take the steps two at time.

Instead of stopping on the floor Elsbeth is on, John proceeds up one more flight of stairs and onto the roof. He sprints to the side and looks down, taking aim with his rifle. Two shots and the men suffering below are no more.

"That was nice of you," Elsbeth says from the door to the stairs.

"A waste of ammo, if you ask me," Critter says, right behind her.

"I didn't ask you," John says. "And I'd hope you waste a bullet on me one day if it comes to it."

Critter just shrugs.

"Are we sleeping inside, or up here?" Elsbeth asks.

"Sleeping? How the fuck can you sleep with those things down there?" one of the men asks.

"I curl up and put my arms under my head," Elsbeth responds, "then I close my eyes. How do you sleep with those things down there?"

"Fucked up, man," the man says, turns, and walks back down the stairs.

The other man looks from Critter to John to Elsbeth and back. "So? Where are we sleeping?"

A scream below sends them rushing inside.

Elsbeth and John look over the railing and can see the first man struggling with a Z two floors below.

"I thought you cleared it?" John says.

"Me too," Elsbeth answers.

"Guess we're sleeping on the roof," Critter says. "I'd love to find a blanket or two, but maybe that ain't such a good idea."

They all head back up, shutting the door behind them. John looks around, but there's nothing to barricade the door with.

"We keep watch," John says. "Two at a time so that way we don't risk someone falling asleep. Two hour shifts. No one's eyes stray from that door."

"I'll take first watch," Critter says. "Who's gonna join me?"

"Elsbeth?" John asks, then sees the young woman curled up all the way across in a corner of the roof, her eyes closed and arms under her head. "I'll join you then. Let your guy here get a little sleep."

"That means I have to stand watch with her," the man says.

"I hire only fucking geniuses," Critter snorts.

***

The gunshots get louder and louder as Melissa and her brothers make their way through the underground cave that connects to a secret entrance inside the Farm. The entire acreage is surrounded by row after row of barbed and concertina wire, so there are only a couple ways in and out other than the main entrance used by vehicles. But that entrance is under siege as the convoy of trucks that passed them earlier in the day tries to push into the Farm.

"Sounds like Daddy is making a stand," Pup says.

"Or trying to," Buzz replies.

"Hush now," Melissa scolds them, "focus."

They get to the door that leads them into the Farm proper and Melissa instinctively finds the latch that's hidden in the rock wall. With a sharp click, the door swings open and the Fitzpatricks hurry through, their weapons ready. After following a long, curving stone corridor, they come to a set of stairs that leads them up into a small, stone shed. They all hurry through and burst into the barnyard.

Fire is everywhere and those that aren't fighting it with hoses and buckets, are fighting the armed men that have abandoned their trucks and are now rushing up the road towards the farmhouse. Melissa puts her rifle to her shoulder and squeezes off round after round as she runs towards the fighting, while trying to ignore the chaos about her.

Pup and Porky follow her, almost mirroring her step for step, but Buzz dashes off to the back of the farmhouse and into the huge kitchen.

"Daddy!" he shouts.

"On the porch!" Stella cries as she huddles with Greta and Charlie by the iron stove.

Buzz looks around and realizes that most of the children that live on the Farm are all inside the kitchen. Probably the safest place for them, he thinks.

"Ya'll stay here," he says, "don't you dare go outside."

"Wasn't thinking of it," Stella says.

"I want to fight," Charlie shouts. "I can shoot. Give me a rifle and I'll kill some of those mother fuckers!"

"You're staying here with your mother, young man," Buzz orders. "You want to shoot?" He pulls a pistol from his belt. "You shoot this. You kill anyone that comes in this kitchen that you don't know. Got it?"

"Got it," Charlie says as he takes the pistol in both hands.

"Safety's on the side," Buzz says, "but be careful, hear me? Don't shoot yourself or any of these kids."

Charlie nods as Buzz runs from the kitchen. He ducks down in a crouch when plaster kicks up by his head as a bullet just misses him. More bullets slam into the wall and Buzz hits the ground, crawling elbow over elbow into the front room.

"There ya are," Big Daddy says from the front window, a rifle to his shoulder. "Your brothers and sister with ya?"

"Yes, sir," Buzz replies. "They're outside in the thick of it."

"Well, I'd be there with them, but I decided to wrassle with a bullet and lost," Big Daddy says.

Buzz can see a dark stain on his father's thigh.

"Ain't nothing but a muscle wound," Big Daddy says, seeing the look on Buzz's face. "Missed the artery. I'll be just fine once I get stitched up."

"Which he won't let me do," Dr. McCormick says from a corner of the room, her hands blood deep in a woman's belly. There are more wounded lying about being tended to by whoever is at hand. "Stubborn old bull."

"You got more important business, doc," Big Daddy says, ducking as a round of slugs slam into the house just outside the window. "Keep that one alive, if you can."

"That's what I'm trying to do," Dr. McCormick snaps. "Not exactly ideal circumstances."

"No, 'spect it ain't," Big Daddy says.

"Ha, your accent gets thicker when you're in pain," Buzz says, crouching next to his father. "Sure you're okay?"

"I'm fine, son. Don't bother about me."

"Fine, I'll take your word for it. How many out there?"

"We counted at least thirty," Big Daddy says. "I think we whittled them down to a dozen or so."

"How many of ours have we lost?"

"More than I'd like," Big Daddy says.

"Fifteen at last count," Dr. McCormick says. "Three children."

"Mother Mary," Buzz says. "Can we hold them?"

"Well, your brothers are out there now trying to flank them," Big Daddy says, "while we keep them distracted up here. Where do you want to be?"

"Sir?"

"You want to help with the distraction or you want in the thick of it?"

"This is the thick of it," Dr. McCormick says as a geyser of blood spurts from the woman's abdomen. "Mother fucking piece of shit!"

"Doctor, language," Big Daddy says.

"Fuck your language!" Dr. McCormick says. "I lost her!"

The doctor shoves the corpse away and turns on her knee, ready for the next person. She dives right in, not bothering with new gloves. In the zombie apocalypse, blood transmitted diseases are the least of one's worries.

"I better get out there," Buzz says. "You've got enough in here."

Buzz works his way back through the house and out the kitchen, giving a thumbs up to Charlie as he goes by. Mainly because he's glad Charlie doesn't accidentally shoot him.

He steps outside and finds Emmanuel Fertig waiting for him, AR-15 in hand. Manny, as he's known, is a tall black man, in his late thirties and in good shape. He and his family have been staying on the Farm since just after Z-Day. Being good friends, it's a nice surprise for Buzz to see him with a big smile on his face.

"Hey, Manny. Sarah and the kids safe?" Buzz asks.

"They are," Manny replies. "Got them holed up in one of the bunkers out in field six."

"Good. What's with the shit eating grin?"

"Don't let your daddy hear you cussing like that," Manny smiles wider. "I think I found their weak spot. Care to join me?"

"Gladly," Buzz says.

They hurry around the farmhouse and back to the stone shed that leads down to the secret entrance in and out of the Farm. Two of Buzz's brothers are waiting for them, rifles ready.

"Gunga, Toad," Buzz nods. The two men, just as big as Buzz, nod back.

"They look like pros, but they don't know shit about the way these hills work. They're thinking linearly. We don't have to," Manny says.

"Show me the way," Buzz says. "We don't need more men?"

"Nah," Manny smiles.

***

I know someone is there without opening my eyes. Living post-Z tends to heighten the senses. But I keep my eyes closed and listen, waiting to see if I can catch any info before the nightmare begins again. My thoughts drift back to Leeds and what I had to do; what Mondello made me do.

President of the United States, my dick. More like President of the Sick Fuckers Union. And that's a pretty fucking big union these days.

"Please open your eyes, Stanford," Foster says. "Your breathing changed exactly two minutes ago. I know you are awake."

"Oh, hey there," I say, opening my eyes and squinting against the harsh sunlight coming in through the windows. I'm back in the same room as before, all alone, strapped to a cot. And my head is killing me almost as much as my hand. "When's breakfast?"

"I have to hand it to you, Stanford," Foster says, "you are something else. Just killed your friend, got the fuck all beaten out of you, and you still find time for sarcasm. That's quite a defense mechanism."

"It's my defense mecha- Oh, right, you just said that," I say. "Way to steal my thunder, Ms. Foster."

"I thought I'd give you a chance to make things right," Foster says. "We are having a tiny bit of a problem with your people out at that farm."

"The Farm," I say.

"Yeah, I just said that."

"No, no, it's the Farm. Big F. Around here, there's only one Farm now."

Foster tilts her head and looks at me strangely. "Why does that matter?"

"Because it matters to Big Daddy," I say, "and he's probably the closest thing to a real President that we have. If it matters to him, then it matters to me."

"Interesting," Foster nods. "So how about a little help then?"

"I'm thinking...no," I reply. "Nothing personal."

"It's very personal to all those poor people you know that are getting slaughtered right now," Foster says. "You help me and I'll make sure no one else is hurt from here on out." She pulls a radio from her belt. "I just give the order and my men stand down, give your people some time to tend to their wounded and get their things in order before we move in."

"Getting your ass kicked, huh?" I smile. Which hurts a lot. "Why else would you need me to help? Let me guess, you want to know another way into the Farm. You're getting picked apart left and right and you can't figure out how. Can I tell you a secret?"

"Sure, please do," Foster says.

"That's how it's supposed to work," I say. "Big Daddy figured out the Z issue right away. You been out to the Farm?"

"I've done some recon."

"Then you know that the Zs can't get through all the fences. You also know there's enough of them at those fences to deter people from trying to get through. You probably tried a frontal assault through the main driveway and then realized just how boxed in you were, right?"

Foster doesn't say anything.

"Then, once my friends had cut your friends down to a manageable size, the flanking attacks began. Am I close?"

"Close," she nods.

"And just minutes before I woke up, you received a report that all of your friends had been overrun and were just trying to get out of there with their skin intact. Now you think you can trick me into giving you information that I don't need to give you, because you have nothing to offer."

"Not so close anymore," Foster smiles. "You're thinking small, Stanford."

"Am I?"

"You are thinking guns and bullets. Which, you are correct, didn't work. But now I'm moving on to the next level. Rockets and fire." She smiles big at the look on my face. "You're smart, I'll give you that, but you aren't a soldier. Leave the warfare to the professionals, Stanford. We're much better at it."

"What are you going to do?" I ask, thinking of Stella and the kids.

"Blow the ever loving fuck out of that farm. Little F, because I don't give a ffffffffffffuck. Whatever is left after the wave of RPGs will be scorched from this earth as we set fire to every single field on that farm. Again little ffffffffffff."

She leans forward in her chair and grabs my bandaged hand. Then squeezes. I'd be lying if I said I didn't scream.

"All President Mondello wanted to do was secure the farm and its resources for our work crews," Foster says. "No one had to die. No one else has to now. Just give us a way in and we'll make sure every single person still alive, stays that way."

"Did you think of asking?" I say. "Maybe send one guy up there to knock on the door?"

"Let's not be naïve, Stanford. I'm sure you know what immanent domain is."

"I'm sure you know what a crock of shit is," I counter. "You should, because one just fell out of your mouth. Go fuck yourself, Ms. Foster. And tell Mondello he can too. Fuck himself, not fuck you. I don't condone necrophilia."

Foster smirks and nods. "Good one. But you can tell President Mondello yourself. I just thought I'd give you a chance."

She gets up and goes to the door. A beefy guard opens it for her. "All yours, sir," she says as she walks past Mondello.

The door closes behind her and the guard follows Mondello right up to my cot. Foster could easily handle herself with me, but it looks like Mondello isn't so sure about his chances. That's one way to boost my spirits.

"Not going to cooperate?" Mondello asks me as he pulls the chair back from the cot a couple feet. "May I ask why?"

"Do you really need to?"

"No, I suppose not," Mondello says. "Ms. Foster told you our plans to destroy the farm?"

"She did."

"And that doesn't bother you?"

"Yeah, it bothers the fuck out of me. But that doesn't matter. You're not going to let anyone on the Farm live anyway."

"That's where you're wrong, Mr. Stanford," Mondello says. "I will let everyone live. They are way more valuable alive than dead."

He shifts in his chair and smiles at me.

"Would you like to know why?"

"Would you like to take a flying fucking leap out that window and kiss your ass on the way down?"

"I'll tell you anyway," he replies. "The world hasn't changed as much as you think since Z-Day. It just reverted to times in human history thought to be long behind us. Do you know what the most valuable resource on this planet is right now and always has been, Mr. Stanford?"

"I'm sure you'll tell me."

"Oh, be a sport and play along. Take a guess."

"Fuck you."

"Close. It has to do with the outcome of that. Still don't want to play? Fine. It's people. People have been this planet's most valuable resource since the species first started walking upright. Think of it, Mr. Stanford. All of the innovations people have made."

"I'm thinking more of the atrocities they have perpetrated."

"Captain Leeds was a soldier. He had one duty and that was to obey orders. Sedition is a capital offense. He made his choice and it was out of my hands."

"What about the people at the Farm? Are they being seditious too?"

"Them? No, they just have what we need."

"Right. Food and water. Building materials. Fuel. All that good stuff that makes dictatorships run."

"I thought you were so much smarter than that, Mr. Stanford," Mondello says, shaking his head. "I'm basically spelling it out for you and you're still thinking small. Yes, food, water, fuel, all of that is helpful. But you know what I really need?"

Shit. I get it. Yeah, I know what he needs.

"People," I reply.

"People," he nods, "exactly."

That slave comment Foster made back in East Asheville by the Parkway entrance comes back to me. Jesus. The workers haven't been hired to repair the Blue Ridge Parkway, they've been conscripted, enslaved. Foster and her people are here to keep them in line, not protect them from the Zs. What. The. Fuck.

Then I have to laugh.

"What's so funny, Mr. Stanford? Please let me in on the joke," Mondello says.

"It's just that you are thinking too big," I say. "You're thinking about the human race over the millennia, when you should be thinking just a couple centuries; not even that. Care for a history lesson a little more recent?"

"Of course," Mondello says, "educate me."

"Did you know that North Carolina had the highest percentage of Union soldiers of all the Southern states during the civil war?" I ask.

"I didn't know that, no."

"Did you know that the majority of those soldiers came from Western North Carolina? And that those that didn't join up hid up here in the mountains, refusing to fight for either side? How about the fact that Western North Carolina hid more escaped slaves than any other region in the South?"

"All fascinating, Mr. Stanford, but not really relevant to today."

"I beg to differ, Tony," I say. "You don't mind if I call you Tony, do you?"

"I do mind," Mondello says, his smile gone, "Mr. President is more appropriate."

"Well, Tony, did you also know that bootlegging began in the late 1800's up here in the mountains? Not during Prohibition, like everyone thinks, but decades before that? It started when the US government issued a tax on all liquor, including homemade stills. That's where 'Revenuers' came from. Agents of the Department of Revenue came up here and tried to enforce the tax. How do you think they made out?"

He doesn't answer.

"They tried hard, but in the end, it proved too costly to fight all the moonshiners. The people up here are resourceful and they don't take kindly to anyone, especially the government, telling them what to do. When Prohibition finally came about, the hollers here were ready for it; there were more stills in these mountains producing liquor than anywhere else in the country. The Department of Revenue thought they could outgun the moonshiners. Not so much. Then they thought they'd chase them down on their delivery routes and confiscate their vehicles and cargo. Know where I'm going with this?"

"I have a feeling."

"Good. Is it a sinking feeling? A feeling of dread? Because it should be. Remember that NASCAR thing pre-Z? Yeah, came out of the bootleggers and moonshiners modifying their cars so they could outrun the Revenuers. Started a multibillion dollar racing industry. Changed the world."

"I'm familiar with the history of NASCAR, Mr. Stanford."

"All of that, from bootlegging in the 1800s, to running moonshine in the 1920s, was done by simple folks, most of whom didn't have a day of formal education. But they had guts, and drive, and a burning need to be free and independent. Just like today. And guess what?"

"What, Mr. Stanford?"

"The people left today do have education. They grew up knowing about the world, technology, and concepts their ancestors couldn't dream of. And they have been fighting to stay alive for years against a menace that doesn't give two shits about what's in their head or hearts except for the tasty meat and blood that make them up. Do you, and tell me honestly, do you really believe you will convince any of them to be your slave willingly? For what? What can you possibly offer them?"

Mondello is quiet for a long time. Long enough for me to get slightly nervous. Shit, did I over play my hand? Did I go too far and embarrass him enough that he'll have the hulk behind him put a bullet in my brain?

"What can I possibly offer? Is that the question?" Mondello finally asks.

"It was kinda rhetorical," I say.

"Well, it shouldn't be," Mondello says. "Are you comfortable, Mr. Stanford? I hope so. You should settle in because now I'm going to tell you my story."

He takes a deep breath and begins.

"Do you know how far down the totem pole I am in the line of succession? The bottom, pretty much. That means everyone above me had to die for me to become President. Not how I wanted it. Actually, I never wanted it. I was happy serving my time as Secretary of Homeland Security. A couple more years and I would semi-retire and rake in the cash on speaking tours, commencement speeches, and possibly a book or two. I'd worked my way up from laying concrete to CEO of one of the largest construction companies in the world. I was ready to relax.

"But, as you know, that wasn't to be. I watched friends, family, and colleagues die horrible deaths. I watched this nation, and the world, crumble. And I had a front row seat. I wasn't some junior senator or congressman, I was Secretary of Homeland Security. That meant I was right there, every step of the way, as the zeds slowly began to win. We threw everything we had at them. By the time we realized numbers were against us, and it was too late to think of the nuclear option, the President was dead and so was her entire cabinet. Congress was massacred on Bloody Wednesday. You know how? Three fat fucks had heart attacks on the same day. They couldn't take the stress. They turned and then turned everyone around them."

Mondello shakes his head.

"We had DC locked down. We had the Capitol building locked down. The zeds may have been winning in the suburbs, but on Capitol Hill, we had them beaten. But that's not how this all works. It isn't us versus them, Mr. Stanford. Know why? Because we ARE them! I kill you now and leave your brain intact and you come back as a zed. You, me, every human being on this planet! We. Are. Them."

"Yeah, I know, trust me," I reply. The look of pure rage on his face tells me he was expecting a different answer.

Mondello gets himself under control and continues, "Of course you do, Mr. Stanford. You're one of the few that has survived and adapted. We've been watching what you were trying to accomplish in your little Whispering Pines. It was impressive. Until that buffoon Vance fucked it all up."

"Wait...you know Vance?" I ask.

"In a way," Mondello says. "There is a business group, a Consortium, if you will, that came together soon after Z-Day. While the US government was busy either tucking its tail between its legs or bickering about who was in charge, they were busy securing resources and the means to survive, and then rebuild once the ashes had settled."

"A Consortium?" I ask. Critter and Big Daddy had mentioned there might be others working with Vance, but I thought more along the lines of criminals, mob bosses, that kind of shit.

"These men and women have been behind most of the big moves this country has made the past few decades," Mondello says. "Oh, I don't have to tell you that this is strictly between us, right? Not to leave this room?"

"Yeah, sure, whatever," I say. He's going to kill me so saying that was just BS to try to get me to relax. How this guy was in charge of anything, I don't know.

"Good...good," Mondello says. He rubs his brow and I can watch the emotions play across his face. "Where was I?"

"Consortium," I prompt.

"Exactly," Mondello says. "The US has always been about business. Even your example of the history around here proves that. The US government wanted in on the moonshine business and the moonshiners didn't want that. Well, the Consortium didn't spend their entire lives building their empires of business to have it all come crumbling down because of some walking corpses. Not these folks, Mr. Stanford."

"So, what, are you their puppet?"

"Puppet? Hardly! I'm the President of the United States. And just like every President before me, I'm a facilitator. Do you think roads were built so everyday people could drive around where and when they wanted? Do you think the interstate highway system; Hoover damn, the Keystone pipeline, any of that happened for the common man and woman? I certainly hope not. All of that happened because business wanted it to happen. Do you remember the dismantling of the educational system that was happening just before Z-Day?"

"Sure, my wife is a teacher," I reply, "it was bullshit."

"Not if you wanted an ignorant, pliable work force that didn't have the education or context to understand just how doomed they were," Mondello smiles. "Keep them dumb and broke and you have democratic, capitalistic slavery at its finest. The wheels were already turning, Mr. Stanford. Z-Day just got rid of the pretext and brought the agenda out in the open."

"I still don't see what that has to do with you," I say. "Or with the Blue Ridge Parkway."

"Oh, that's simple," Mondello laughs. "The Parkway is an almost direct route from Charlottesville, which is where the new capital of the United States is, down to Atlanta, which is where the new center of business is."

"Wait…what?" I ask. "Atlanta is a wasteland. The place is nothing but Zs."

"Really? Have you been there since Z-Day?" Mondello asks, a sly smile on his face. "You've seen it yourself?"

"Well…no."

"Then you are only repeating to me what the Consortium wants repeated. Quote un quote 'survivors' were sent out as far as they could get to tell people to stay away from Atlanta. Woe unto those that venture into the Hell of that city! Nothing but the undead everywhere!" Mondello starts laughing. "It was just too easy."

"Jesus…"

"Yep," Mondello says, wiping tears from his eyes. "Atlanta never fell. It came close, but it survived. The Consortium is based there and they need a working supply line between Atlanta and Charlottesville. They also need a safe travel route. The Blue Ridge Parkway is perfect. Sure, there's some space between it and Atlanta that still has to be dealt with, but that will happen. For now, we are clearing and repairing the Parkway. Pretty easy since it is so remote. Not many Zeds except for tourists trapped in their RVs and the stray hiker or camper. Almost impossible for herds to get to because of the mountains. The perfect trade route."

"And Asheville is the perfect base to set up operations and repair and maintain the Parkway," I say.

"Yes, it is. Which is why we went into business with Vance. He was going to secure Asheville for us."

"But you didn't count on the crazy," I smile.

"Oh, on the contrary, we factored that in," he answers. "Trust me, you don't make plans post-Z and forget about the crazy. We just didn't know the crazy would get him killed so quickly. And unite all of you fine folks. That's the real issue."

"Because you wanted us beaten and broken so you could swoop in and show us a 'better' way," I say.

"Now you're getting it," Mondello says, touching his finger to his nose.

"Slave labor to rebuild the country in the image the Consortium had been planning on in the first place," I say. "I do get it. And the US government-" I use air quotes on that one. "-makes sure the infrastructure is in place to make it all happen."

87

"You are smart, Mr. Stanford."

"So now what? You kill me?"

"Kill you?" Mondello asks, truly puzzled. "Why would I do that?"

"Isn't that how it goes? The bad guy fills the good guy in on his plans since he's going to kill him anyway?"

"Well, the first flaw in that assumption is that I'm the bad guy," Mondello laughs. "The second flaw is that you are trying to apply what happens in the movies to what happens in real life. Killing you, after I have spent all this time and energy educating you, would be a massive waste. I have zero intention of killing you, Mr. Stanford. I'm going to keep you alive as long as I can."

"Then I guess I'm not as smart as you think, because I'm lost here."

"Oh, I'm going to kill your family. One at a time. Unless you agree to help me take that farm and secure those resources we need to finish our job with the Parkway. That is why I told you everything. I wanted you to have that big picture in your head so you know that even if you kill me, which is possible, and somehow manage to stop Foster and her people, which is the real hard part, you're only chopping off heads of the hydra. And there are so many more heads to replace us."

At this point, I am glad I haven't had breakfast. I can feel the bile build up in my stomach and I want nothing more than to turn my head and puke. Mondello sees this and that smile takes over his face. He pats me on the leg and stands up.

"I'll let you think it over," he says as he walks to the door. "Someone will bring you food soon and you're welcome to take a shower. I'll have Foster's people find you some fresh clothes. You have today to run it over in your head. I expect an answer by this evening."

"You have my family?" I ask.

"No, not yet," he says, "but it won't be hard to get to them. Your people on that farm are probably pretty proud of themselves. Maybe too proud. They'll be exhausted, scared, confused, and many will be over confident." He stops, his hand on the door handle. "The perfect recipe for extraction. Don't forget, Mr. Stanford, while Foster is the expert, I was Secretary of Homeland

Security. I know how to acquire assets and how to use them. It was my job after all."

Then he's gone, leaving me to my physical pain and my emotional turmoil.

I get up, slowly, since I feel like I've been hit by a truck, and go to the window. It's locked and secured and three stories up. I'm not getting out that way. I have some skills, but scaling the rock and brick face of a hotel is not one of those skills.

I look out at the Grove Park grounds and watch as dozens of people hustle about. Foster's private contractors, construction crews gearing up, obvious administrative types working for Mondello, all the cogs in the machine.

And fuck, it sounds like quite the machine.

A knock at the door makes me turn, which I regret as I twist something in my side. I'm a fucking mess, as usual.

"Food and clothing," Foster says.

"Didn't expect you to deliver it personally," I reply.

"Go take a shower and then let's talk," Foster says.

"About?"

She shrugs and motions towards the bathroom.

I'm not one to argue against a free shower. So I take the clothes and step in. I try to close the door, but she blocks it with her foot.

"I'd feel better with this open," she says. "I won't look, I promise. Just don't want you using that brain of yours without supervision."

"Well that brain of mine, as you all keep calling it, isn't running at full steam right now," I reply. "I think you're safe."

"I'm never safe," she says, then walks away, out of sight.

I turn the water on and wait for it to get hot. And wait. And wait. Fuck.

"No hot water?" I call out.

"You have to be up earlier than this," she says from the room. "Only two boilers working at a time. It helps motivate the crews in the morning. First ones up get hot water and bigger portions. You should see the lines."

"Great," I mutter.

"What was that?"

"Nothing," I reply.

Cold shower it is. I suffer through, still glad to get the dirt and blood washed off me. There was a lot of blood. I get dressed in the black cargo pants and black t-shirt Foster gave me and walk back into the room. She hands me a small bottle and I sniff it.

"Mouthwash?" I ask.

"All out of toothpaste. Thought you'd like this," she replies. "Socks and boots are over there. Get them on. Eat fast. We're going for a walk."

I comply. What the fuck else am I going to do?

Boots on, food in my belly, and we are walking. We get downstairs and outside and I can't help but take a deep breath of the late fall air. Sure, it's tinged with the smell of death and ash, but still it's nice.

"The President told you that we're going to use your family as leverage, right?" she asks finally as we make our way down to the golf course.

"He did," I reply, "do you have them?"

"Maybe," she shrugs.

"Then I don't know what we have to talk about," I say.

"There's a girl, a young woman, that you've taken in," Foster says. "Do you know who she is?"

"Nope, don't know who you are talking about," I say.

"Cut the crap, Stanford," Foster laughs. "I know who she is. I know she means something to you. Maybe not as much as your family does, but she's part of your life now. So answer my question: do you know who she is?"

"She was a canny, a cannibal," I say. "She saved my ass. Despite the fact that my good friend killed her father."

Foster stops and I stop with her. She turns and looks at me and I'm pretty fucking confused by the look on her face.

"That wasn't her father," Foster says. "Just a man that took her when Z-Day hit."

"Hold on...what?" I ask. "What are you telling me? Why? What the fuck is going on?"

"I want that girl," Foster states flatly.

"I'd hardly call Elsbeth a girl," I say.

"Elsbeth...," she says, "that's what she calls herself?"

"That's the name her father said when they had me tied up in a basement and were ready to carve me up for dinner," I say.

"He wasn't her father," Foster growls, "got that?"

"Yeah, yeah, sorry," I say. "So I'm guessing you know her real name and where she's from and who her real father is and all that crap?"

"I know everything about her," Foster says. "I just need to get her."

"What does that have to do with me?" I ask. "Go get her. I dare you."

This makes Foster smile. "She trusts you. You can get her to me without anyone dying, especially her. I send in my people and there will be blood."

"You aren't wrong there," I say, "and if I get her to go with you, then are you going to harm her?"

"Not a single hair on her head."

"And you'll make sure my family isn't harmed?"

"That's the deal."

"Say it," I insist.

"Stanford, I promise your family won't be harmed and none of you will end up on Mondello's slave crews. I can't say the same for the rest of your Whispering Pines neighbors or for those on that farm. But the Stanfords will be free to go."

"Go where?"

She shrugs. "That's not my concern. You figure that part out. Uncertain freedom is better than certain slavery."

"Ha, not always," I laugh. "Have you seen the world lately?"

"More than I care to. So do we have a deal?"

I look over at the four guards that have accompanied us. "You aren't afraid they'll talk?"

"Not in the least," she replies. "Governments come and go, as do clients, but I'm a constant. My people know that if they stick with me, they'll have the best shot at a life in this world. Mondello is a bureaucrat; the Consortium is just a bunch of greedy fucks. They don't understand what life is like on the ground. Maybe at one time, some of them did, but not any longer. Plus, we're all that stands between the zeds and Mondello's ass. The Secret Service was never reinstated. Easier just to hire us."

"Why do you want Elsbeth?" I ask. "Tell me that, at least."

"No," she states flatly, "do we have a deal?"

"No," I state flatly in the exact same way. "I'm not selling that young woman out. Not unless you give me something. Some reason I should do that."

"You mean besides the fact that I can save your family?"

I don't answer.

"Fine. Why do you think I'm in Asheville?"

"To do your job helping Mondello run his slave labor and secure the Parkway."

"Good. That's what he thinks too," Foster says. "I'm actually here for a different reason. I took this contract because I knew it would be based in Asheville and not one of the other sites. I'm actually very familiar with this area."

"Other sites?" I ask. "What other sites?"

She shakes her head. "Not your concern now. What is your concern, is your family. And my concern is the young woman you call Elsbeth. We can help each other with those concerns."

"I don't know..." I really don't.

Foster holds out her hand and one of the guards gives her a radio. "This is Foster. Do you have the Stanfords?"

"We do," a voice crackles.

Foster hands the radio back to the guard.

"Your move, Stanford," she says.

"Jesus fuck," I whisper, "what is wrong with you people?"

"Do we have a deal? Yes or no?"

"Yes, of course we do," I say now that I have no choice, "but there's one problem."

"What's that?"

"I have no idea where Elsbeth is," I say.

"Oh, that's not a problem," Foster replies, "I know exactly where she is."

CHAPTER SIX

The group stands before Stuart, their expectant faces watching him closely. Julio in turn studies them, trying to figure out the mood. It's obviously one of apprehension with a healthy dose of fear. But is it fear that will lead to panic or fear that can be turned to resolve?

"Last night was quite a night," Stuart says. "I know you heard the gunfire and I know you heard a crowd cheering, because I heard that too. I don't know the source of either of those things, but I do plan on finding out."

Stuart watches the people in the group nod their heads in agreement and understanding.

"As much as I'd rather stay here and keep working on the stairs and deck, I believe I need to head into town and have a look," Stuart says. "I'm taking a small team with me. Just two guys. Harlan and Shep."

"Whoa! What?" Julio exclaims. "That's not what-"

"I know, but we'll move faster," Stuart says. "If we run into any trouble, then we'll double back and get help."

"What if you're hurt or captured?" someone asks. "Shouldn't we send more with you?"

"Exactly," Julio says, "at least take me, Stuart. Come on!"

"I need you here supervising," Stuart says to Julio.

"He's not even part of Whispering Pines," Carl Leitch, Whispering Pines' electrical grid expert says from the group. "No offense, Julio."

93

"None taken, man," Julio says. "He's right, Stuart. I'm good for security and clearing out Zs, but I ain't no supervisor. What the fuck do I know about building stairs and a deck?"

"You'll do fine," Stuart says. "Carl knows what needs to be done. I'll leave him in charge of the actual building. You just keep things cool here."

"What if you don't come back?" someone asks. "What then?"

"We go back to the Farm?" someone else asks.

"We lost communications with the Farm late last night," Landon Chase says, the head of Whispering Pines's tech. "Normal chatter, then it went dead. Someone jammed the signal."

"You don't know that," Carl says.

"I sure as hell do," Landon replies. "If the system had gone down, there would have been signs. There weren't. One second it's up, the next nothing."

"Maybe the cell tower they're bouncing off was damaged? Or the battery bank fried? Both possible," Carl counters, "did you think of that, genius?"

"I did, dumbass," Landon says. "And that isn't what happened. I can still catch wave form, but no real signal. The cell tower is working, just not receiving the Farm's communications."

"Don't you ever call me dumbass, dumbass!" Carl snaps. He stomps over to Landon. Julio instantly gets between them.

"That's why I need you here," Stuart says to Julio.

"Right," Julio nods, staring the two bickering men down. "We cool, gentlemen?"

"That old shit will never be cool," Landon snorts.

"Says the twenty-something with teenage acne," Carl laughs.

"Fuck you, faggot," Landon mutters.

"What did you say?" Carl's partner, Brian, snaps. "You fucking apologize now, geek!"

"HEY!" Stuart shouts. "Everyone shut the hell up! Landon, you ever say that again and I'll leave you out there for the Zs, got it?"

"Whatever," Landon says.

"Two seconds to agree with me, son," Stuart says.

"Okay, I'll never say it again," Landon says.

"Apologize," Stuart orders.

"I'm sorry I called you a faggot," Landon says to Carl then looks at Stuart. "That good enough? What about what he said to me?"

"You deserve that," Julio smiles. "You do have teenage acne, geek."

"Jesus," Stuart mutters.

"Don't you say the Lord's name in vane!" a crusty old voice snaps from behind the group. Preacher Carrey, the head and only member of the Church of Jesus of the Light, steps into view, making Stuart sigh.

"This is Whispering Pines business, preacher," Stuart says. "How about you go back up to your church and let us handle this how we handle it."

Preacher Carrey points a gnarled finger at everyone. "The Lord has cursed you because of your wicked ways! Homosexuals! Immigrants! Godless believers in technology and false idols! You deserve everything you get!"

The only reason Stuart doesn't knock the guy out, is that his church, a building grandfathered in when Whispering Pines was built, has the only water source in Whispering Pines- the well on its grounds. Sure, Stuart could take it by force, but the man is a preacher and the building is a church. He'd be cheered by some, but condemned by most.

"Preacher, you've said your part," Stuart says, rubbing his temples. "Can you let us get on with business?"

"Devil's business," Carrey sneers as he walks away towards his church. The building survived the destruction that leveled Whispering Pines, a fact he never tires of pointing out. He continues to mutter about the devil and the homosexuals and immigrants as he shuffles off.

"What the fuck did he mean by immigrants?" Julio asks. "I was fucking born here, man."

"Let's forget Carrey for now, okay? We have other things to deal with," Stuart says. "You all have your day's assignments. Can I count on all of you to do your part and try to stay on schedule without bickering and killing each other?"

"Or making me kill you," Julio ads.

"Goes without saying," Stuart says, looking at the group. Slowly, one by one, they all nod. "Good. Harlan? Shep? Ready in five. Pack light so we can move quickly."

Stuart looks about at the neighborhood that used to have cookie cutter houses built on it, but is now ruins.

"We'll get everything back, folks, we will," he says, "we just have to work for it."

***

"You are obviously giving preference to your people," Brenda Kelly snarls at Big Daddy. "I have members of Whispering Pines that are wounded and have been waiting for attention for hours! I know you are holding back treatment to them so you can keep your workforce strong! This is not how we agreed to run things, Mr. Fitzpatrick! You are in violation of our agreement!"

Brenda Kelly, Chairperson of the Whispering Pines HOA Board, stands in front of the rocking chair Big Daddy is seated in. Her hands are firmly planted on her hips and righteous indignation and rage radiate from her short, fat, homely body. Despite the night's battle, and other than some dirt scuffs on her pants, Brenda looks like the fighting passed her by.

Big Daddy wonders where she was during the thick of it all. He doesn't wonder too hard, knowing the coward she is, but he logs the thought away to be brought up another day.

"I would appreciate it if you moved to the side," Big Daddy says, "so I can supervise the clean up."

"Supervise?" Brenda snorts. "You have a bullet in your leg and are sitting on your front porch! You are hardly supervising anything, Mr. Fitzpatrick! That is why I should be in charge right now and make sure that services are equally distributed between your people and the members of Whispering Pines!"

"Members that are guests on my land," Big Daddy says, sick of having to remind the abominable woman. "Guests at my invitation. An invitation I can rescind at any time, Ms. Kelly."

Brenda puts her hands to her heart like she's been stabbed. "How dare you? How dare you! You would kick innocent women and children out into the Z ridden wilds! What kind of monster are you?"

"Oh, shut the hell up, Brenda," Dr. McCormick says as she shoves her out of the way so she can get to Big Daddy's leg. "No one is getting any special treatment, you fat cow. Sergeant Stillwater and I have been taking care of everyone equally, depending on the severity of their wounds. I would have liked to look to Mr. Fitzpatrick's wound hours ago, but he insisted I tend to everyone else first."

"Well, you should be tending to Whispering Pines people first, is what you should do!" Brenda snarls. "If you know where your loyalties are!"

"Someone get this bitch away from me," Dr. McCormick says.

"Doctor, while I appreciate the work you do, I hate to have to ask you to watch your language time and time again," Big Daddy says. "I don't ask much, but that is one thing I insist on."

"Why don't I take you over here and you can go see to the Whispering Pines people?" Sergeant Alex "Reaper" Stillwater says, placing a hand on Dr. McCormick's shoulder.

"That's the first smart thing I've heard around here all day," Brenda snaps. "Why didn't you offer earlier? Would have saved us all a lot of trouble."

Dr. McCormick is about to respond when Big Daddy takes her hand. "Laura, go ahead. You aren't breaking any doctor's oath by keeping the peace."

"That's right," Brenda says. "You swore an oath as a doctor to uphold the covenants of the Whispering Pines's HOA-"

"I did no such thing!" Dr. McCormick shouts.

"Has anyone seen Charlie?" Jennifer Patel asks, running up onto the porch, looking frazzled and desperate. Which is pretty much how everyone looks. "I can't find him anywhere."

"Young miss, adults are speaking here," Brenda growls, turning on the teenager. "You just march yourself down those steps and away from here right now. I'm sure you are needed elsewhere."

"Have you asked his mother?" Big Daddy asks, concerned.

"I can't find Mrs. Stanford or Greta," Jennifer says. "I've looked everywhere and no one has seen them since this morning."

Big Daddy and Reaper share a look. "Someone go get one of my boys," Big Daddy says. "Have him get those that have the energy to scour the area."

"I hardly think that's a good use of manpower at this time," Brenda says.

"You hardly think at all," Dr. McCormick says.

"Ladies," Big Daddy says. He looks at Jennifer. "You go find Buzz or Gunga, okay? Tell them I want them to start looking for the Stanfords."

"Yes, sir," Jennifer smiles and hurries away.

"Radios still down?" Big Daddy asks Reaper.

"They are," he nods.

"But we've got all of those men in custody, right? The ones we found with the rockets?" Big Daddy asks.

"We do," Reaper replies. "And Master Sergeant Platt has gone through every truck looking for a jamming device. Nothing."

"Can you ask your superior officer to join me here?" Big Daddy asks. "I'd go find him, but I'm incapacitated."

"I'm right here," Platt says from the farmhouse doorway, a corn muffin in his hand. "Just trying to put something in my stomach."

"Good idea," Big Daddy says. "Wouldn't look right having a Special Forces soldier passing out in front of everyone."

"What can I do for you, sir?" Platt asks.

"I have a sinking feeling we have been duped," Big Daddy says. "While I am sure the objective was to take the Farm by force, I have to wonder if there wasn't a second objective. Or perhaps taking the Farm was the second objective."

Platt looks at everyone, puzzled. "Care to fill me in on what I missed?"

"The Stanfords are missing," Reaper says.

"They could just be hiding," Platt says.

"Not Stella," Big Daddy says. "You know the woman; she'd be in the thick of all of this. That's one A-type woman there."

"You aren't joking," Platt nods. "What are you saying? That all these people died for a snatch and grab?"

"Like I said, I think taking the Farm was the objective," Big Daddy says, "but it sure did provide enough chaos for us all to miss a significant presence here. None of us even noticed Stella and her children are gone."

"If they are at all," Brenda says. "Could be that Patel girl is just too stupid to find them."

"That does it," Dr. McCormick says and hauls off and punches Brenda in the jaw, knocking the woman to the porch. "Crap! I think I hurt my hand!"

"Let me look at that," Reaper says. "Sir, would you mind escorting Ms. Kelly away before she gets herself hurt further."

"Gladly," Platt says, "you take care of the doctor. I'll bring Ms. Kelly with me as I have a chat with the prisoners. I believe she has a certain skill set that could prove useful."

"You want me to what?" Brenda asks as she's helped to her feet by Platt. "I'm not speaking to those men! They tried to kill us! With rockets!"

"Yes they did," Platt agrees, "and don't you think they deserve a piece of your mind? They can't just sit there and be comfortable after what they did, can they?"

"Comfortable?" Brenda asks as she walks down the porch steps. "Why are they comfortable? I won't stand for that! Those men should be shackled and strung up for what they did! This is unacceptable! They killed and wounded members of the Whispering Pines HOA! They will answer for that!"

"Damn," Reaper says, then looks at Big Daddy. "I mean darn. Glad I'm not those guys."

"Me as well, Sergeant Stillwater," Big Daddy says. "But let's hope Master Sergeant Platt is correct in using her. We could certainly do with more information about why we were really attacked."

***

Her stomach lurches as she rocks from side to side. She tries to open her eyes, but just that small effort sends waves of nausea through her. She takes a couple of deep breaths through her nose, realizing her mouth is taped shut.

"This one is moving," a gruff voice says, "put her out again?"

"Nah," another voice replies, "just keep an eye on her. What about the kids?"

"They're still out," the first voice says. "Doubt they'll wake up for a while. She should be out too, but guess she's a tough one."

"Body chemistry, man," the second voice says. "You just never fucking know. Remember that time in Bahrain when we had to remove that sheik? Gassed the whole damn palace and still one of his whores was up walking around. Half naked and jabbering about something in that high pitched Arabic voice. I passed right by her, she could have reached out and touched me, but she didn't even know I was there. Just kept jabbering, jabbering, jabbering. You just never know, man."

"Foster say what she wanted us to do with them?" the first voice asks.

"Not yet. Secure them and bring them back to Asheville."

"We going to put them in one of the rooms in that Grove Park place? Or are they going into the general population?"

"Neither, man. Foster said to bring them to her. She'll radio Horace with the location. If he hasn't heard from her by the time we hit the city, then we're to hold tight and wait by the river until we do."

"What's she up to?"

"Not a clue, man. But it's Foster, so I'm sure she has a plan."

"She better not fuck up this contract," the first man says. "I haven't slept in a bed this many nights in a row in a long fucking time. I could get used to this gig."

"Tell me about it, man. But we do what the woman wants, am I right? She hasn't steered us wrong yet."

"Tru dat, brother," the first man laughs. There's silence for a minute. "You think we'll get to have some fun with the woman?"

"Don't be a scumbag," the second voice snaps. "We ain't survivor trash. Fuck one of the workers if you need to get your rocks off. Foster doesn't want her or the kids harmed, so don't even think about it."

"Jeez, I was just talking out loud."

"Maybe you shouldn't," the second man says, "if you know what's good for you. Those thoughts get back to Foster and she'll publicly cut your balls off, roast them over a fucking fire, and then feed them to you. And you'll fucking thank her for it by the time you finish eating. Don't fuck with that woman, man."

"Fine, fine, I hear ya."

Stella just lies there, paralyzed with fear. She doesn't know where she is or what's happening, but she prays that her children will be safe. Despite what the one man said, she has no illusions as to her own safety. And she will do whatever it takes, no matter how horrible, to keep her children from harm. There is no doubt in her mind about that.

***

We stand in the shadows of an old Victorian house on Charlotte St. It used to be gorgeous, colored in dark purples and greens, but now it just sits there, sad and decrepit. Much like the rest of Asheville.

"Visual confirmation," Foster's radio crackles. "Twenty yards south, east side. They're keeping to the houses."

"That's across the street," I say.

"Thank you for that assist, Stanford," Foster mocks. "I'm so new at this I never would have figured it out."

"Fuck you, Foster," I say.

"Be nice, Stanford," she replies, "I have your family, remember."

"There's three- two males and one female," the radio voice states. "Orders?"

"Three?" Foster asks.

"Affirmative."

"There were four, where's the third male?" Foster asks. "I want descriptions, now!"

The man describes Elsbeth, Critter, and probably one of Critter's guys. Who's the other guy that is supposed to be with them?

"Where's the fucking sniper?" Foster growls into the radio, her eyes darting around, scanning the area. She pushes her hand on my chest, shoving me against the house and deeper into the shadows. "I swear I'm gonna cut a bitch if I find out we lost the sniper."

John. Did he get hurt? Taken down by Zs? Or is he on the offensive? I'm hoping for the latter.

"This is not good," Foster says, looking at me. "I need you in the middle of the street now. If that sniper is out there, I want him to know there will be consequences if he starts firing."

"What sniper?" I ask. "I have no idea-"

She grabs me by the front of my shirt and yanks me to her. "Stop. Right. Now. I know you know exactly who I am talking about. I know all about Leeds's team. I have access to their dossiers. Weapons Sergeant Sammy "John" Baptiste. He's a deadly mother fucker. I want you in that road and calling to Elsbeth in thirty seconds. At thirty-one seconds, I call my guys and your family dies. Are we clear, Stanford?"

"Crystal," I reply, trying to pull her hand from my shirt. Not happening. This chick has one fucking strong grip. "What about the others? Critter and his guy?"

"What about them?"

"I don't want them killed either," I say.

"Not part of the deal," she replies. "The deal is set. Elsbeth for your family. Critter will have to take care of himself."

"You're one cold bitch," I say.

"You know nothing about me, Stanford," she glares. "Now get your ass out there."

Finally, she lets go and shoves me towards the road. I stumble as I get up, but quickly get my balance and walk casually into the middle of the road. I shield my eyes and look towards where I think they should be.

"Elsbeth!" I cry out. "Elsbeth, it's me! Long Pork!" Ugh, I hate that name.

I wait, but there's no reply.

"Elsbeth! It's safe! You can come out!" Still no reply. "Please! They have Stella and the kids!"

"What's that?" Elsbeth calls as she steps from behind a large oak. "Who has the kids? Who has Stella?"

"Just come down here and I can tell you," I say, feeling like the shittiest person in the world. Seriously, I would consider Mondello a saint compared to the person I am right now. "We don't have much time."

Elsbeth watches me for a minute then shakes her head. "Why, Long Pork?" she asks. "Why down there? That's stupid. No cover. Get up here with me."

Hmmm, a problem...

"Come on," I say. "It doesn't matter. I just need your help. Please. Come down here."

She watches me again.

She knows. Even from here, I can tell she knows I have betrayed her. Come on, come on. I really don't have time. The seconds are ticking away. She has to get down here or Foster will kill my family.

"Please!" I beg. "Just come here."

Hisses get my attention and I look over my shoulder to see a group of ten or twelve Zs shambling out of an old ice cream shop. The entire front of the building is busted in, like a car rammed it. But there's no car. Just Zs.

"Shit," I mutter.

Elsbeth sees them and she pulls her blades, stepping further away from the tree and towards me.

"Get up here, Long Pork," she says, motioning towards me, "they'll eat your ass."

Where the fuck is Critter? Why hasn't he said anything?

Because he knows it's a trap. She knows it, he knows it, and that's why John is missing. He's probably watching this all play out from on top of one of the houses, his scope centered on my forehead. Or maybe on Foster's forehead. I would like to think that's how it is. Yes, on Foster's forehead.

I don't really care about Critter's guy, wherever he is. Not trying to be callous, just being honest. A man can only worry about so much in the zombie apocalypse. Gotta pick your worries carefully, if you know what I mean. Otherwise, you're just a constant ball of nerves; twitching and flinching like a stray dog.

"Long Pork!" Elsbeth shouts, pointing behind me.

Oh, right, the Zs. What do I do? If I run towards her, then Foster could give the order to kill my family. But stay here and I'm Z chow. Fuck.

I rub my face with my non-throbbing hand and look back at the Zs. Twelve. Yeah, I for certain count twelve of them. Without a weapon, I could maybe get lucky and kill two, possibly three. Possibly...

"I'm fucked!" I shout. "This is all fucking bullshit!" I point towards Foster. "You! Get your fucking ass out here! This whole situation has gone to shit and it's your fault. Get out here and fix this."

"Who are you talking to, Long Pork?" Elsbeth asks, her voice cautious and cold. "That the person you're working for now?"

"Working for?" I ask, "What the fuck? I don't work for anyone, El. I'm just trying to keep my family alive! There's a woman here that knows you and wants to meet you. I said I could help if she doesn't kill Stella and the kids."

Elsbeth walks completely away from the tree and down the yard towards me. Her eyes scan the area, focusing on the shadows I pointed to.

"A woman? What woman? I don't know a woman," Elsbeth says.

As soon as she's in the street, SUVs come barreling from all directions, surrounding us. Elsbeth freezes, her eyes locked on mine. Jesus, I suck. The pain, the betrayal I see. She'll hate me forever.

"Hold!" Foster shouts as she walks into the road, her hands out towards the SUVs. "Do not engage!"

"Tough shit," Cowboy says as he steps from one of the SUVs. "You fucked up, Foster."

"Jameson? What the hell are you doing?" Foster asks, marching up to him. "You're supposed to be with the President!"

"Oh, he is, Ms. Foster," Mondello says from inside the SUV. He leans across the seat and waves. "Hello there, Mr. Stanford. Sorry my former employee got you mixed up in all of this. I'll try not to let it reflect too poorly on you."

"Long Pork?" Elsbeth asks, her eyes taking it all in. "What's happening?"

"I don't know," I say. "Honestly, El, I'm just as lost as you."

"I'm not lost," Elsbeth says, looking around. "I know exactly where I am."

More men jump from the SUVs and surround Foster, Elsbeth, and myself.

"What the fuck have you done, Jameson?" Foster asks her man.

"Just what you would do in my situation," Cowboy replies. "I took an opportunity to advance my career."

"It's true, Ms. Foster," Mondello says from inside the SUV. "Please say hello to the new head of the Secret Service. Mr. Jameson put on a great presentation on why he was the most qualified person for the job. I had considered you for the position, but as always, you are strictly in this business for yourself."

"Jameson," Foster says. "You're making a mistake. What have I always said?"

"We work for anyone, but are owned by no one," Cowboy snorts. "Which is pretty fucking stupid. They mean the same thing."

"No, they don't, you fucking moron," Foster says. "God, you royally fucked this up. We could've had it all. Now what do we have? Jack shit."

"No, you have jack shit," Cowboy smiles. "I have a sweet new gig. And get to keep from being tonight's entertainment."

"What?" Foster asks, looking at Mondello. "You fucking bastard. Just put a bullet in my head."

"And waste your talent?" Mondello laughs. "Please, Ms. Foster, be practical. At least you may have a chance to live. Until you lose, that is."

Groans get my attention. Oh, right, those Zs. Twelve of them.

"My family," I say to Foster. "What about my family?"

"Oh, don't worry about them," Cowboy says. "We intercepted the van a few blocks over. They're on their way back to the Grove Park right now." He looks over his shoulder at Mondello. "And I believe you have them scheduled for tonight also, is that right Mr. President?"

"You fuck!" I yell and dive at the SUV. Cowboy drops me hard.

"No!" Elsbeth shouts and then the shit hits the fan.

I try to push myself up, but Cowboy really walloped me upside the head. Dizzy and shaky, all I see are legs moving about me and all I hear are shouts and then gunshots. But even through the haze of my confusion, I can make out one steady sound of gunshots; systematic and perfectly timed.

I push up again and am able to reach up and grab the side mirror of the SUV in front of me. Pulling myself to my feet, I watch as one, two, three, four men fall, blood spraying from their heads. John. Gotta love a sniper.

Then rapid fire from across the street. Critter and his guy. Oh, snap, well there goes Critter's guy. Half his head vaporizes as Cowboy returns fire.

"Go! Go!" Cowboy shouts, slamming the SUV door closed and slapping the side. The vehicle with Mondello inside speeds off, mowing through the Zs, and squeals around a corner towards the Grove Park.

Cowboy is running one way, his rifle held tight, firing round after round, while Critter runs the other way, a 9mm in each hand. I happen to be right in the fucking middle.

I hit the ground and do what any self-respecting hero would do: I cover my head with my arms. Men are shouting, cursing, screaming, and dying. I do notice I haven't heard a woman scream or call out, so Elsbeth, and I guess Foster, must be doing alright. Not really going to look up and find out. Just fine cowering right here for now, thank you very much.

A man falls dead next me, most of his head gone, and I snag his rifle and roll over on my back, ready to shoot any mother fucker coming at me. Except there aren't any. Oh, there's plenty of men I could shoot, but they aren't coming after me; they're busy with Elsbeth, Foster, Critter, and John. No, what I get to deal with are the Zs that didn't get run over.

And, hey, look! They brought friends!

Fifteen is my quick guesstimation. Fuck it. I start firing.

Now, I have fired a lot of weapons since Z-Day. Sure, I'd fired a couple hand guns before that, but you don't really get familiar with firearms until you're thrust into the middle of the apocalypse. But, despite my experience, I am not ready for what I am holding in my hands.

Especially since the thing is set to full auto. I have no idea what kind of rifle it is, some special boom boom stick that contractors use, I guess. But with just the press of my finger it unloads everything on the Zs. And whatever is behind them. Because, honestly, I miss completely.

Oh, don't get me wrong, I hit the fuckers, for sure. Hard not to with all those bullets. But, I don't get a single headshot. Not one. I just shred some already shredded looking rib cages and kill empty air. Good one, Jace. Way to be a hero.

The rifle clicks empty, but I don't waste time. If everyone is too busy shooting at each other to take care of the undead fucks, then I guess I'll have to do it. I get up, turn the rifle around, burn the fuck out of my hand on the smoking barrel, scream, and cover my burnt hand with my sleeve, take hold of the barrel (Ow! Still hot!) and start swinging.

Really, I'm better with melee weapons. I can crush a Z's head like a mother fucker.

I take two down before I have to retreat backwards to avoid getting caught and surrounded. I feel the hot sting of a bullet graze my cheek and cry out. Okay, I scream. Fucking hurts!

"Just get down, Long Pork!" Elsbeth yells, shoving me to the pavement. She leapfrogs over me and takes off six Z heads before she has both feet back on the ground. It still leaves plenty of Zs, though.

I look about for another weapon, but there's nothing within reach. A hand grabs me and I almost start to pound the face that goes with it, but stop as Critter yanks me to my feet.

"Good to see ya, Long Pork," Critter grins. "I'll add this ass saving to the list."

"List? What list?" I ask. "There's a list?"

"There is now," Critter says.

"Look out!" I shout, but it's too late. Critter takes the butt of Cowboy's rifle to the back of his head and crumples.

He swipes at me, but I stumble back and trip over my own feet, landing right back on the pavement. Cowboy just smiles and takes aim, but the smile falls away quickly as he ducks under a blade that just misses his head. I look up and see Elsbeth standing over me, plenty of Z goo dripping off of her. Which drips right onto me. Dammit.

"You get to running, Long Pork," Elsbeth says. "I got this. Toy soldiers don't scare me."

"Toy soldiers?" Cowboy laughs. "Girl, I'm about to teach you how scary toys can be."

"I know how scary they can be," Elsbeth replies, her lips pulled back into a snarl. "I had a clown once."

"That's scary," I say. "Can't deny that, Cowboy."

"The name is Jameson, you little annoying bitch," he snaps.

"Don't call her a bitch!" I shout. He just shakes his head. "Oh, you were calling me a bitch. Right. Elsbeth kill him."

She steps past me, but stops as Cowboy presses the barrel of his rifle to Critter's unconscious temple.

"You sure you want to do that, girl?" Cowboy says. "I mean, go right ahead. I don't really care. Of course, if you take one more step, I blow his fucking head off."

Elsbeth stops.

"He isn't a very nice man," Elsbeth says.

Cowboy looks at me. "Who's she talking about? Me or the hillbilly here?"

"Both," Elsbeth says, "but he's helped me. What do I do, Long Pork?"

I glance around and see that the fighting has stopped. There are bodies everywhere; blood coats the asphalt. On her knees, with one eye already swollen shut and blood pouring from a gash on her scalp, is Foster. The one eye she has open is burning a hole in the back of Cowboy's head.

"I'll count to three, girl," Cowboy says. "At three, this scrawny fuck dies. Then you and your buddy on the ground die. You may be able to get to me, but you won't get to everyone behind me. You don't stand a chance."

I make a quick count and realize he's right; even with Elsbeth's speed and skills she can't take them all. We're dead.

"Put them down, El," I say.

"But, Long Pork," she protests, "I can do this."

"No, you can't," I say.

She glances down at me and I see the wounded hurt in her eyes. Fuck, I'm just crushing her soul today.

"Why?" she asks.

There's so much in that one word that I don't know how to answer. So I shrug. It's the go to gesture when you've betrayed one of your closest friends.

The blades clatter against the pavement and Cowboy smiles.

"Good," he says, "the President will be pleased. Foster and now this chick in the arena? Talk about entertainment."

"Fuck you, Jameson," Foster spits behind him.

"Shut her the fuck up," he orders, his eyes still watching Elsbeth.

A pistol slams into the back of Foster's head and she collapses. Cowboy steps away from Critter, his rifle to his shoulder.

"On your knees, bitch," he says to Elsbeth. A low growl comes from her throat. "Do it or you and your Long Pork die!"

"Please, El," I say. "They have Stella. They have Charlie and Greta."

"I know," Elsbeth says as she gets on her knees.

Cowboy rushes forward and nails Elsbeth in the face with the butt of his rifle. She goes down, but she's not out. For a split second, I think she's going to fight back, but she just looks at me as the second blow comes. Then her eyes close and I look up at Cowboy.

"You gonna smack me too?" I ask.

"You gonna be trouble?" he replies.

"I always am," I say. "Don't try to be, but fuck if I don't just breed trouble."

Cowboy watches me a second then smiles. "Nah, I'll let you get into the vehicle on your own steam," Cowboy says. "Easier that way. Plus, I want you to be thinking about what a fucking cowardly little pussy you are while we drive back to the Grove Park. And also think about what it's going to be like to watch your family get eaten by zeds tonight. That's gonna be a show and a half."

"What?" I shout, getting to my feet in an instant. Where the fuck is John? Why hasn't he put a bullet in this fucking asshole's head?

"You didn't think you were getting out of this unscathed, did you?" Cowboy asks as he shoves me towards an SUV that isn't shot to shit. "Everyone pays the piper, pussy. And you are going to be paying for a long time."

I want to fight; I want to kill the fuck. But all my strength just leaves me as Cowboy pushes me into the SUV. What can I do? I'm good at killing Zs and I know how to fight cannies and even crazies like Vance and his goons. But professional soldiers? People, man. People.

They suck.

***

The working SUVs speed off down Charlotte St and around the corner, heading up to the Grove Park Inn. John counts out the seconds, double checks the area, and then cautiously makes his way down to the street. One hand is holding his empty sniper rifle, while the other is clamped to his wounded left shoulder. He kneels next to one of the dead PCs and rifles through the man's vest.

He finds extra magazines and checks the cartridges inside.

"Fuck," he mutters. Not compatible with his M110. He looks at his weapon and shakes his head. "Sorry, girl."

He picks up the rifle lying next to the PC. He grunts in disgust at the imperfect weapon, knowing he can still be lethal with it, but won't have anywhere near the range and accuracy that he needs. He slings the rifle over his shoulder, gets up, and gathers as many magazines as he can. Once he has them jammed into his pockets, he starts to go through the dead men's gear until he finds what he's looking for.

He hops into the backseat of an SUV and closes the door behind him, his eyes catching sight of a new group of Zs heading his way. He sets his gear down on the floor of the SUV and pulls his uniform away from his shoulder.

Grimacing at what he sees, he readies himself for what he has to do. Pulling two shotgun shells from his gear, he cracks them open and pours the powder into his wound. It's a through and through, luckily, so he doesn't have to worry about a stray slug stuck inside. But that's little comfort as he picks up a glove and jams it into his mouth. He mentally counts to three and then lights the powder.

God, he tries not to scream too loudly, but there's no way to stay quiet as the flesh around and inside the wound is cauterized by burning gunpowder. The Zs in the street hear him and start their slow shuffle towards the SUV. John knows he has to move or he'll be trapped, but he can't get his legs to work.

The wound keeps burning and burning and soon his head is spinning. He leans back into the seat, planning on resting for just a second, just enough to catch his breath. But his eyes instantly roll up into his head and he passes out, slumping down out of sight.

The Zs make it to the SUV and their undead hands claw at the windows. They groan and hiss, trying to get inside at the source of the smell of burning flesh. They smack the glass, the doors; they rock the SUV, but they can't get in. And John isn't coming out. As the sun starts to dip lower in the sky, and John hasn't moved an inch, more Zs crowd around the SUV. One by one, they shamble up to it, called by the swarming of their kind, continuing their never ending search for food, for the flesh that drives their hunger.

CHAPTER SEVEN

Stunned into silence, Big Daddy reaches back, catching Pup's hand so he can be helped onto the bale of hay behind him. *Not* stunned into silence is Brenda Kelly as she rails at him, pacing back and forth, her hands moving frantically, alternating between pointing at the PCs trussed up on the barn floor and the now seated Big Daddy.

"The President of the United States! We fought against the President of the United States! How are you not full of shame? Why are these men still tied up? We need to free them immediately and contact President Mondello!" Brenda shouts, turning to the bound men. "What kind of name is Mondello? Is that Mexican? Italian? What?" She then spins about, glaring at Big Daddy. "Why are these men still tied up? I just asked you that and you refuse to answer! If I have to have my Head of Security come in here and untie them I will, Mr. Fitzpatrick! Mark my words, I'll have Mindy Sterling set these men free!"

"Are you quite finished, ma'am?" Big Daddy asks, a sheen of cold sweat on his forehead. "Because I have similar questions, just without all of the spit and vinegar."

"Spit and vinegar? Spit and vinegar! What are you babbling about now, you dumb redneck?" Brenda yells. "There's a reason I wanted Whispering Pines secure! And not just because of the Zs! It was to keep away from ignorant yokels like you, Mr. Fitzpatrick! Spit and vinegar!"

"Ma'am, please calm down," Pup says. "And don't be insulting my daddy. You're our guest here, but not for long if you continue to act like a-"

"That's enough, Pup," Big Daddy says, "she's a silly fool and fools can't help what they are."

"How dare you? How dare you!" Brenda screeches.

"Ma'am, please be quiet," Big Daddy says. "I shouldn't have to remind you every single, gosh darn time I see you that there is no need for this behavior. We can all be adults and discuss this without resorting to hysterics and name calling."

"Oh, hysterics is it? Why? Because I'm a woman and lesser than you? You think any time a woman exerts her power she's hysterical?"

"Well, I think you're pretty hysterical," Melissa Fitzpatrick says from the barn door. "A down right hoot. Personally, I could laugh at your pompous face all day long. There's just something about the way you look. Kinda like a watermelon with legs and arms."

Brenda tries to respond, but just sputters and fumes. Melissa smiles at this. The designated head of the Whispering Pines scavenger crew, Melissa, has seen horrors that Brenda can't imagine. While protected in the relative (and former) safety of Whispering Pines, Brenda Kelly used her bluster and ruthlessness to intimidate most of the residents and HOA; especially since the majority of them didn't set foot outside the gate, ever.

But Melissa does step outside, risking her life to obtain desperately needed supplies and materials for the benefit of Whispering Pines. Being Big Daddy's only daughter, raised with six brothers, a woman like Brenda Kelly is an inconvenience only, not a source of intimidation or fear. And Melissa has no problem reminding the HOA Board Chair of that any chance she gets.

"The fact that Whispering Pines was destroyed should be evidence enough that you have no place criticizing others for the decisions they make," Melissa states. "So just close your mouth and listen. Or I'll close it for you, Brenda. I will promise you that. And then you'll wish things were hysterical."

"Sweetie Mel," Big Daddy says, "I believe you've made your point. Unfortunately, I think you added to the spit and vinegar." He holds up a hand to stay his daughter's objections. "So how about you ladies let me handle this for a minute? If I don't do an adequate job, then I'll let each of you have your turns, your ways."

Melissa nods while Brenda just snorts in disgust.

"Good enough," Big Daddy says getting back to his feet with Pup's help. His leg throbs and sharp pains make him want to cry out, but he's a lifetime farmer and it isn't enough to slow him down, even at his age.

"Gentlemen," Big Daddy addresses the men at his feet, "I'm sure you have been listening to what Ms. Kelly has been railing on about. This is wholly unbelievable, to say the least. I'm sure you can appreciate that." He smiles down at the men; they do not smile back.

"Anthony Mondello is the Secretary of Homeland Security," Platt acknowledges, having been silent until now. Standing above them all at the edge of the hayloft, Platt has his arms behind his back, his face showing zero emotion.

"Thank you, Master Sergeant," Big Daddy says. "So we know that part is true. The rest? Can't be verified. Not right this moment, you understand. While I'd like to believe you, the problem I have is that you've already admitted you're hired guns."

"Private contractors," one of the men replies.

"I believe that there is known as splitting hairs, sir," Big Daddy responds. "Whatever you boys like to be called, you and your boss have been paid to provide a service to a man that calls himself President. I'm fairly certain that if he paid you enough you'd call him the Easter Bunny. Although I believe that particular holy day should be reserved for the memory of our Lord and Savior, and not a rodent handing out chocolates."

"We knew he was President before we were hired," another man says. "He's been President for over a year now."

"At least," a third man agrees.

"Funny," Platt says, "I don't remember voting for him."

"I don't neither," Big Daddy says. "But I do believe that is besides the proverbial point."

"This is *all* besides the point!" Brenda snaps. "So how about you get to it, Mr. Fitzpatrick!"

"Shrill," Big Daddy says.

"Tell me about it," Melissa agrees.

"But, to satisfy you, Ms. Kelly," Big Daddy continues before she can protest further. "I will get to the point. Why were the Stanfords taken? What does this so called President want with them?"

"Don't know," the first man answers, "I didn't ask him."

"Did he give you the orders or did your boss?" Big Daddy asks.

The men stay quiet.

"Their boss," Platt says. Big Daddy nods at this.

The men all look up at Platt, their eyes filled with malice and anger.

"What?" Platt asks. "Are the private contractors afraid of regular military?"

"We may be hired," the first man says. "But you aren't. Pretty sure President Mondello is your Commander-in-Chief. Pretty sure that this is sedition. Considering he knows your team has been here. I doubt you didn't know about him."

"This true?" Big Daddy asks.

"Irrelevant," Platt says. "It takes more than just saying so to be President. If he knew about us, he could have reached out at any time and made contact, showing proof of his right to the presidency."

"An argument can be made both ways," Big Daddy says.

"Hardly," Platt replies. "Making contact would have compromised the team. Through some convoluted back channels we heard what was going on in Charlottesville-"

"Charlottesville?" Brenda Kelly snorts. "The man doesn't even know where the capitol is!"

"He's right, lady," the first man says. "Charlottesville is the new seat of the government. But Atlanta is where the action is at."

"Dumb shit," the second man says.

"What? Atlanta isn't a secret."

"It is to us," Platt says, "what's in Atlanta?"

"Fuck," the first man says.

"We're gonna be here a while," Melissa says, plopping down on a bale of hay. "Guess I should get comfortable."

***

"Why are we hiding here again?" Harlan asks, as he and Shep stay hidden under the rhododendron bushes next to one of the mansions on Kimberly Ave, across the road from the Grove Park Inn's golf course, and in sight of the Inn itself. "Didn't the gunfire come from over on Charlotte? Sounded like it to me."

"Do you still hear gunfire?" Stuart asks, binoculars to his eyes, focused on the Grove Park. "I don't. We'll check it out soon, but right now, I want to watch the GPI."

"Entrance is on the other side," Shep says. "All we see here are the same guards walking back and forth."

"No, Shep, not the same guards," Stuart replies, handing him the binoculars. "Take a look."

Shep takes the binoculars and has a look, but just shrugs and hands them back. "They all look the same to me, man. Black armor and big guns."

"You like those biceps, eh Shep?" Harlan laughs.

"Knock it off," Stuart says. "They changed shifts, trust me. Those are new guards." Stuart checks his watch. "Two hours early."

"How the fuck do you know that?" Harlan asks. "How many times have you come here?"

"I've been a few," Stuart says. "So have some of Leeds's team. Between us, we've figured out a schedule. They've stuck to it until today."

"What do you think it means?" Harlan asks.

"I don't know," Stuart says, "but it's strange. There must have been a disruption somewhere."

"Like all that damn gunfire?" Harlan laughs. "That the disruption you're looking for?"

"That could be," Stuart says. "But it can't just be that. Something else is going on."

"We gonna find out?" Shep asks. "Or we gonna go check out Charlotte St?"

"Both," Stuart says. "The entrance is easier to observe if we come at it from Charlotte."

"Yeah," Harlan agrees. "But we could take Country Club Dr and go up the back way."

"More patrols that way," Shep says. "Right?"

"Right," Stuart says, thinking it over. "No, we go Charlotte. See what the dust up was over. Then to the Grove Park."

"Lead the way," Harlan says.

Stuart does.

***

The sun beams down on John as he kicks back in the deck chair, his feet up, and a cold beer in his hand. He hasn't caught a thing all day, but the fact that he's on leave and away from Fort Bragg for a few days makes up for that. He's happy just to enjoy the gentle rocking of the small boat on the intercoastal waterway as he sips his beer and watches the swaying of the fishing pole locked in place. Gulls fly overhead, making strange, low noises, but again, John is just happy to be somewhere that isn't overrun by Zs.

By Zs?

He sets his beer down and shields his eyes. Why would he think of Zs? He's on leave, enjoying some much needed rest and relaxation. Zs aren't his problem. Then more gulls fly overhead and the sounds coming from them chill John's bones. Gulls don't moan. They don't hiss and snarl. And are they getting louder?

He starts to stand up, but the gentle rocking of the boat turns into some seriously rough rocking, and he falls back on his ass. Pain shoots out from his shoulder and he glances down, surprised at the blood blooming through his t-shirt.

What the fuck? Is there a storm coming? He crawls to the side of the boat and looks into the water. It is completely still and calm, not a wave. Yet the boat keeps rocking. He starts to look away then realizes the reflection in the water isn't of his face. The face staring back at him is missing one eye and most of its nose. And it isn't alone. More faces stare back at him, their mouths opening, timed with the sounds of the groans and hisses.

John scrambles back from the side, his hands frantically searching behind him for his pack and his cell phone. He has to call this in. Something is very wrong in the North Carolina outer banks. Crazy sounding gulls? Dead people looking at him from under the water? What the hell?

His hand finds his pack, but something finds his hand. He looks back over his shoulder as a shadow passes over him. Looking up, against the sun, he can barely make out the features of the person that has taken hold of his arm.

"What the hell is going on?" John shouts. "Who are you?"

The person leans forward and John wants to scream. The face that is pressing close to his doesn't have any flesh; nothing holds its jaw on except for a couple strands of dry tendon. Its tongue is black and swollen, coated in wiggling maggots that squirm off of it and fall onto the boat's deck. John finally does scream as he sees the thing's eyes.

Eyes he has seen in the mirror every single day of his life.

Still screaming, John bolts awake, thrust back into the true nightmare of real life. Panicked, he looks around, realizing he's still in the SUV, surrounded by Zs, with a shoulder that, while no longer literally on fire, fucking hurts like it.

Oh, and the SUV is rocking back and forth rather violently as dozens and dozens of Zs try to break inside to get at John's living tastiness. The windows are holding fine even with the pounding they are taking from the Zs due to the bulletproof glass they are made from. John is pretty sure the SUVs are reinforced, so he doesn't think there's any way the Zs can get to him. But that doesn't solve the problem of being surrounded by the undead without any supplies. He forces himself to move and search the vehicle, but he comes up with nothing; not even a canteen of water. Which he so desperately could use right now.

"Fuck," he croaks, his throat raw and dry. Then he looks at the undead faces. "I thought you guys would have left by now." He figures he must have been making noise in his sleep, which kept the Zs interested. That and the smell of his burning flesh.

The sound of his voice just eggs them on. The Zs double their attack, clawing over each other as they catch sight of him inside. He tries to slide down in the seat and rest in the shadows of the fading evening light, but it doesn't make a difference. As long as one Z sees him and shows interest, then they all will. Zs aren't known for their independent thinking abilities.

There is one thing John is happy about: all the ammunition he has. He knows that when the time comes, he can shoot his way out of the SUV. He has no idea how far he'll get, but he doesn't have to die trapped if he doesn't want to. No, he has lots of choices. Such as dying out in the street, or making it to a house and dying there, or possibly being picked up by some of the private contractor fucks and dying in a brutal firefight.

He is busy thinking through his next move, separating the full magazines from the partial ones, when he stops and cocks his head. The light outside the SUV has almost completely faded, so it's hard to see, but John swears there's movement out there. Movement not very Z-like. He picks up the highly modified M4 rifle he snagged from a dead PC and slaps a magazine home.

Some of the Zs start to hiss loudly and turn from the SUV, their attention drawn to whatever is out there. John keeps the rifle butt pressed to his right shoulder, glad that it's his left that is wounded. Well, not really *glad*... He watches carefully, tracking the changing behavior and movements of the Zs. Soon most are gone from the SUV and John can hear the distinctive sounds of skulls being crushed and bodies dropping to the pavement.

The sun has hit the crest of the mountains and the bright sunset glare nearly blinds him as he tries to make out what is happening outside the tinted windows of the SUV. Not all of the Zs have left the vehicle; some just refuse to give up, knowing the prey inside is theirs for the picking if they could just get in.

But even those drop and John takes a deep breath and slowly, very slowly, lets it out as his finger lightly touches the trigger of the rifle. A light knock at the driver's window, makes John turn quickly, ready to fire.

"Hello?" a voice calls quietly, trying not to draw more Zs to the SUV. "Is someone alive in there?"

John knows that voice, but can't quite place it.

"Hey! Whoever is in there, don't shoot!" the voice says. "I'm going to open this door and check on you. Just hold your fire, okay?"

John is about to place the voice when the door opens. He readies himself and is one squeeze away from blowing away the head that looks inside.

"Fuck me, Stuart," John says, "am I glad to see you."

John lowers his rifle and lets out a grateful sigh.

"John? What the fuck?" Stuart asks. "How'd get yourself stuck in here? And what the fuck is that smell?"

"Needed a secure place to pass out," John says, nodding his head towards the mess that is his left shoulder. "Had to perform some emergency surgery."

"Smells like you cauterized the wound," Stuart replies, his nose crinkling even more from the stench. "Damn, soldier, that takes guts."

"I was passed out until you showed up," John says. "I was about to make my move when you took care of the Zs for me."

"Yeah, you were," Stuart laughs. "No offense, but you wouldn't have made it ten feet before they would have taken you down. At least in the state you're in now."

"No offense taken," John smiles. "You're probably right."

"Hey, dude, why ain't you using your own rifle?" Shep asks from behind Stuart, looking at John's M110.

"I'm out of ammo," John says. "Critter has some back at his holler, but doesn't do me any good out here."

"Carry that," Stuart says to Shep. "He'll want it later. That M4 he's holding will just piss him off."

"Already has," John says. "You guys come for me specifically? Or is this just a happy accident?"

"On our way to scope out the entrance to the Grove Park," Stuart says. "See what they are up to there."

"They are up to a lot," John replies. "I'll come with and fill you in." He looks past Stuart at Shep and then Harlan's face. "You trust these two to be stealthy? We're gonna have to go in full silent or we'll be spotted before we hit the main road."

"Why? What do you know?" Stuart asks, looking over his shoulder at the carnage around them. "I'm guessing all of this is connected to the Grove Park?"

"They have Elsbeth, Long Pork, and his family," John says. "And I think the President is there."

"What?" Stuart exclaims.

"Help me out of here and I'll fill you in," John says. "And please tell me you have some water."

***

Normally, I would be glad I'm not the one in the fight cage, but tonight there is no normality or gladness to be fucking found.

Not when I'm looking at the terrified faces of my family pressed against the chain link, their eyes darting to the crowd, to the Zs moaning inside the cage, and at each other. The floodlights that shine down on the cage make it impossible for them to see me, and I have been told that if I cry out to them, they'll die right there, so I have to just sit here, my hands tucked away, my mouth shut, and watch in horror.

"Look, Mr. Stanford," Mondello says from my side. "I'm a fair man. Tell me why Ms. Foster needed you with her and I'll let them go."

"I already told you," I reply, "she wanted me to draw in my friend."

"This Elsbeth woman?" Mondello asks. "Why her?"

"I don't know," I say, "honestly, man, I don't."

"I can't believe that," Mondello says. "Do you believe that, Mr. Jameson?"

Cowboy is standing two feet from us, his rifle in the crook of his arm, his eyes tracking the Zs inside the cage.

"Could be he's telling the truth," Cowboy says. "Foster did have his family. Now we do. I say we send them in one at a time. I'm sure once he sees that little girl of his go down as zed chow, he'll remember a few things. But if he doesn't, then we'll know he's not lying. Ain't a father in the world that will stay quiet after watching his daughter get torn apart."

"Don't you fucking dare," I snarl.

"I will dare," Mondello says. "But I'm not cruel like Mr. Jameson here. I'm going to put them in there together. The family that fights zeds together, may not die together."

"Come on!" I say. "Charlie is sixteen! Greta is thirteen! Don't do this! You can have the Blue Ridge Parkway. Do whatever the fuck you want! Make it your slave highway and move supplies back and forth from Charlottesville to Hotlanta! Fuck if I care. Just let my family go. We'll slip away and you'll never see us again."

"Right," Mondello says. "Do you think you're the first man to beg in front of me? You'll say anything. But as soon as I let you go, you'll crawl back to your subdivision, regroup, and make my life difficult. I didn't just come here to secure the Parkway. You seem to forget that. I came here to secure a labor force. This Foster business is just a distraction." Mondello leans in close to me, his eyes intense and hard to look at. "I am not a man that has time for distractions. But I'm also not a man to let loose threads unravel everything. I need to know what Ms. Foster is up to. And you will tell me."

"I don't fucking know!" I shout.

Even over the loud chatter of the crowd, Greta hears me. I see her elbow Stella and point up towards where I'm sitting.

"Dad!" Greta calls out. Stella tries to hush her, but she keeps it up. "DAD! HELP US!"

"Dad! Help us!" the crowd starts to mock until it becomes an unbearable chant.

Dear God, people are fucked up.

"Oh, now look what you did," Mondello says. "Mr. Jameson? If you will."

Cowboy lets out a long whistle and guards open the cage, shoving my family inside. They toss in a few weapons as an afterthought, and then secure the cage and step back, ready to watch the show with everyone else. I want to close my eyes and let it just be over, but I can't. I have to watch. I have to do something. I have to think.

"Have you talked to Elsbeth?" I ask.

"What's that?" Mondello replies, turning from the cage. "The canny woman? Of course we have. But she refuses to say anything. Just keeps asking to be fed."

"She what?" I ask, my eyes tracking my family's movements. The Zs have spotted them, but Mondello obviously put slow ones in there.

"She keeps saying she wants long pork," Cowboy laughs. "How fucked up is that? Like we're going to feed her human flesh to get her to talk."

There it is. I smile.

"What?" Cowboy asks. "What did I say?"

"She's not asking for long pork to eat," I say. "She's asking to see me. I'm Long Pork. That's what she calls me."

"She calls you Long Pork?" Mondello frowns. "Do I want to know?"

"Doesn't matter," I say, trying to keep my anxiety under check as I watch the Zs get closer to Stella and the kids. Stella is holding a cracked baseball bat while Greta has a length of rebar and Charlie holds a 2x4 with a nail in it.

Are you fucking kidding me? They actually gave him a fucking board with a nail in it? What the fuck is this? A Simpson's Halloween special?

"Let them go and I'll talk to her," I say. "Do it now. If they are harmed one bit, then fuck you."

"I don't think that will be the case, Mr. Stanford," Mondello says. "I'm fairly certain that you'd still help if only two of them are left."

"Take them out of there," I say. "The only way Elsbeth will talk is if she knows my family hasn't been harmed. She loves them. Got that? She may want to talk only to me, but she won't say shit if she knows I let them get hurt. She'll blame me for it. Trust me on this shit, man. Don't fuck up your chance."

Mondello studies me for a moment then nods. "Tell you what, Mr. Stanford; this is what I'll do." He looks at Cowboy and some hidden communication passes between them. Cowboy starts to speak into his com while Mondello turns back to me. "I'll have the young canny woman join us here and she can decide your family's fate. She talks to you and they are set free. She doesn't and they have to fight. I will make this very clear to her in simple terms she can understand."

"She isn't stupid," I say, "she'll understand complex terms too."

"No need to get ahead of ourselves," Mondello says.

He stands up and raises his hand. Instantly, the cage is opened and guards rush in to separate my family from the encroaching Zs. The Zs are secured with catchpoles and my family is pushed back against the fence. For a split second there, I swear Stella is going to bury the broken baseball bat in the skull of the guard that grabs her, but luckily, she restrains herself.

The crowd boos and calls out, aiming their disappointment at Mondello. He takes it in good nature, but guards step forward and the crowd quiets down.

"Ladies and gentlemen, please," Mondello says. "Not to worry, tonight's entertainment will commence shortly. In fact, we'll add to it."

The cage is opened and Critter and Ms. Foster are pushed inside. No extra weapons are offered to them. But, from the other side of the cage, guards with several more Zs enter, adding to the numbers of undead.

Critter looks about, his eyes taking everything in. He looks pretty badly beaten, but he holds his head up and doesn't even flinch as some of the guards let a couple Zs get close to him.

Ms. Foster, on the other hand, looks like she's had better days. Just as beaten as Critter, she hangs her head, refusing to look up at the crowd or over at Mondello. She just lets a guard lead her to my family and stays still as the restraints on her hands are cut loose. Critter walks up to Stella, but he's told to shut the fuck up by one of the guards.

This is getting better and better by the second. Fuck.

"Long Pork?" Elsbeth asks as she's brought over to us. "Why are they doing this? Are they gonna eat us up? Those people look like cannies." Her hands bound in front of her, she nods towards the crowd. "I'd know that crazy anywhere."

"Please, Ms. Elsbeth, is it? We do not feed human flesh to our labor force," Mondello says. "Too much of a chance for the spread of disease. A sick worker is a useless worker."

"This man says you want to talk," Elsbeth says, looking over her shoulder at Cowboy. "What you want to talk about?"

"You see that woman down there?" Mondello asks, pointing towards Foster. "She was very keen to get a hold of you. I'd like you to tell me why."

"I don't know her," Elsbeth says.

And for the first time since I've known her, I think Elsbeth is lying. Or at the very least, unsure of the truth of her answer.

"El," I say. "I know you're mad at me right now-"

"I'm hopping pissed as shit at you," Elsbeth says. "This is your fault."

"I don't' know about that," I say. "I was taken prisoner. I haven't exactly had freedom of choice the past couple of days."

"You messed with the gas," Elsbeth states. She leaves it at that.

Fuck. She's right. I did mess with the gas, which led me to get captured by Cowboy in the first place, and taken to Foster. It did all snowball from that moment where I thought flipping switches would fix things. I officially fucking hate switches and swear on my soul I'll never flip them again.

Unless I have to.

"I need to know why that woman wants you," Mondello says, focusing on Elsbeth. "You tell me and Mr. Stanford's family is set free. Don't tell me and they start fighting some zeds. Even with Ms. Foster's help, they won't survive."

"Please, El, if you know her, just tell him how," I plead. "Think of Stella and the kids."

"I don't know her," Elsbeth says. "I've never seen her before."

Again, I don't believe her. Mondello doesn't either.

"That is just too bad," Mondello says. "Mr. Jameson?"

The whistle again and the Zs are set loose. Stella and Critter get in front of the kids, but Foster just stands there, looking at her feet. The Zs shamble their way across the cage; eager for the free meal they've been offered.

"Don't'!" I cry. "Please! What else do you want? How about the Farm? I can get you in there! I can take you to some of Critter's caches! There has to be something else! PLEASE!"

"You'll do all of those things eventually, Mr. Stanford," Mondello says. "Mr. Jameson is very persuasive."

"You won't get fucking shit from me if my family is harmed!" I yell. "Stop this now or you get nothing!"

"Is that your only family, Mr. Stanford?" Mondello asks. "Or were there more of you on Z-Day?"

"There were more," I answer. There were, but Stella and I don't talk about it. It's too painful what happened and what we had to do.

"Then you know what it is like to see family turned, don't you?" Mondello says. "I know what it's like also. I know the conflict that sticks in your very soul as you watch what used to be a person you loved turn into a flesh eating monster. I know that conflict very well. I also know the pain of having to make the decision of what to do with them."

Fuck.

"Did you make any of those decisions?" he asks.

"Yes," I say very quietly.

"What was that?"

"Yes, I made those decisions," I reply.

"Do you want to have to make those decisions again?" Mondello asks. "I can arrange that for you. You see, Mr. Stanford, your pain won't end when your family dies. It will just begin. You'll watch them turn, then you'll watch them suffer as zeds in this very cage. Night after night, I will make sure you are forced to witness them fight humans. And I'll make sure they win. I'll make sure you see your beautiful little girl eat the intestines of a worker that strayed from the rules. I'll make sure your son's first taste of a woman is her bloody throat. I'll make sure your wife eats the privates of every man that is put in there. You'll get to watch her chomping cock and balls for the rest of your life."

"No, no, no," I say, shaking my head, "don't. Please."

"Pleases get you nowhere," Mondello snaps. "Nowhere! I only want answers, not pleases!"

"El?" I ask. "Tell him what you know."

Elsbeth shakes her head. "I don't know anything."

"But you've seen that woman before, right?" I ask. "Be honest. Just tell the truth on that. I know you've seen her before."

Elsbeth looks from me to Mondello and then down at the cage. She starts to get fidgety and shakes her head.

"Elsbeth!" I shout. "Please! For fuck's sake!"

The Zs are almost to Stella and Critter. They are ready for them, but there are too many. I count twenty Zs. No way Stella and Critter can fight off that many, even if Greta and Charlie help. Maybe if Foster joins in the fight, but she isn't looking useful right now.

"Elsbeth!" I shout again.

Her eyes lock with mine and I see nothing but fear. This is a woman that I have personally witnessed kill fifty Zs by herself. She's saved my ass more times than I'm proud to admit. She stuck with us, with the people of Whispering Pines, even though Stuart killed her father. Which may or may not be her actual father. But, that's beside the point.

The woman I know as Elsbeth, is one badass mother fucker. She's a killer, through and through.

But the young woman I see before me isn't that Elsbeth. She looks ten years younger. Her fear is almost coming off her in waves. Whatever she knows terrifies her. But I have to ignore that.

I have to think of my family. I have to do whatever it takes to help them.

"You have to tell me, Elsbeth," I say, getting up and walking down to the chain link fence.

"Whoa there!" Cowboy shouts.

"Let him be," Mondello says as I get to the fence.

I start to climb it, getting to the top and swinging a leg over. The crowd, which had been cheering and yelling, goes silent as they watch me do something very stupid.

"Elsbeth, tell him how you know her," I say, "or I jump in with them. You'll be alone again, El. I'll be dead, Stella and the kids will be dead, everyone you've come to know will be dead. Just tell him the truth."

"I don't know her," Elsbeth replies.

"But you've seen her before?" I ask.

There's a long pause, but then she nods.

"You have? Where?" Mondello asks. "Where have you seen her?"

Elsbeth stays quiet, her eyes locked on mine. I nod. She shakes her head. I nod again. She shakes her head. I swing my other leg over, wincing at the pain in my fucked up hand. She better answer soon or I have totally fucked myself. I can't hang on much longer, even with my feet wedged into the holes in the chain link.

"Just fucking kill her," Cowboy says. "We're wasting everyone's time. This chick is not part of the job. Who fucking cares if Foster wants her? Foster's done. Look at her. None of this shit matters."

"It matters to Ms. Foster so it matters to me," Mondello says. "And you work for me so it should matter to you, as well. Got that, Mr. Jameson? We'll waste as much time as I'd like."

Speaking of wasting time, I can hear my children whimpering behind me. I'd love to turn and look, but my balance on the fence is pretty fucking precarious. If I even turn my head, I'll fall in there. Which does no one any good. As long as I'm in Mondello's good graces, I have a chance of saving my family. I just don't have much time.

"Where have you seen her?" Mondello asks Elsbeth. "Tell me. Tell me now!"

"In my dreams!" Elsbeth says.

That's not the answer any of us are expecting.

"What was that?" Mondello asks.

"Huh?" I say.

"See? Fucking waste of time," Cowboy states.

Mondello looks from Elsbeth to Foster and back. "Your dreams? Why do you see her in your dreams? What is she doing?"

The Zs are getting closer, I can tell from the sounds. In just seconds, Stella and Critter will have to start fighting. I have seconds to fix this shit.

"Elsbeth, tell him about your dreams," I say. "Tell him everything."

"We're gonna listen to some wackjob's dreams? What the fuck?" Cowboy complains. "Maybe we should get a psychic up here. Do a tarot reading or two. Fucking A…"

"Mr. Jameson, I won't warn you again," Mondello says. He reaches for Elsbeth, but she shrinks back. He smiles at her and if I didn't know he was a total asshole, I'd think the smile was genuine. "Ms. Elsbeth-"

"Just Elsbeth," she says.

"Okay, Elsbeth," Mondello says. "What is Ms. Foster doing in your dreams?"

"I don't know," Elsbeth shrugs.

"I think you do," Mondello says.

"Jace!" Stella calls out. Elsbeth looks down there immediately, her face filled with concern. Mondello's smile widens.

"Tell me, Elsbeth," Mondello says. "And all of this can be over. Tell me what Ms. Foster is doing in your dreams."

"She's…," Elsbeth starts.

"Yes?" Mondello pushes. "Go on."

"She's…well…she's," Elsbeth stutters. "She's singing. To me. She sings to me in my dreams."

"She sings to you?" Mondello asks. "In your dreams you see Ms. Foster? And she sings to you?"

He looks down at Foster and narrows his eyes. I can't see what she's doing, I'm too focused on Elsbeth and the fact that my arms are starting to shake uncontrollably. I won't be able to hang on much longer, so I try to swing my leg back up and hook it over the top of the fence.

Yeah, that doesn't work so well.

You see, part of surviving the zombie apocalypse is being very aware of your surroundings. Sounds simple, but it's not. There are so many things in life that can distract you from the task at hand. Like now, for example, I should be thinking about the Zs inside the cage. You know, the cage that I am most of the way inside, hanging from the top of the fence. But I am distracted by the sounds of my family, by the look of fear on Elsbeth's face, by the incredible revelation she's just told Mondello, and by the fact that Cowboy keeps moving ever closer to where I am. I'm pretty sure the fucker wants to push me all the way in the cage.

So, those are the distractions. What did they distract me from? Oh, just two Zs that have shambled over to my position and are reaching their putrid hands up to grab me.

Which is what they do. Grab me.

"FUCK!" I yell as I'm yanked down into the cage. "OH, SHIT FUCKING COCK SHIT FU-!"

The last fuck is cut off as my back slams into the ground and all the wind is knocked out of my lungs. The two Zs are on me in an instant. I slam my good fist into the face of one, knocking it back, and then slam my bad fist into the other, doing nothing but causing some serious fucking agony to radiate up my arm.

"FUCK!" There's that last fuck. It came back.

"JACE!" Stella screams.

"DAD!" the kids yell.

"YAY!" the crowd cheers.

"LONG PORK!" Elsbeth cries.

"Rocky!" I shout. I just can't help myself sometimes.

Sploosh goes the Zs head. And then crack goes a gunshot.

Wait…what?

"Who's firing?" Mondello yells. "Hold your fire!"

The Z I knocked away doesn't care what's going on and lunges for me again.

Sploosh. Crack.

"WHO IS FIRING?" Mondello roars. "HOLD YOUR FUCKING FIRE!"

Then the opposite of his order happens and the night is filled with the sounds of automatic gunfire.

CHAPTER EIGHT

I roll to my side, see Foster lift her head, a seriously scary, and fucked up smile on her face. She actually winks at me as she takes off for the fence, leaps at it, grabs the top, and swings herself over. Landing right in front of a shocked Cowboy.

The two go at it fast, almost faster than I can keep track of. Not that I need to be paying attention to that. I should really be paying attention to the screaming coming from my family. Or the gunfire that's taking out the guards that ring the outside of the fight cage.

I'm gonna go with family first.

I push myself to my feet and head straight for Stella and Critter as they start killing Zs. I come up behind a Z and reach out, snapping its neck as I sprint past. Doesn't kill it, but it immobilizes the fucking thing. Its jaws snap at my ankles. Fuck you, ankle biter!

Another Z turns and tries to grab me as I come up on it. How'd the fucker know I was there? Doesn't matter since I slam my fist into its face. I grab its lower jaw and yank it right off, then jam it in the mother fucker's eye socket. Down the bitch goes!

Fuck yeah!

Ooof.

Two Zs come at me from each side. I'm tackled and then pinned, barely able to keep the things from biting me. I punch and punch, knocking the biting heads back and away, but they just

131

keep coming back. What can I do? They're pretty fresh Zs, so they have some meat still on them. And meat is weight. I'm stuck.

"Hey!" Greta screams. "Get off my dada!"

Aw, she called me dada. Holy fuck, she just stabbed one through the back of the head!

She yanks the rebar free and slams it into the skull of the second Z, crushing the bone and splattering rotten grey matter all over me. The Z shakes for a minute and then is still, forever. Greta flicks the gunk from the rebar and holds out her hand. I take it.

"Thanks, sweetie," I say.

"No problem," she shrugs, "you need a weapon."

"Yeah, I do," I say.

"Can't have mine," she smiles then turns and runs at an oncoming Z. That's my apocalypse girl!

The gunfight intensifies as Cowboy's men return fire, finally seeming to get a bead on the location of the shooters. I glance over and see Foster and Cowboy in a deadly duel. Hands and feet are flying and meeting each other. Cowboy uses his strength and size while Foster uses her speed and agility. When he lands a punch, she stumbles back; when she lands a punch, he cries out in pain.

In the pre-Z days, you could have charged money on pay per view for this shit!

But, this is post-Z and they aren't battling it out in the Octagon for a stupid belt. They're trying to kill each other. I, however, am in a fight cage and need to fucking pay attention to that fact.

A Z snarls at me and I sweep its legs. Before I can stomp its face in, Charlie slams that board with a nail in it down hard. Splat goes that fucker. He pulls the board, with the nail, free and looks at me, a satisfied smirk on his face.

"Behind you," I say.

His smile fades and he spins around, bringing the board up. Then down as the Z that was reaching for him meets some serious nail action. More splat. He looks over his shoulder, an eyebrow raised.

"Good one," I smile. "Wouldn't want to give your old man that board with a nail in it, would you?"

"Don't think so," Charlie says. "Behind you."

I smirk. "Ha ha."

"No, seriously Dad, behind you!" he yells. "Duck!"

I do and board with nail swings over my head. I hear a Z grunt, then look to my left and see a head tumble away, its eyes wide and jaws snapping open and closed. Charlie chases it down and crushes its skull, ending its bodiless existence.

"You better go get that one too," I say, pointing to a Z creeping up on his sister.

Charlie nods and runs over to Greta, knocking the Z away and then standing with her back to back. My children haven't had to fight like this in a long time; not since the early days of Whispering Pines. But, unfortunately in this world, they have had to fight like this. More times than I care to think about. So I watch them briefly (Head in the game, Jace!) and I feel pride swell inside me.

We may be from a subdivision, but damn can we kick ass.

"Jace!" Stella yells.

I look around and see her trying to free Critter from the corner he's gotten himself backed into. Six Zs are after him and he's doing a great job fighting them off, but they are too much for him. I see what Stella sees: he's going to lose.

I dig deep and run hard, leaping and tackling two Zs before they can get to Critter. We go down in a tangle of living and undead limbs. I feel teeth try to bite into my arm and I yank back hard. Panic sets in and I look at my forearm, but there are no puncture marks, just some bruising. Thank God.

I drop an elbow on one Z's head while I plant my knee in the chest of the other. Ribs start to crack and my knee sinks, sending me off balance as I try for another elbow blow. The first Z hisses at me and lunges, going for the kill bite. I'm able to get my bad hand up under its chin and I push, keeping its face away. But the second Z, with the smooshy ribs, is twisting its torso about, ignoring the damage it's doing to itself, and tries to chomp on my side.

I don't hear the gunshots, simply because there are too many to sort through, but I do see the results as both Z heads explode all over me. I'm coated in Z brains as I shove the bodies away and get to my feet, wiping the gunk away and flicking it into the dirt. I try to see who just saved my ass, but there is too much chaos.

Guards are firing and screaming; the crowd is panicked and running for their lives; Foster and Cowboy are involved in some serious mortal combat. But where's Mondello and Elsbeth?

Stella is at my side and hands me the baseball bat, since that's kinda my thing.

"What about you?" I ask.

She raises a Beretta 9mm and grins, then nods her head towards the far side of the cage. There stands Stuart with a quick wave and a nod. Then he's burying a knife in the gut of a guard and tossing the man to the side while he jams his own 9mm up under another guard's chin and pulls the trigger. Fuck, living blood is bright. You get used to seeing the dark, black blood of Zs so much that you forget what real blood looks like sometimes.

Not that I don't have plenty of chances to witness it tonight. It's fucking everywhere.

The bat feels good in my hand (don't tell The Bitch) and I take a couple swipes before I step up to the last few Zs that are after us. Swing and a hit! Oh, another! That's a double, folks! Z heads are crushed and their corpses fall, truly dead now. I look around and see Charlie and Greta finishing up the last Z that's after them, each taking turns bringing their weapon down on the thing's head. Pretty sure it was done for ten smacks ago, but why ruin their fun? They earned it.

"You okay?" I ask Stella.

"No, I'm not fucking okay!" she yells as she wraps her arms around me and kisses me hard. "Don't ever ask a stupid question like that again!"

"No promises, baby," I smile. "You know me and my penchant for stupid questions."

"Come on!" Harlan yells from the cage gate. "Move ass, people!"

We do. I grab onto Charlie and Greta as we run by, headed for the gate. But dirt kicks up in front of us and we skid to a stop. Two guards, close to where Mondello had been standing, are aiming right at us. They open fire again and we jump back, burying our faces in the dirt.

"Fuck you!" Stella screams and I look over at her.

She takes aim and fires until the 9 is empty and just clicking. I wait for the bullets to shred our bodies, but they don't come.

Rolling over, I look and see the two guards crumpled in the seats, blood pouring from them.

"Damn," I say, "nice shooting, Tex."

"Wasn't me," Stella frowns. "I think every one of my shots missed."

"Then who was it?"

Stella points to the far end of the cage and I see John leaning against the chain link, the barrel of his rifle resting through one of the holes. He smiles and nods, then raises his eyebrows and looks towards the gate.

"Right," I say. "We better go."

We get to the gate and Harlan shoves us along, back around towards John.

"Where's Elsbeth?" I shout. "Have you seen her?"

"The canny? No," Harlan shouts back. "Was she here?"

"Yeah, she was here!" I say. "We have to find her!"

"We have to get out of here first!" Harlan yells. "We didn't come here to look for that canny! We came to get you!"

"Fuck you, Harlan!" Greta yells. "She's family and we save family!"

"She ain't my family," he replies.

"She's mine," Greta says, smacking the rebar in her palm.

"Hey, calm down," Stella says. "Both of you. Harlan? Where are the vehicles?"

"What vehicles?"

"The vehicles you came in," Stella says. "Don't tell me you walked."

"Then I won't tell you," Harlan frowns. "But we did."

"Shit," Stella says. "Then we need vehicles if we're to get away from here."

"What about all of these people? And what about Elsbeth?" I ask.

"I'm getting the kids in a vehicle and back to the Farm," Stella says. "Are you coming with us?"

"Yes, of course!" I say.

We head around the cage towards the front entrance to the Grove Park and the parking lot. Pretty good assumption that's where the vehicles are. We get to the walkway that leads to the front and stop.

Cowboy.

He lifts his hand and Stella screams, holding her hand over Greta's eyes.

"Stop, Mom!" Greta yells and shoves her hand away.

In Cowboy's hand is the severed head of Foster, dripping blood from her ragged neck.

"Didn't kill the brain," Cowboy says. "She's gonna turn soon. Want to watch? Ah, fuck it. I think I'll just kill you."

In his other hand is a machine pistol and he takes aim at us. Stella and I shove the kids to the ground, with Critter following right on top of us, but Harlan doesn't make it. His body dances and shakes as he's torn apart by automatic fire. The machine pistol jams and Cowboy swears, tossing it aside.

Chunks of pavement spray up between his feet and he leaps back, his eyes searching for the source before he drops Foster's head, turns and runs. The head rolls down the slight incline and stops right by us. I kick it away and get to my feet, helping Stella up as Critter helps the kids up. The head just keeps rolling down the hill, lost in the darkness.

"Guess she lost that workplace dispute," Critter cackles.

"Jesus," I say, shaking my head. "Not now, Critter."

"Got to give an old man his due," Critter says.

"Vehicles!" Stella shouts, pointing up ahead. She takes off with the kids.

"What about-" I start, but a hand on my back, pushing me forward answers my question.

"Right here," Stuart says.

"John?" I ask.

"Already on it," Stuart says, nodding up ahead where John is standing, laying down covering fire while Stella and the kids, with Critter behind, sprint to an SUV.

"Anyone else?" I ask.

"Shep," Stuart says, "but he didn't make it."

"Neither did Harlan," I say. "Sorry."

"What for?" Stuart asks. "They were good men, but they knew what they signed up for. It was just a matter of time before something happened."

"Yeah, but I'm still sorry," I say. Stuart nods.

We get into the SUV and Stuart takes the front, while John takes the passenger's seat. Stella and the kids cram into the middle seat and Critter and I hop into the fold up backseat. Gunfire follows us and Stuart gets the SUV started, finding the keys already in it. John leans across Stuart and rests the barrel of his rifle on the open windowsill.

"Sorry," John says. "This will be-"

We don't hear the rest of what he says because we all have our hands jammed against our ears as he opens fire. A man screams and then John pulls his rifle back, turns about and points it out his window, firing again. Another man screams. Fuck, Special Forces folk don't fuck around. And I'm very glad for that.

Stuart slams the accelerator down and the SUV rockets forward. We dodge the laborers running here and there, but barely stop in time as another SUV cuts us off.

"There!" I shout. "That was Elsbeth! And Mondello!"

"Who?" Stuart asks.

"The fucking President of the United States," I say.

"If that's true," Critter says, "you may want to be a might more respectful."

"Fuck him," I snarl. "He's a false leader set up to be the Consortium's puppet."

They all look at me like I'm crazy.

"It's a long fucking story," I say.

"He's right," John says. "We heard chatter that the Secretary of Homeland Security was taking the office. Just never had a chance to verify."

"Oh, it's fucking verified," I say. "Follow that fuck!"

"Jace, the kids," Stella says. "We need to get back to the Farm."

"No, we need to get Elsbeth," Greta says. "We save family, right?"

"Sweetie," Stella starts, but Greta holds up her hand.

"Can it, Mom," Greta says. "We save family."

"I sure as shit don't want to be the one to tell Julio we watched his lady get taken and did nothing about it," Stuart says, hitting the accelerator again. "Let's get that girl."

"And don't ever tell your mother to can it, you hear me?" I say.

Greta nods.

Mondello's SUV is already up the drive and speeding around the corner by the time we negotiate our way through the chaos. I see taillights in the distance, then they are gone.

"We're gonna lose them," Greta says.

"No, we aren't," I reply. "I know exactly where he's heading!"

"Enlighten me, Jace," Stuart says, taking a curve and nearly sending the SUV up onto two wheels.

"Buckle up," Stella tells the kids. She doesn't get an argument over that one.

The road may be a residential switchback, but it's still a switchback. We all try to brace ourselves to keep from rocking into each other as Stuart cranks the wheel one way then back the other way. He follows the same route up that Foster used when bringing me to the Grove Park.

"Just keep going as fast as you can," I tell Stuart, "the road is clear all the way."

"All the way to where?" he asks.

"The Blue Ridge Parkway," I say. "Mondello is going to make a run for it. He's heading back to Charlottesville."

"We are not following him all the way to Charlottesville," Stella says. "No fucking way, Jace."

"Won't have to, Mrs. Stanford," John says. "If gunny here can get me in range, I can take them out."

"And by take them out you mean the tires, right?" I ask.

"Exactly," John says, "although these SUVs have run flats, so it won't stop them completely."

"But it'll make things very hard on them," Stuart says. "Giving us time to catch up."

"What about gas?" Charlie asks, shoving his hand against the roof of the SUV to keep from flailing into his sister. "Do we have enough?"

We all wait for the answer.

"Depends on how much they have," Stuart says. "Half a tank in here."

"So they better have less than that," Charlie replies.

"Good math, genius," Greta smirks.

"Shut it, you two," Stella says. "Not in the mood."

"None of us are," Critter says. "Ain't nothing worse than the bickering of siblings. My mother used to smack me and Hollis upside the head every time we started in on each other."

"That explains a lot," Stella says.

Critter doesn't respond. Damn, she really doesn't like the guy.

"There," John says, pointing ahead and above us.

We see taillights take a turn and then they are lost. But at least we know we're on their trail.

"Why do you think they're heading for the Parkway?" Stuart asks. "And why Charlottesville?"

"That's the new capitol," I reply. "It's the seat of the US government, whatever that may be."

"Sounds like you learned a little while you were gone," Stuart says.

"Where's Captain Leeds?" Charlie asks.

"Looks like we done forgot someone," Critter said. "We going back or is he expendable since he's not family?"

"Oh, just shut up, you old coot," Stella says.

"That's the best ya got, missy?"

"Not now," Stuart says. "Jace? Where is Captain Leeds?"

John looks back at me and can instantly tell by the look on my face what happened.

"He didn't make it, huh?" John asks.

"No," I reply, "he didn't."

"Was it a good death?" Stuart asks.

"How can any death be good?" Stella asks.

"There are some better than others," John says. "Trust me."

"It was the best death possible," I say.

"Care to elaborate on that?" Stuart asks.

"No," I state flatly, "not right now."

"Fair enough," Stuart nods as he takes a seriously sharp curve.

We all rock into each other and I feel the SUV's tires slide some. This isn't going to be fun when we hit the parkway and only have a guardrail between us and several hundred feet of open air. Hey, maybe the trees will catch us and we'll only fall fifty feet. One can only hope.

"Back, back, back!" John yells as Stuart rockets past the turn.

"What? Where?" Stuart yells, slamming on the brakes, putting the SUV into reverse.

"I see them!" Charlie yells, pointing towards red lights between the trees.

Stuart speeds backwards and cranks the wheel hard as we get back to the turn.

"A little heads up would have been nice, Jace," Stuart says, putting it in drive and moving ass.

"Sorry," I say. "I was coming down last time. And it was light out. Couple big differences."

"Excuses, excuses," Greta says.

"Damn, you're just busting balls left and right tonight," Charlie laughs.

"Getting drugged and kidnapped brings out the snark in me," Greta says.

"I thought just waking up did that?" Charlie replies.

"Stop," Stella says.

The kids shut up.

And then we are at the Blue Ridge Parkway. And one shitty decision: right or left?

"You see them?" Stuart asks, craning his head back and forth. "I don't."

"Charlottesville is north, y'all," Critter says. "Ain't hard to figure out."

"Unless he's going to Atlanta," I say. "Which he could be too."

"Atlanta?" Stuart asks.

"Another long story," I say.

"Hold on," John says and hops out of the SUV. He sweeps the area, always ready for Zs, and steps out into the middle of the Parkway. "Turn off the headlights!"

Stuart turns the headlights off, plunging everything into pitch darkness. Pre-Z the glow of Asheville city lights would have provided some illumination, if slight. But, post-Z there's nothing, just pure darkness. We all lean forward, trying to get our own look.

"There!" John says. "Charlottesville!"

He hurries back into the SUV and Stuart is turning and speeding north before he even has the door closed. Doesn't even faze John.

Stuart presses the accelerator pedal all the way to the floor. Or at least that's what it feels like as we are shoved back into our seats. I'd love nothing more than to just close my eyes and wait for it all to be over as we take curve after curve at speeds I'm pretty sure are not safe on the Parkway. Or safe on any road, really.

"How close do you need to be?" Stuart asks John. "What's the range on that thing?"

"The range is shit," John replies. "But at least the stability sucks."

"Great," Stuart says. "I'll get as close as possible. I highly doubt Mr. President can outrun a marine on the open road."

"Even though I root Army, I won't argue with that," John says. "I don't think the man did military duty in any branch. Pretty sure he was in construction."

"So don't get in a game of bulldozer chicken with him," I say. No one responds. "You know, like in Footloose."

"Jace," Stella says, "not now, honey."

"Fine. Whatever," I sigh. "I thought it was funny."

I have to say that during the day the Parkway can be intimidating, let alone at night, what with the sharp curves and constant change in elevation. Oh, and there are the tunnels. Yep. Tunnels. Like the one we're coming up on now.

"Hold on," Stuart says. "John?"

"On it," John says, rolling down the window. He settles the M4 on the side mirror, trying to steady it as much as possible.

"On what?" Stella asks then belches. "Sorry. I get car sick."

"Well ain't that just wonderful," Critter says. "We coulda dropped ya off, ya know? Ain't no cowardice in sittin' this one out."

"Stop being an idiot," Stella says.

"Lost cause, ma'am," Critter laughs. "Been tryin' my whole life."

The tunnel is freakishly dark. It's like driving in ink made of rock. The only evidence there is a world is by catching the sheen of water on the sides of the tunnel. Otherwise, you'd just think you were driving into nothing. Good thing Stuart's at the wheel. Bad thing is that he hasn't slowed down. Not. At. All.

"Ohhhhhh, shiiiiiiiiiiiit," Charlie and Greta say at the same time as we take one last turn in the tunnel.

I'd laugh, but I'm too busy keeping the piss in my bladder and not all over the seat. Would suck to piss myself. Especially with

Critter in the SUV. Jeez, he'd tell everyone and then I'd be called Piss Pants or Piss Seat or just Pissy. Critter's good that way.

Not that Long Pork is any great thing.

"There," Stuart says as we shoot from the tunnel.

John leans out the window, his eye to the sight. How he can track anything at night, I have no idea. It doesn't look like a night scope is on that rifle. Maybe he's tracking by the tail lights? But they keep disappearing as Mondello takes the curves just as fast as we do. But then John is a trained sniper. He's the man.

Two shots and we all hold our breath as we come around the next curve. Nope. Mondello is still going. We see his taillights speed away.

"Fuck," John says. "This piece of shit isn't worth, well, shit."

"Nice oxymoron," Charlie says. "Shit not worth shit."

"He's a genius like my dad," Greta says.

"Thanks," Charlie and I answer at the same time.

"Hey!"

"Wait a minute!"

"Dial it back, sweetie," Stella says to Greta. "They're sensitive."

"Can you catch them?" John asks Stuart.

"I'm trying," Stuart replies. "But looks like this asshole has some training."

"He probably got some from the private contractors," John says. "They will train clients in defensive driving and weapons. Makes their jobs a little easier."

"It's making my job a little harder," Stuart says. "And where's the pick up on this thing? I thought they put supped up engines in these vehicles?"

"They also armor them with some heavy duty plating," John says. "Adds weight and reduces speed."

"Just give me a Humvee, any day," Stuart says.

"There," John says and leans back out the window. He fires once, twice, three times. "FUCK!"

"How do you know you missed?" Charlie asks.

"I missed, trust me," John says. "I need a different rifle."

On a whim, and since I have nothing better to do, I look in the very back cargo area. There isn't much room since the extra seats are up (which Critter and I occupy, thank you very much), but there's enough room for something interesting.

"Holy shit," I say, reaching back for what I find. Then the rear window explodes and reinforced glass shatters all over me. "HOLY SHIT!"

"Well, ain't that a kick in the dick?" Critter says as he holds his hand to the back of his shoulder. "Looks like I caught something."

"Oh, God!" Stella cries as she turns and looks.

I glance over at Critter and see that the bullet that took out the back window also went clean through Critter's shoulder.

"Ah, crap," I say, ripping his shirt in half. "Hold this on there. Tight."

"Headlights!" Stuart yells. "Looks like we're the meat in a shit sandwich."

"Lame analogy," Greta says.

"Get down!" Stella shouts at Charlie and Greta. "And stop being a snarky twat!"

I feel the heat of a second bullet and then a third whiz by my head as I try to reach what's in the back.

"I thought the windows were fucking bulletproof!" I shout. "How'd they shoot out the back one?"

"Probably AP rounds," John yells.

"So what's the fucking point of any of this shit?" I yell back. "Might as well not reinforce anything!"

"That's one way to look at it," John says. "But does help with your average crazies."

"I don't think average crazies exist anymore," I say. "It's all uber crazies these days."

The windshield cracks as another bullet enters the SUV.

"Fuck," Stuart says. "I caught the ricochet."

"You gonna make it, gunny?" John asks.

"Just a nick," Stuart replies. He sees the look John gives him. "Honest. I'm not gonna pass out and send us over the side."

"Okay," John says then turns and takes aim. "Everyone may want to close their ears. Oh, and get the fuck down."

He barely waits for us to do either of those things as he opens fire. Even with my hands pressed to my ears it's so fucking loud!

I'm willing to bet most old soldiers are stone fucking deaf. I'll be deaf in about ten seconds, I do know that.

John stops and we all wait, then when we know it's clear we sit up and look behind us. We wait…wait…wait…fuck! Headlights. John curses and ejects the magazine so he can throw a fresh one in. He pulls back the slide and smiles.

"One more time, folks," John says. "Cover your ears and get down."

We do. He shoots until the gun clicks empty. Again, we wait then pop back up and look behind.

Waiting…waiting…waiting…waiting…

"I think we- Shit fuck!" I yell, turning to John. "You sure you know how to use that thing?"

"Fuck you, Long Pork," John says, replacing the magazine.

The headlights behind us are gaining quickly. I see muzzle flashes and shout, "Get down!"

Everyone does, but it doesn't matter. The bullets weren't for us, they're for the tires.

"Fuck!" Stuart yells as he struggles to keep control of the SUV.

I know what a run flat wheel is. It's reinforced with a band of steel covering the rim so that if the tire is shot out the vehicle can still keep going. I used to watch a lot of Discovery Channel. In theory, run flats are great. Especially during the day. On an open, flat, wide road.

Not so much on the Blue Ridge Parkway.

Stuart keeps struggling, but then a second tire is shot out and it's goodnight, Irene. The SUV fish tails and for one second, I'm pretty sure we're going right over the edge. But Stuart is able to twist the wheel and send us the other way. Right into the side of the mountain.

The impact is insane. You know those slow motion crash test dummy videos? Yeah, that. Time completely slows down and it's like I'm watching every single molecule, broken down to its atoms, flying by me as we slam into nothing but rock. Everyone strains their seat belts then bounces back, slamming into their seats.

Glass and metal protest then break and tear. Shards slice my cheeks, my forehead, my arms, and my neck. I hear screaming, but have no idea if it's mine or someone else's. Probably both. Pretty sure we're all screaming, but I'm also close to deaf from the gunfire and the big crashing and smashing, so who fucking knows.

The SUV careens off the mountain and rolls backward, spinning completely around. Oh, hey, look...now we're heading for the edge! Fucking joy of joys.

I watch in horror as the SUV slides closer and closer and closer and OH, FUCK WE'RE ALL GONNA DIE!

But we don't. We hit the guardrail and crumple it, the nose of the SUV teetering over the edge. I can feel blood flowing from the hundreds of cuts I've sustained. My hands come away bloody as I feel myself to make sure I don't have any serious injuries. Not that bleeding like a stuck pig isn't serious, just not broken bone or ruptured spleen serious.

The headlights are getting closer.

Shit.

"Crawl out the back," Stuart says as he unbuckles and carefully pushes himself into the back seat, helping Charlie and Greta climb over to me. "John? You cool?"

"As a mother fucking cucumber," John says. "Right behind you."

I crawl out of the broken back window and help Stella and the kids out onto the shoulder of the road. Stuart helps Critter out since he's pretty fucking banged up and dazed. I'm guessing he's losing a lot of blood from that shoulder wound.

"What the fuck?" Stuart says as he climbs out, looking from the back of the SUV and then to me. "That would have been nice to know about."

"I was trying to tell everyone when all the shooting and the crashing happened," I say. "I'm guessing John can use that?"

"Use what?" John asks as he gets to the way back seat and looks into the cargo area. "Holy shit. Yeah. I can use that."

"Use what?" Charlie asks.

"The big gun we crawled over to get out," Greta says. "How have you not been eaten yet?"

"Kids," Stella warns. "Shut the fuck up."

Stuart gets the tailgate open and John is just one big smile as he pulls the very large gun out of the SUV. His smile gets even bigger as he sees the box of magazines that go with it.

"Fucking Barret M82 or Army XM107, if you want to get specific," John says. "Whoa, wait, this is the upgrade. A mother fucking M107A1! Hell yeah to the might of the .50 caliber, bitches!"

John doesn't even hesitate, just walks out into the middle of the road, lies down and sets the rifle up. He pulls back the slide, secures the rifle against his good shoulder, which, lucky for us, is his shooting shoulder, takes aim and fires.

HOLY CRAP THAT THING IS LOUD!

If he'd shot that inside the SUV our eardrums would have burst.

We watch as the approaching headlights (plural) turn into headlight (singular). John laughs then squeezes off three more rounds. Then giggles and fires a fourth. We see sparks and fire erupt from under the hood of the SUV and the vehicle swerves to the left, slamming into the mountain. But unlike our fun-filled thrill ride, it just smashes and doesn't bounce back.

John repositions the rifle and opens fire until the magazine is empty. As he's busy replacing it, gunfire comes from inside the SUV and we all hit the ground. Stella covers the kids with her body and I cover her with mine. Stuart drags Critter over around our SUV as bullets kick up dirt right next to them.

"Fuckers," John says then unloads the new magazine.

There's a couple screams and then the enemy fire stops. We all wait, our heads still down.

"Clear?" Stuart asks.

I take a peek and see John still aiming at the SUV. He's put a fresh magazine in the rifle, but he holds his fire.

"John?" Stuart calls out.

"Hold," John says. "Sniper senses are tingling."

And he's right as bullets crack the pavement next to him. He shoves up to his knees and grabs the rifle, crouch running his way over to the SUV.

"Get better cover!" John shouts at me. "Jesus fuck, Long Pork! Move your family!"

I scramble up and help Stella and the kids find cover by sliding over to the side and ducking behind a row of rocks set to help reinforce the guardrail. We get there just in time as bullets shatter parts of the rocks, sending chunks flying into the air. Stella and the kids are screaming as the gunfire continues. Yes, I'm screaming too.

"I can do this all day, fuckers!" Cowboy shouts from the enemy SUV. "You even peak that rifle out and I'll send a round straight down the barrel, sniper boy!"

"Gonna run out of ammo some time!" Stuart yells. "Then we come for you!"

"Not likely!" And just to make a point he unloads on us again.

"I think he's the only one left," Charlie says to me, barely heard over the rifle fire.

"Your point?" Greta asks.

Charlie does point, into the darkness to our left. "If we get around there we can come at him from behind."

"There's no place to go," Stella says. "It's just rock and a cliff."

"No, there's a ledge," Charlie says. "See? You can just make it out."

"Great," I say, knowing whose job it will be to make that trip. "Keep him talking and focused this way."

"What the fuck are you thinking?" Stella says. "I do not see a ledge."

More gunfire and chips of rock shower down on us.

"I have to do this," I say. "Mondello is already way ahead of us. We can't just wait here."

Stella grabs my arm, pulling me close to her. "She's gone, Jace. He took her. Even if you stop this guy, we have no vehicle. We're walking home as it is. You think we can run and catch up? Are we going to hitchhike to Charlottesville? She's gone."

She's right. I know that. Elsbeth is long gone by now. But Cowboy isn't. If I can't save Elsbeth, or at least be a member of the saving party, then I'm going to put a fucking bullet in Cowboy's brain. He's got it coming. The fucking asshole has really ruined the past couple days for me.

I kiss Stella hard then slip from her grasp, focusing on my feet and hands. Well, hand. My broken one isn't much help other than to steady me and help keep my balance. As for the gripping? Yeah, not so much.

My toes are wedged against the rock and I shuffle slowly, inch by inch, carefully making my way to the curve of the road beyond.

Did I mention the shuffling slowly? Damn right. Not even my whole feet fit on the ledge and I have to press my chest against the rock to keep from tumbling backwards. Not my favorite thing in the world. But, at least it's so fucking dark that if I make the mistake of looking down I won't see anything. Not that I'm looking down, no fucking way, I'm looking directly at the rock while I pray to every deity, including the Flying Spaghetti Monster, to get me safely to the other side.

And…I make it. Barely. My right foot slips just as my left hits solid ground. I start to slide, but grab onto the guardrail in front of me. I hold my breath; pretty sure Cowboy heard the little squeal of terror that escaped my lips. When the gunfire comes, I'm pretty sure I catch every single bullet.

But I don't.

He's still firing at the SUV. I'm able to crawl under the guardrail, keeping my belly to the ground. Arm over arm, I wiggle myself across the road, stopping every couple of feet to make sure I'm not spotted. There's really no way Cowboy can see me. The light from the muzzle of his rifle is blinding in the pitch darkness of the night.

Just a few more feet. Five. Four. Three. Click.

"Hey, Long Pork," Cowboy says.

Even in the dark, I can make out the outline of a 9mm pointed at my head.

Fuck.

"Didn't think I would just ignore my surroundings, did you?" Cowboy asks.

"I was kinda hoping you would," I say. "My whole plan really hinged on it."

"How about you crawl your worthless ass over to me?" Cowboy asks. "I could use the company."

Double fuck.

CHAPTER NINE

"I have your precious Long Pork here!" Cowboy shouts, the muzzle of his 9mm pressed to my temple as Cowboy stands us both up. "Bring that .50 caliber out, will ya? Just set it in the road, nice and gentle."

"Fuck you!" John shouts.

"JOHN!" Stella cries. "Do it!"

Stuart and John's voices carry over to us, but I can't make out what they're saying. I'm pretty sure it must be something like, "We can't let Jace die! He's the best guy in the whole wide world!" Or maybe, "Oh, that Jace. Always getting into trouble. That scamp. Well, better just do what the crazy Cowboy wants and then he'll let Jace go!" Right? Yeah, sure, that's what they're saying.

"Go fuck yourself, you piece of merc shit," John says. "The second I show my face you'll blow it off."

"Mrs. Long Pork?" Cowboy says. "Yoohoo! I could use your assistance. You seem to have a more rational grasp on what's about to happen if sniper boy doesn't comply with my orders. Are you listening, Mrs. Long Pork?"

"My name is Stella," Stella says, "and yes, I'm listening."

"Stella, don't!" Stuart cries. "Whatever he tells you is a lie!"

Cowboy fires up into the air then jams the scalding hot muzzle against my temple. The pain is excruciating and the smell of my flesh burning is almost as bad. Stella and the kids both start screaming, calling for me.

"I'm fine!" I shout. "I'm fine!"

"And if you'd like him to stay that way then I suggest you listen," Cowboy says. "Are you listening, Stella?"

"I said I was, you fucking cocksucker," Stella growls.

Oooh, I know that growl. She's really pissed. The problem is, I don't know who she's more pissed at: Cowboy or me. I know I'm going to catch some serious shit for getting caught. There will be months of "I told you so." Of course, I have to get out of this alive. If I do, I will gladly, and I do mean gladly, take the "I told you so's. Living in embarrassment is better than dead in…well, better than dead.

"This is what you are going to do, Stella," Cowboy says. "You will come out from your hiding place and slowly walk over to that SUV. You will relieve that fucking sniper of his weapon and you will then slowly walk it into the middle of the road. There will be no sudden movements, no tricks or plans. All you have to do is set it down and back away. Got it?"

"Then what?" Stella asks. "Then you let Jace go?"

"No, then I start walking with your hubby in tow," Cowboy says. "I will be walking back to Asheville. You will not. All of you will stay right where you are, you won't follow, you won't move a muscle, you won't even fart. I catch a hint of stank gas and I blow his head off and toss him over the edge. Are we clear?"

"When will you let him go?" Stella asks. "I'm not doing this unless you actually plan on letting him go."

"I'll let him go once I feel secure," Cowboy says. "That could be a long while. It's gonna be quite the hike back to Asheville. I'm thinking you folks should just get comfortable and maybe not move until noon tomorrow. Sound good?"

"No!" Stuart yells. "See Stella? He has no intention of letting Jace go. You do this and he's dead."

"You don't do it and he's dead," Cowboy says, pushing the 9 against my temple even harder, making me cry out. "I will guarantee that. Sure, you have no idea if he'll live once I'm all secure in my safety. But wouldn't you rather risk it and help me out than not risk it and listen to the sound of your husband's brains splattering against the side of this SUV?"

"I'd rather none of that happen," Stella says. "That's what I'd fucking rather." I hear the shifting of gravel. "Fine. I'm going to get that rifle and do what you ask."

"Good girl," Cowboy says.

"Fuck you," my wife responds. "But if you think you can just get away, you're a fucking idiot. You hurt him and I will track you down, mother fucker."

Cowboy starts to laugh. It builds and builds until I think he's going to stop breathing.

"Oh, man, oh, wow," he says, finally able to get control of himself. Don't' get me wrong, it's not like I can make a move. Cowboy is a fucking professional. Even during his little laugh fest he kept that 9 firmly against my temple. I'm just glad he didn't laugh too hard and accidentally pull the trigger. "Damn, Long Pork, that wife of yours is something else."

"Yeah, she is," I say. "I'm fond of her. I'm really fond of the idea of spending the rest of my life with her."

"Stella, think this over," Stuart says.

"I'm not giving this to you," John says.

"You have other guns," Stella snaps. "Give me the fucking sniper rifles, John!"

"Oh, yeah, toss those other guns out too, will ya?" Cowboy says.

"That wasn't the deal," Stella replies. "You have to stick to the deal!"

"Do I? Do I really?" Cowboy asks, laughing again. "I'd really like to hear what your reasoning is, Stella. Tell me why I have to stick to the deal? Why exactly can't I switch the deal as I see fit?"

Stella is silent.

"Yeah, that's what I thought," Cowboy says. "The other guns."

"Please," I hear Stella beg of Stuart and John. "Please just give Jace a chance."

There are some mumbled words and I wait; it's all I can do. My fate is in the hands of two soldiers and my wife. Not really my ideal situation, but I gotta just roll with it. Shit happens. Serious mother fucking shit happens in the apocalypse. It's good to remember. I should learn to do needlepoint and put that on a doily or something. What the fuck is a doily anyway?

"There," Stella says, "the rifle is in the middle of the road."

"And those other guns we spent so much time renegotiating about?" Cowboy asks.

"Screw you," Stuart calls out.

"Dammit!" Stella shouts. "Give me the fucking guns, Stuart!"

The strain in her voice nearly breaks my heart. How could I have been so stupid to bring my family with me? We should have just driven them off to safety. I have risked everything, put everyone in danger, to chase after a canny girl. Yes, she has saved my ass plenty of times; yes, she's one of the most trusting people I know; yes, I hurt her badly when I betrayed her back at the Grove Park; yes, I owe her.

But my family…

Is she worth their lives? No, she isn't. And I'm a fucking fool for thinking so.

"STUART!" Stella screams. "GIVE ME THE MOTHER FUCKING GUNS!"

Cowboy chuckles at this. It takes all of my willpower not to strangle the fucker. Even with the pistol pressed against me, I still think, just for a stupid split second, that I can take him. I'm actually about to go for it, willpower be damned, but then I hear the clatter of metal on asphalt.

"Done," Stella says. "No more guns."

"You sure about that, Stella?" Cowboy says. "I have a very sensitive trigger here. I'd hate to stand up and start walking away and find out you're wrong. That would just make me mad and when I get mad I start squeezing things."

"Like that trigger," Stella says. "Yeah, I get it. You can knock off the cheap bad guy lines, ok? I've seen this fucking movie, dickhead."

"Damn," Cowboy snorts. "I like you, Stella. You are one tough broad."

"What did I say about knocking off the cheap lines? One tough broad? What, were you raised on black and white gangster movies?"

"Get up slowly," Cowboy orders me.

He grabs my left arm and yanks it up behind my back, making me stand up with him instantly. He yanks even harder when we're standing and I cry out.

"Jace!" Stella calls.

"I'm fine, I'm fine," I say. "Just establishing who's in charge, is all."

"That would be me, right Long Pork?" Cowboy asks, his sour breath hot against my ear. "Say it."

"Yes, Cowboy, that would be you," I say, regretting it instantly. The pain in my arm shoots into my shoulder and it feels like he's ripping me apart.

"I'm sure I warned you about calling me that already," Cowboy says.

"Did you? You probably did," I reply, gasping. "Sorry, Mr. Jameson, sir."

"Don't lay it on too thick," Cowboy says. "Mr. Jameson is just fine. No need for the sir part."

"How nice of you," I say as we start to walk backwards, away from the SUV.

"I have him right in front of me," he calls out. Which he does. If Stuart or John still have a weapon and try to take a shot in the dark they'll nail me first. "You all just stay put. What time did I say you could come looking for him?"

"Noon," Stella replies, "tomorrow."

"Exactly," Cowboy says. "Not a minute sooner."

"How are you gonna know?" I ask. "I've always wondered that. Why do villains tell people to wait for an hour or two? How will you know they don't come looking at like 11:30 or 11:45?"

"Because maybe I'll be waiting down the road," Cowboy says so only I can hear. "Maybe I'll snap your neck and get comfortable. Just wait until that gutsy wife of yours comes walking down along. Put some bullets in the heads of those soldiers and have my way with sexy Stella. How is that for an answer?"

"Not really liking that answer," I say. "Can we forget I asked the question?"

"Maybe," Cowboy says as we get further and further away. This guy is pretty good at walking backwards. I, on the other hand, am using every skill I have not to trip on my own feet.

"Maybe?" I ask. "Can't do better than that?"

"I don't know," Cowboy says. "The more I think of it, the more I like that idea. Kill you, get some rest, wait and rape your wife. I'll make your kids watch too."

I start to struggle at that, but he pulls my arm up even harder and I feel it pop. Well, I feel more than it just pop as I scream. Yeah, he dislocated my fucking shoulder.

"Shut the fuck up," he snarls, flipping me over his leg and down onto the ground. In one motion he shoves my arm back into the socket then yanks me up by it and we're back where we started. Just with a fuck ton more pain. "I can do that to you all night long. Want to test me?"

"No," I gasp. "No...that's fine."

"Then keep still, Long Pork. Make this easy for me and I make it easy for you. I'm not the fucking villain here, just a guy hired to do a job."

"But your boss is long gone," I say. "Why bother?"

"You think Mondello is my only boss?" Cowboy laughs. "You think this is just about him? Yes, I was hired by the guy, but there are bigger fish than him. I fuck this all up and I'm dead, Long Pork. I'm zed food. Mondello is a fucking bureaucrat, that's it. He knows rules, procedures, and shit like that. He's happy playing President. And I'd be happy playing Secret Service, but I'm not an idiot."

"You sure?" Pain! "Sorry, kidding, kidding!"

"Don't," he says. "Mondello is a means to an ends, just like Foster was. I keep climbing the power ladder until I hit the top. That's when I find my real boss. Whoever that is."

"You don't know?" I ask. "You're talking about the Consortium, right? The power players living in Atlanta?"

"That's them," Cowboy says. "And no, I don't know who the top dog in that pack is. They keep their cards close to their chests. As far as I know, he or she could be part of my crew. Wouldn't that be a fucking hoot?"

"Yeah, I highly doubt that," I say.

"Me too," Cowboy says. "Just proving a point."

"What point? You already said you don't know. You don't have to prove that. And even by saying what you said you aren't proving it. There's no way I can actually know if you are lying or not. You should really-"

Pain!

"Shut up," he says.

I do. Quickly. And stay shut up for a long while until he stops walking.

"What? Why did we stop?" I ask.

"Shhh," he warns. I shhhh.

We listen for a long time, but hear nothing.

"Good," Cowboy says. "Looks like your wife kept the men in line. She always been a ball buster like that? Or did she come into it after Z-Day?"

"I wouldn't call her a ball buster," I say, "but, yes, she has always been like that."

"Damn," Cowboy laughs, "doesn't take a big brain to figure out who wears the pants in your family."

He turns us around and we get to walk in a normal forward fashion finally. I'm glad since walking backwards was just awkward, especially with my arm jammed up between my shoulder blades. After a few yards, Cowboy eases up and lets me go.

"Don't think I can't still rip that arm off," he says, "because I can. You won't get more than two steps before I make you scream like a little girl. Got it?"

"Got it," I say. "I do. Seriously. All got and shit."

"Man, there is something wrong with your mind," Cowboy says. "You're like those smart ass punks I used to kick the crap out of in high school. That happen to you, Long Pork? You get the crap kicked out of you a lot?"

"No, not really," I say. "I had a good time in high school."

"Right," Cowboy chuckles. "Sure you did. I'll bet you had a shitty time in high school and are just one of those losers that has invented some pretend life you've told your kids. Is that it? You tell your kids you were part of the popular crowd? Make them think their daddy wasn't the total loser that he actually was?"

"What the fuck are you talking about?" I ask. "Where did this come from? Who cares what I was in high school?"

"You brought it up," Cowboy says, giving me a little shove from behind.

"No, I didn't!" I protest. "You brought up high school. You asked me if I was one of the smart asses that got his ass kicked by bitches like you."

"Oh, right," Cowboy says. "And then you lied to me."

"Fuck you," I say.

"Say what you want," Cowboy says. "Doesn't change the fact that you were a loser. Still are. Can't even protect your family right."

"Fuck you!" I yell and whirl on him. Then keep whirling as he pistol whips me across the face. Said face smashes into the pavement and my nose explodes in pain. Hot blood pours from it as I struggle to get up, but I'm pushed down by Cowboy's foot in the middle of my back. And then the muzzle of his pistol is against the back of my head. Awesome.

"You figure out how stupid that was?" he asks.

"I'm getting the picture," I say, blood coating the back of my throat. I spit a bunch out and nod. "Yeah, that was stupid."

"You going to play nice?" Cowboy asks. "Because, frankly, I don't have to keep you alive."

"Then why are you?" I ask, slowly, cautiously, getting to my feet.

Cowboy shrugs. "You're alive because I'm still working the angles of this scenario."

"What the hell does that mean?"

"It means I won't put a bullet in your head until I know for sure that I don't need you," Cowboy says. "I'll keep you posted."

"Funny," I say. "You know, I don't mind going back and waiting with my family while you decide. Seriously, I don't."

"Now look who's being funny," Cowboy says, shoving me down the road. "Keep walking, Seinfeld."

We walk for a few more minutes, making our way slowly down the Parkway. The road is more than a little creepy as tree branches sway in the slight breeze and dry leaves blow across the road. With no moonlight to see by, every shadow looks like a Z ready to grab us when we pass. Turns out they're really just rhododendrons. But scary rhododendrons.

Maybe twenty minutes go by and we come to the first tunnel.

"Flashlight?" I ask.

"No," Cowboy says, "didn't get a chance to grab one."

"You don't have one on you? That seems like bad planning."

"Wasn't completely geared out since we were at the FOB," Cowboy says. "Just had my rifle and sidearm."

"Well, live and learn, right?"

"If you live," Cowboy chuckles.

"Ouch," I say, "that's harsh."

"March it, Long Pork."

I take a deep breath and step into the tunnel.

If I thought it was dark before, I was wrong. This is dark. Super duper, mother fucking dark. Outside the tunnel, I could at least make out shapes and see Cowboy next to me. But in here? Nothing. I wave my hand in front of my face and don't see a thing. Crazy.

"Make any stupid moves and I'll just start shooting," Cowboy says. "And hitting the ground won't make a difference. I'll shoot the ground too."

"Damn, you're brutal," I say. "What did the ground ever do to you?"

"Just keep walking," Cowboy says. "As long as I hear your footfalls then you get to stay alive."

"But only until you decide to kill me," I reply.

"We've already been over this," Cowboy responds. "I hate repeating myself."

"Right. Sorry."

I make my way to the side until I can run my hand on the wet rock of the mountain. Our footsteps echo around us, joining the sound of dripping water...and something else.

"Stop," Cowboy orders. "Just hold up."

I do as ordered since I have no plan on being randomly fired at. I can hear Cowboy breathing, the water drip, drip, dripping and that other sound. It's like...I don't know. It kinda sounds familiar, but I can't quite place it.

"What the fuck is that?" Cowboy whispers. "Long Pork? If it's your buddies coming for a rescue, you're dead."

"Maybe it's Zs," I say.

"Doesn't sound like shuffling feet," Cowboy answers. "It sounds like...like...tires?"

"Tires?" I ask. "But wouldn't there be an engine sound to go along with that?"

"There should be," Cowboy says. "There really should-"

Then we are blind. Headlights illuminate the tunnel, only a couple feet from us. I'm not stupid, I know when I'm supposed to hit the deck. And I do just as the gunfire erupts. Bullets ricochet around the tunnel and I say a small prayer I don't catch a stray.

"Fuck you!" Cowboy yells as he unloads his 9 at the vehicle, shooting out one of the headlights.

I take a peak and it looks like one of the SUVs, but how is that possible? Cowboy's was toast and so was ours. The only SUV it could have been was maybe… Nah…

Cowboy starts running towards the SUV, taking the fight to whoever is inside. His pistol clicks empty, but that doesn't stop him. I can see the driver door open, but Cowboy leaps at it, knocking it into whoever is trying to get out. A brief cry of pain tells me exactly who that is.

"Stay there, Long Pork," Elsbeth shouts. "I'll get you when I'm done."

"Fuck you, girly," Cowboy says, swinging at her head.

Elsbeth ducks and shoves him away from the SUV. She doesn't waste any time and goes right for him, kicking the door closed with her foot. Why? Maybe it makes for fewer obstacles? Fuck if I know. I'm just the guy splayed out on the wet ground.

Cowboy lands a solid punch to her gut and I hear the breath leave her as she falls to a knee. She blocks a blow as he tries to bring his fist down on the back of her neck. Grabbing his arm, she twists as she comes up fast, spinning him around. I know that move! Elsbeth has his arm up behind his back and he grunts as she pushes harder and harder.

But he's got a little more size than she does. Instead of fighting back he rushes forward towards the tunnel wall. Elsbeth tries to counter, but before she can, Cowboy has used his momentum to swing her around and slam her against the rock. He closes fast and lands a punch to her gut, her head, and her chest. She drops again and Cowboy is smiling, thinking he has her.

Until she nails him in the nuts.

The huge, private contractor, military mother fucker, squeaks. Yep. He squeaks. Both of his hands go to his crotch and this time he falls, coming down hard on both knees. He's pretty much eye to eye with Elsbeth and I think it's about done.

Except he head butts her, his forehead slamming into the bridge of her nose. She cries out as blood sprays everywhere; the crack of bone and cartilage echoes in the tunnel.

"How you like that, bitch?" Cowboy yells, head butting her again. "Nice, right?"

Elsbeth falls back against the tunnel wall. She shakes her head a couple times, but I can tell she's pretty dazed by the slow way she brings her hands up to shield her face. She does get them up in time, I'll give her that. Cowboy tries to finish her off with a punch to the face, but he hits forearms instead.

"Come on, bitch!" Cowboy yells. "You wanna fight? Let's fight!"

He gets up, steadies himself, then pulls Elsbeth to her feet. He grabs her by the hair and slams her face down as he brings his knee up. She screams, he laughs. He tries it again, but then he screams, while she laughs. Well, she sort of laughs; hard to tell with her mouth full of leg.

Elsbeth spits the chunk of Cowboy's leg and pants onto the ground. He hops back, screaming at her, his hand trying to slow the blood that is gushing (and I do mean gushing) from the wound. He gets a foot back then slips in his own blood and comes down hard in front of the SUV. Right next to him is his pistol and he grabs it.

Why? The thing is empty. Oh…

The tunnel is plunged back into darkness as Cowboy slams the butt of the pistol into the one working headlight. I try to slow my breathing so I can hear what is going on. I hear footsteps and someone sliding around. I'm guessing the footsteps are Elsbeth's and the sliding is Cowboy. I can't tell.

Then I hear them. Something hits flesh, a cry of pain, more impacts, more cries. I'm pretty sure the cries are coming from Cowboy, but I can't say for sure. Punch, punch, cry; punch, punch, cry.

Smack! Smack!

"Please," Cowboy croaks.

Smack! Smack! Smack!

"Okay…okay," he begs. "You…win."

"Not yet," Elsbeth says.

I hear dragging sounds and Cowboy choking. Then the dome light inside the SUV comes on. Elsbeth has the driver's door open and she wedges Cowboy's head in there. I turn away as she slams the door closed. I keep my eyes averted as the door slams again and again.

Slam! Slam! Slam! Slam!

I can tell by the sounds that Cowboy's head is mush on the third slam, but Elsbeth being Elsbeth gives it one extra just for good measure. Or fun. I don't think she knows the difference.

"You alright, Long Pork?" Elsbeth asks.

"Yeah, I'm fine," I say as I get to my feet. I look at the pulverized head of Cowboy and the brains dripping off the running board of the SUV. "I don't think he's coming back a Z."

"No," Elsbeth says, "he's not."

Her face is all blood and shadows and I reach for her. "Let me look," I say.

She flinches, but lets me take her head and check out her face.

"It's broken," she states. "I've broken it before. It feels broken."

She hocks up a gob of bloody phlegm and spits it on the pavement. I look at the SUV and shake my head.

"I didn't know you could drive," I say.

"Julio has been teaching me," she says. "But I didn't really drive. I just steered and used the braking pedal."

"Just brake pedal," I say. The look on her face makes me cringe. "Or braking pedal. Whatever works. All the same in the end."

"I let the car take me here," she says.

"You just coasted down the road so he wouldn't hear you," I say. "Brilliant."

"What? No," she says, shaking her head. "It's out of the gas."

"Oh," I say. "Well that works too." Then it hits me. "Wait, where's Mondello?"

She walks to the back and opens the tailgate, showing me a bound and gagged Mondello, blood trickling from several cuts on his face.

"He's stupid," she states. "Car runs out of gas and he orders me to stay in it while he gets out." She laughs and a blood bubble pops from her nose. "I didn't stay. Stupid."

"How'd you get it turned around without gas?" I ask.

"I pushed," she says. "Not that hard."

"No, no, not at all." Damn. "Did you pass the others?"

"Yes, they are on the way," she says. "Stuart said not to slow down and keep going until I find you. He was right. I found you." She nods at Cowboy's corpse. "And killed him. Asshole."

"Yeah, tell me about it," I say.

We stand there, looking at each other for approximately forever.

"Listen," I start, "I owe you an apology."

"Yes," she says.

"Right...so, I'm sorry," I say.

"For what?"

"Not going to make this easy for me, are you?"

"No."

"Okay, fine, I deserve the rough treatment," I say. "I'm sorry I let you down. I didn't want to betray you, honestly. It's just, well, I was...I was..."

"Scared?" she asks, cocking her head.

"Yes," I agree. "Scared. Scared I wouldn't ever see my family again. Scared they would be killed once I did see them again. Watching Zs go after your family in a cage makes you do things you didn't think you'd do."

"I don't know," she says.

"Don't know what?"

"Don't know if it would make me do strange things," she says. "Maybe."

"Yeah, well it makes me do strange things," I say. "But I came for you."

Elsbeth looks around. "No. I came for you."

"What I mean is we were chasing you," I say. "That's why we're up here. To get you from Mondello. To save you."

"Oh, I was fine," Elsbeth says. "I just wanted to hear what he had to say."

"What? What does that mean?" I ask.

"He told me that if I wanted to know more about Foster I should go with him," she says. "I did want to know more. That lady is in my dreams."

"Yeah, you said that. You said she was singing. What does she sing?"

Elsbeth shakes her head. "I don't know the song."

"You don't remember your dreams?"

"I don't remember the song," she says quietly. "I remember my dreams. I don't want to, but I do."

"What did Mondello say?" I ask. "About Foster?"

She shrugs. "Not much."

"Well, he had to have said something," I push. "You two were in the car for a while together."

"He was driving fast," Elsbeth says. "Because we were being chased. He didn't say a lot. I asked questions, but he told me to be quiet. I don't think he was a very good driver."

"Huh, okay," I nod. "Hold on. You did want us to come after you? You did, right? You wanted us to rescue you, right?"

She shrugs again.

"Elsbeth, come on," I snap. "You can't be telling me you actually were planning on going with him all the way to Charlottesville."

"I don't know," she says. "Nothing for me here."

"What about me? What about Stella and the kids?" I ask. "We're here!"

"You gave me up," she says. Ouch. That smarts.

"Okay, true, you get that one," I say and hold up my hand before she can speak again. "But what about Julio? He would have thought you were kidnapped or worse. If you hadn't come back we would have all assumed you were dead."

"Maybe it's better to be dead," she says.

"No, it's not!" I shout, my voice bouncing up and down the tunnel. "It's better to be alive!"

"I don't know that," she says. "The dreams I have…"

"What about them?"

"If that lady that sings to me is real, then what else is real? What if my dreams are real?"

"Dreams are just our subconscious exercising itself," I say. "That's all. Some can be real, in a way, but it's mainly just symbols and stuff. It's how our subconscious stretches its legs."

"Sub...sub...subconscious? I don't know that."

"You know how you are thinking right now?" I ask.

"Yes," she nods. "I'm thinking of hitting Mondello in the face. Because I don't want to hit you in the face, but I want to hit someone's face."

"Okay, well thanks for not hitting me," I say.

"I still might."

"Great. Well then thanks for the warning. Can we get back to the subject?"

"You asked what I was thinking. I told you. That's the subject."

"Not gonna argue that," I say. "The subconscious. It's the part of your mind you can't hear thinking. If you are thinking about punching me, then the subconscious is what put that thought there. It's the deep part of your brain."

"Deep? Like a hole?"

"Yes, kinda," I reply. "People do say they bury things deep in their subconscious so they don't have to think about them."

"That's dumb," she says. "You don't bury anything in your mind. Your mind is in your head. If you bury something in your head, like a shovel or a knife, then you die. But you don't come back, so maybe that is what the people mean? Bury something in your head so you die and don't come back?"

"No, no, that's not it," I say. I can see her getting frustrated so I back off. "Don't worry about it. We'll get to the bottom of it all later. Just know that your dreams are just dreams; they aren't real."

"They feel real," she says. "They make me cry sometimes. I don't like to cry."

"I know. I don't like to cry either."

We stand there a little longer then she grabs me and hugs me so hard I'm actually afraid she's cracked a rib. I take the discomfort and hug her back, glad to be on her good side again.

"I'm family?" she asks, finally letting me go. "You came to get me because I'm family?"

"Yes, that's exactly why I came to get you," I say. "It's why we all came to get you. You're our crazy canny girl. Life would be boring and suck without you."

"I'm not crazy," she states, fire in her eyes. "And not a canny anymore."

Fuck.

"No, you're right. Sorry. I just meant that you are who you are and we love you for it. It's all good. When the others get here, we'll hop in this SUV and roll on down the mountain back home. How does that sound?"

"Sounds good to me," Stuart says from back in the tunnel, Critter thrown across his shoulders. The man doesn't look too good; too pale, even taking into account the dim light.

"Daddy!" Greta yells and rushes into my arms. Stella and Charlie are right behind her. We all hug and it's the best feeling in the world.

Greta pulls away first and jumps at Elsbeth, wrapping her arms around her. Stella smiles at me and we all give her a huge hug, wrapping her up with Stanford love.

"Sorry to cut this love fest short," John says, "but we aren't out of the woods yet."

"We aren't in the woods," Elsbeth says. "We're in the mountain."

"That is both true and observant," John nods. "But what I mean is, do you hear that?"

We all go quiet and listen.

Yes, I think we do hear that.

The shuffling of feet and the low moans of Zs reach our ears. It sounds like a lot of feet.

"The tunnel amplifies the sound, right?" Charlie asks. "There aren't as many as it seems? Right? Hello? Right?"

Man, I wish I could tell him he's right. But as the things start to reach the dim circle of the SUV's dome light, I realize he's wrong. Very wrong.

"Tell me you brought guns," I say to John and Stuart.

"We brought guns," John says. "But it's gonna get close in here. We're just as likely to shoot each other."

"Fuck," I swear. "So we crush skulls?"

"We crush skulls," Stuart nods, setting Critter down against the SUV.

"He going to make it?" I ask.

"Maybe," Stella says, "he's lost a lot of blood."

"Shit," I reply.

"Help me get him inside," Stuart says.

I grab Critter's legs as Stuart crawls into the backseat of the SUV. He pulls, I lift and push, and we manage to get Critter settled. Damn, for a skinny guy that's leaking blood, he's fucking heavy. It's that dead weight thing.

Speaking of dead weight...

"You guys got Sleeping Beauty taken care of?" John asks.

"Good to go," Stuart replies. He has a rifle in his hands and he turns it around like a bat as he ejects the magazine, letting it clatter to the ground. John does the same thing. I look at them and frown.

"Have an extra?" I ask.

"Here," Elsbeth says, handing me a tire iron. "It was in the car."

"Great," I nod. "Thanks. What are you going to use?"

"Me," she says then walks towards the Zs.

"Right," I say. "How stupid of me."

The Zs see her first and they groan and hiss, all closing in on her. Elsbeth takes two down with well placed elbows then kicks out, knocking one back into the others, creating a domino effect. None are hurt, but they get tangled in a knot of undead arms and legs.

"Get in the SUV," I yell at Stella and the kids.

"But, Jace!" Stella cries.

"Do it!" I shout. "We'll be fine!" But I don't really know that; there are a lot of Zs and more and more seem to be coming.

How? I thought Mondello said they had cleared the Parkway. Or maybe he said they were *clearing* the Parkway. Damn, I need to listen better. Which is something Stella is always saying, so I'll just keep that self-admission to myself. No need to let her score spouse points. She's already way ahead.

John and Stuart rush the Zs, with me right behind. I glance back for a brief second and see Stella and the kids jumping into the SUV. The door closes. And the dome light goes out.

Ah, fuck me...

"Open the door!" I yell. "Stella! Open the door!"

She does and the light comes back on. Just in time for me to see three Zs coming at me. They don't seem to have a problem seeing in the dark. It's part of the whole Z thing. Dead grey eyes, but with night vision! It's an undead trade-off. I look back at Stella and give her the thumbs up as she turns the dome light on manually and closes the SUV's door.

I take the tire iron and jam the pointy end through a Z's eye socket. I yank back and the thing drops, black blood oozing from its skull. The other two Zs are too fast and I can't get the tire iron back up before they are on me. One grabs me and I spin about, letting it stumble against the tunnel wall. The other grabs my shoulders and comes in for the neck bite, but this time I am able to get the tire iron up. Over my shoulder, I shove it into the thing's mouth and out the back of its head.

It stumbles back, its hands swatting at the iron as the metal bounces up and down in its mouth. I guess I didn't hit brain or sever the spinal column because the fucker is still up and moving.

"Gimme that," I say and pull the tire iron free.

It brings the Z with it, though, and I lower my shoulder and ram the thing, knocking it away. I go in for the kill, but hands snatch my shirt and I stumble, nearly falling right into the Z's mouth. I slip to the side and come down hard on my hip, letting out a little cry. The Zs rush me, seeing easy prey on the ground, and I kick out, sweeping their legs.

This is good because of the knocking them down part. But bad because now I'm under a pile of Zs. You take the good, you take the bad…

My arms and the tire iron are free so I get to the stabbing. I plunge the iron into a Z's skull, pull it out, plunge, and repeat. Over and over I do this until the pile on me stops moving. Maybe I can play dead and just wait this fight out? No? Fuck. Okay, I'm up!

Elsbeth is doing her berserker fast kill thing, while John and Stuart do their military kill thing. Many Zs are crushed and killed. I jump into the fray, ready to add my boring, normal suburban kill thing to the fight. And, of course, I slip on some stray intestines and fall hard on my ass. The smell of shit is overwhelming and for a split second, I think I crap my pants. Then I realize it's the shit from the intestines I slipped on. Phew. Don't want to die with crap in my pants. Or live and have the kids know I crapped my pants.

Stuart reaches down and pulls me to my feet while smacking a Z in the head and knocking it aside. I nod my thanks and swipe at a Z coming at us. Its skull caves in and a new smell is added to the shit and blood smell that is filling the tunnel. That's the problem with being in a tunnel, or any enclosed space, when fighting Zs: the smell. You think you get used to it, but you don't. There's some primal response to the stink of death and decay. It makes your gut clench and your balls shrink. Or other parts shrink if you do not have the testicles.

Ignoring the stankety stank, I bring the tire iron down again and again, smashing skull after skull. John is rocking it, taking Zs down left and right. Stuart is kicking ass too, sending the undead to the Big Sleep in Hell. And Elsbeth is Elsbeth, so her body count eclipses ours.

Yet -and that gut clench gets worse as I realize it- we aren't making a dent in the numbers. Z bodies are piling up around us, hindering our ability to move around, but more and more keep coming. I don't know how many there are since the lighting is less than adequate to say the least. But I keep fighting; I keep swinging; I don't stop.

At least until Stuart calls out, "Get back to the SUV! There's too many!"

"We can do this," John protests, but his attacks are obviously getting weaker and weaker as he favors his wounded shoulder, his left arm almost useless at his side.

"No, we can't!" Stuart yells. "Move! Get in there!"

John starts to protest again, but I grab him, pulling him back to the SUV. "Don't waste time arguing! Come on!"

Charlie opens the door and we scramble inside. Charlie jumps into the far back seat, and I join him, as John pushes Critter's legs aside and gets in to the mid-back seat. So many fucking seats in these things. Stuart opens the other back door and hops in, shoving Critter in between him and John.

"He say anything yet?" Stuart asks Stella, who is sitting in the driver's seat with Greta in the passenger seat.

"No, he's been out the whole time," Stella replies.

We watch as Elsbeth continues to fight the Zs, somehow managing to keep from getting surrounded. She spins and kicks, punches, grabs, twists, cracks, breaks, snaps, kills. She's a dervish of violence, whirling in every direction at once. But even she is human and the Zs are just too much.

The horn blares and we all jump.

"Greta!" Stella shouts, shoving our daughter's hand away from the wheel. "Jesus! You nearly made me piss myself!"

Elsbeth turns to us, her eyes wild and filled with menace.

"Come on!" Greta shouts through the windshield. "El! Get in here!"

We all watch the conflicted thoughts fly across Elsbeth's face. She jams an elbow into a Z's cheek, crushing the rotted flesh and bone. She throws another over her back, snapping it in two as it hits the pavement. Yet another goes down as she slams her fist into its skull over and over. And her eyes are watching us the whole time.

"Elsbeth!" Stella yells. "Stop it! Get in the car!"

She keeps watching us.

"Tell her she's family," I say.

"What?" Stella asks.

"Tell her she's family," I say. "That's the only way she'll get in."

"Elsbeth! You get your butt in here right now, young lady!" Stella shouts, her hands cupped to her mouth. We all cover our ears. "You get in this SUV with your family this instant! Don't make me come out there and get you!"

Stella actually grabs the door handle and starts to open the door, but Elsbeth is at the side of the SUV in a flash, a wide smile beaming at my wife.

"I'm family?" she asks.

"Damn right," Stella says, shoving over to let the young woman in. "And you better start acting like it and listen to me when I tell you to stop killing zombies and get your ass in the car."

"Yes, ma'am," Elsbeth nods and smiles.

"Haven't we been through this before?" Charlie whispers. But his version of a whisper is like a quiet yell.

"Hush," I say, "she has trust issues."

"Shhhh," everyone says.

"What?" Elsbeth asks. "The Zs know we're here."

"Yeah, they do," I say as we watch the things begin to surround the SUV. They swarm us and soon we see nothing but open, rotted mouths and decayed flesh. "It's like that time we went to the wildlife park and the llamas surrounded the car wanting alfalfa pellets."

"No, Dad, it's not like that at all," Greta says.

"Should I turn out the light?" Stella asks.

"No, leave it on so you can see this," Mondello says as he hooks his arms over Charlie's head and pulls back, the wire tying his wrists together digging into my son's throat. "Now, let's talk about getting me out of here."

Mother fucker!

CHAPTER TEN

"I count two pistols aimed at your noggin," I say, so close to reaching out and grabbing Mondello by the throat. But if I do he could pull back and snap Charlie's neck. "Said pistols are in the hands of men who know how to use them."

"Your point is made, Mr. Stanford," Mondello says. "But no matter how good they are, the way my weight is balanced even if they miss your son and only hit me, well, young Charlie will die. I'll fall back and it will be all over."

"Maybe, maybe not," I say. "I'm thinking maybe not."

"Don't kill him," Elsbeth says. "He knows more about me."

I look at Mondello and he has a cat that ate the shitty canary grin on his face.

"What do you know?" I ask. "Tell us."

"And lose leverage point number two? I don't think so, Mr. Stanford."

The Zs get more aggressive, their hands —and heads- slamming harder and harder against the SUV. The vehicle starts to shudder under their mass. We don't have forever to negotiate with Mondello. Soon we'll be trapped forever in this fucking polyester upholstered piece of crap. Not that it's actually upholstered in polyester; fuck if I know what it's upholstered in. Probably some super secret military fiber that lets you get blood stains out while keeping that new car smell.

"So what do we do?" I ask. "Where do we go from here?"

"That's for you to figure out," Mondello says, taking a quick glance out the window. "Someone will need to clear a path for us."

"For us?" Stella asks. "No. No, you will not take my son with you."

"I'm sorry, Mrs. Stanford, but that is the only way this works," Mondello says. "I have to take your son or you will kill me the second I'm outside the SUV."

"Are you paying attention?" John asks. "There's like a hundred Zs out there."

"Where'd they all come from?" Greta asks quietly then looks at us. "Sorry. I was talking to myself."

"They probably came from the pens," Mondello says. "We had holding pens stationed along the Parkway. Easier just to contain the zeds than slaughter and dispose of them. Throw some meat inside a fence and they walk right in."

"But then you have pens filled with Zs," I say. "What then?"

"Security," Mondello says. "They can be released strategically if a convoy is being chased or under attack. We use them against highwaymen."

"Did you just say highwaymen?" Stuart asks. "I just want to be clear that I heard that part."

"Of course I said highwaymen," Mondello says. "Your friend Critter Fitzpatrick here has one of the most notorious crews in the area."

"One of?" John asks. "Who are the others?"

Mondello shrugs. "Hard to say. They come and go quickly due to the nature of the job. Most don't last long. They are eaten by zeds or killed by other crews. Some even have tried to venture into territory they shouldn't. If anyone is caught stealing or robbing in Charlottesville they are hanged on the spot, quartered, and their body parts are put on public display."

"Uh-oh," I say. "The Dark Ages is calling and wants its judicial system back."

"Laugh all you want, Mr. Stanford," Mondello says. "But it is effective. Chaos became order within the week after the first few executions."

"Is that your re-election slogan?" I ask. "Teaching voters a lesson, one hanging at a time?"

"You have had it easy, Mr. Stanford," Mondello says, looking around the SUV. "None of you have a clue what it has been like out there. You've had glimpses, but you can't even fathom the hell I've seen. Not unless you've watched a city of millions turn on itself; watched governmental organizations go rogue; watched as other countries resorted to the nuclear option on their own people. I envy your mountain life."

"Is that really why you set up shop here?" I ask. "Not just to oversee the repair and securing of the Parkway, but to have yourself a long term presidential vacation?"

"Asheville has been a favorite vacation spot for many presidents," Mondello says. "But I don't think the word vacation applies to anything these days."

Charlie gasps and I look him in the eyes. Fear and anxiety look back at me, but something else…resolve? No, what is it? His eyes dart from mine to the front. I rub my forehead and turn, making it less obvious I'm looking at what he's looking at. I see Greta staring at me then her eyes dart to the back of the SUV and then up front and down.

What the fuck are my kids trying to tell me?

They obviously have some plan worked out between them, but fuck if I know what it is. And I'm not even sure I approve of them coming up with plans. I have two highly trained military men in the SUV with us, and I'm no slouch at the thinking gig, so what could two teenagers figure out that we can't?

"He's turning purple," I say to Mondello, "ease up."

"Get me out of here," Mondello replies.

"We can't," Stuart states. "We're all stuck in here until the Zs go away."

"Which won't happen until we can turn out the light and stay very quiet and still," John adds.

"And you won't let us turn out the light," I say. "So I guess we're fucked."

"Let me tell you how I interpret all of that information," Mondello says. "Basically, I let you turn out the light, we are plunged into complete darkness, and you come after me, hoping you can overpower me before I kill Charlie. Or we stay like we are until we die of thirst and starvation. Either way, I die."

"Please, President Mond-," Stella starts.

"Don't," Mondello says. "Just don't. I die in all of your scenarios. I die in pretty much every single scenario except for mine. The one where you clear me a path, create some type of diversion, and I escape out of this SUV and out of this tunnel. I take Charlie for as far as I need to, and then let him go. I live, Charlie lives, a couple of you may die clearing the way, but the important part is that I live."

"You're really a for the people kind of guy, huh?" I say. "I have another slogan for you-"

"Shut the fuck up, Stanford," Mondello snarls. "Your mouth has stopped being cute."

"Dude, I'm like forty, my mouth stopped being cute in my early thirties."

Mondello pulls back on the wire and Charlie begins to choke, his eyes bugging out, spittle foaming at his lips.

"Jace! Shut up!" Stella screams. "Charlie!"

Mondello eases up slightly, but only slightly, so Charlie can take in short, raspy breaths.

"I'm not going to wait anymore," Mondello says. "Get me out of here or Charlie dies."

"How?" Stuart asks. "They way you present it sounds so simple, but it's far from that. How do we even open these doors?"

"Like this!" Greta shouts and slams her hand against the dashboard at the same time Charlie throws his head back into Mondello's face.

The man cries out as blood squirts from his nose, his eyes glassy and confused from the impact. Charlie throws his head back again and again until Mondello is reeling, his body swaying back and forth, close to unconsciousness.

Great plan except now Mondello is sliding down into the back, and pulling Charlie with him.

"Jace! Get him!" Stella shouts as I reach for Charlie.

I hook him under the arm pits and pull forward, but my leverage is shit. I don't know if I'm doing any good or making things worse. Charlie is gasping and spitting, the life being choked out of him right before my eyes. I'm frantic and I tug at him, trying to pull him up, but he's just getting pulled farther and farther into the back.

I let go of Charlie for a second, just long enough to slap Mondello across the cheek a couple of times. It rouses him enough that he steadies himself, taking the weight off Charlie's throat.

"Good," I say. "Now listen you stupid fuck. I'm going- Fuck!"

Greta had hit the automatic tailgate release. In my desperation to save Charlie, I didn't notice, or hear, the back doors opening wide. None of us did. But we fucking do now as Zs start to reach inside, their hands snagging Mondello's pants, pulling him towards their hungry mouths.

More and more of them wedge themselves inside, all trying to get at Mondello, and then us. Charlie starts to choke again, even more now, as Mondello is pulled from the SUV.

"No!" he screams. "NONONONONONONO!"

But there's nothing any of us can do even if we want to. He is taken quickly; his screaming body pulled into the mass of undead that is fighting over each other to get the first bite. I think it's the lady in the old jogging suit that wins that honor as she tears a hunk from his ass cheek and begins to chomp away. Mondello's screams are piercing until they are cut short, his throat shredded by several mouths.

There's just one problem: Charlie.

My son is dragged up and over the back seat and into the cargo area as he pushes himself along, trying to keep from getting his head ripped off. I jump back there with him, alternating between kicking Zs in the face and trying to free his neck from the wire and Mondello's wrists. The Zs aren't pulling at Mondello anymore, they've got his body right where they want it. Which is draped across the back bumper, innards exposed and being strewn about.

"Give me something to hack with!" I yell as Charlie stops choking. That's not a good thing. He's stopped because the wire can't go any further and because he has run out of air. I have seconds to free him or he's dead.

"Here!" John says, slapping the handle of a very large knife against my shoulder.

I take it and plunge the blade into Mondello's wrist then turn and twist, slicing through tendon and muscle. It takes me less than two seconds to sever the wrist, but it feels like an eternity as I watch Charlie's eyes bug from his skull and turn glassy. The hand comes free from the arm and I get the wire away from Charlie's bruised and bleeding throat.

As I shove Charlie over into the back seat, and Johns starts CPR, I feel the grip of fingers around my ankle.

Ah, fuck me.

Instinctively, I kick out, landing a hard blow to some fucking Z that can't take my yelp of surprise as the no it was intended to be. Kicking again and again, I try to scramble up over the seat, but I'm caught as dozens of hands pull me in the opposite direction.

"A little fucking help!" I scream.

"Daddy!"

"Jace!"

"Long Pork!"

"Hold on!" Stuart shouts, reaching for me over John and Charlie. "Just take my hand!"

"Oh, just do that!" I yell. "Fucking brilliant, Stuart! The most brilliant idea you've ever had!"

"Here!" screams Elsbeth as she tosses the tire iron to me.

It hits me in the forehead. Fucking awesome.

Shaken, I slip further back and now hands are gripping my calves, my knees, pulling me to them, adding me to the Mondello buffet. It is gonna be quite the spread tonight, folks! All you can eat asshole and dumbshit! Well, not all you can eat. That's just marketing, really. Eventually I'll run out of meat on me.

"FUCK!" I scream as I turn and just start flailing, slamming my fists against every Z face I see. My good hand cries out as I feel bones bend. My bad hand hasn't really stopped crying (fucking baby hand) so it starts wailing. The pain drives me on, though. With every sharp shock up my arms, I just double my efforts. Teeth are bared, wanting to bite down and get through my jeans at the chicken legs underneath. But I won't let them. Those are my chicken legs, mother fuckers!

"Dad!" Greta screams. "Break the sensors and I can shut the doors!"

Break the sensors? What the fuck is she talking about?

"I'm a little busy, sweetie," I screech. "Maybe speak fucking English please!"

"The sensors that keep the doors from closing on people!" she shouts. "Should be one on each side, down towards the bottom! Probably red plastic!"

Oh, well that makes fucking sense. Why didn't she just say that?

I grab a Z's head and twist, popping it off like a mother fucking grape, then use it to batter the other Zs, moving them from one side of the SUV. There. I see it. I toss the head, which is still trying to bite at me, at the Zs and pick up the tire iron. Slam! Slam! Slam! Crack!

"One down!" I shout. "Try it!"

Maybe it's like a garage door opener where all you have to do is disable one sensor. The doors start to close, the top folding down, while the bottom starts to lift. Then they stop and a loud buzzing fills the SUV. The loud buzzing also pisses off the Zs and they hiss and growl at me. Sensitive fuckers.

"The other one!" Greta yells.

"Yeah, yeah, thank you, I figured that out!"

I smack at the other sensor, but a stubborn Z just won't move. Every time I slam the tire iron down, the fucking Z gets in the way and I just end up slamming it. And the fucking thing won't die! It must have a steel plate in its...oh, yeah, it does. The gleam of metal winks in the weak light as its scalp is torn away. Jesus.

Here is one bummer of the zombie apocalypse after almost an entire generation has been at war halfway across the planet against enemies that use improvised explosive devices: reconstructed skulls. You come across it every once in a while out in the field. Go to crush a Z's skull and your weapon just bounces off. Sometimes the metal is easier to get through than the plastic; that shit is seriously high impact resistant. And a crow bar counts as high impact.

So here I am, slamming a tire iron against a Z that doesn't give a fuck. I reach down with my bandaged hand and shove the Z's head away, stabbing it though the eye with the tire iron. The fucking thing finally dies, but the iron slips from my grasp and goes out the door with the Z.

"Fuck!" I scream as more Zs start to wedge inside.

Only one thing to do...

I smash my bandaged hand against the sensor over and over and over until I hear loud cracks from both hand and plastic. My hand is fuckered as I see bone shards sticking out from the gauze. At least the sensor is busted and the doors start to close finally.

But not before a Z grabs my fuckered hand and takes a hard chomp. I scream as the bones grind against each other and against the teeth of the Z. It may be wrapped in gauze, but I did so much damage to it that the Z's teeth get through, piercing my flesh, tearing into my hand.

"No!" I yell, as I yank my hand back. The tearing sound of my flesh almost makes me vomit. With every ounce of my strength, I kick and kick and kick at the Zs, sending them tumbling from the back of the SUV. The doors are almost closed, but jam as a Z gets its head stuck. I rip the fucker from its neck and the doors close. The Z looks at me, jaw snapping my face. I grip it by the back of the head and smash it into the floor over and over until its brains explode everywhere.

Then I look at my hand. And over my shoulder at everyone in the car.

Their face tells me all I need to know. I'm fucked.

Maybe...

"Where's that knife?" I say, looking around the cargo area for the blade I used to sever Mondello's wrist. "Where the fuck is it?"

There. In the corner, in a pool of blood and ick. I pick it up, take a last look at everyone else, then cut.

"JACE!" Stella screams as they watch me slide the blade into the soft flesh of the inside of my elbow.

The pain. Holy fuck. Holy, holy fuck. My mind detaches from my body and it's like I'm watching a TV show. I know I'm cutting through my own flesh and muscle and tendons and shit, and God does it hurt like nothing else I have ever felt before, but at the same time, I'm able to think through every single turn of the blade. I have a pretty decent knowledge of anatomy and I know just where to slice, cutting up then down and around until my forearm is hanging by threads of sinew. A quick flick and it falls to the floor of the SUV.

Then everyone in the SUV springs into action.

Charlie is pulled up front with Stella and Greta, as John, Stuart, and Elsbeth crawl back to me. Elsbeth hands Stuart a belt and he tightens it around my upper arm while John is busy jamming his torn shirt against the stump that is spurting blood. Fuck if I know where Critter is.

"Greta!" John shouts. "Look under your seat! There should be a breakdown kit!"

"This?" Greta asks as she holds up a large metal box.

"That!" John nods.

Woo, is the SUV spinning or is it just me?

"Pull out the flares that are inside and toss them to me!" John says, looking directly into my eyes. "Jace? Buddy? You hear me?"

"Yep," I nod. "I hear you loud and clear. Clear as a bell. Loud as a whistle."

Stuart slaps me.

"No going into shock!" he shouts in my face. "You fucking hold on!"

"Shock bad," I say. "Fucking holding on good."

I look hard at John and he is very serious.

"Why so serious?" I laugh. That's funny shit right there. Comedy gold, bitches!

"This is not going to be fun for either of us," John says as he holds up one flare so I can see it. "Do you know what I'm about to do?"

"Cook some Jace meat?" I say, reality taking hold a little. Ah, shit…

"Yep," he nods as he pulls the cap and strikes it against the end of the flare. The whole SUV is bathed in a red glow. Like blood. Glowing blood.

In all honesty, I don't think there is a way to describe what I feel. Cutting off my own arm was excruciating. Having a flare jammed into the open wound? Excruciating times eleven. Off the mother fucking scale!

"FUUUUUUUUUUUUUUUUUUUUUUUUUUUUUUUUU UUCK!"

The smell of my flesh burning makes me gag and I turn my head and puke while Stuart and Elsbeth hold my arm still. I kick out against the sides of the cargo hold, my throat raw from screaming. But I can't stop. I have to keep screaming. If I stop, I know I'll die.

The flare fades and John doesn't hesitate as he strikes the next flare and goes back at it.

"THROW ANOTHER SHRIMP ON THE BARBY!" I scream. I don't know why. It seems appropriate. Shut up.

The pain builds, which I didn't think was possible. It builds and builds and builds and then is gone. Well, that's the mother fucking whopper of all lies, it isn't just gone. But the searing pain that was stabbing through my brain, spine, ass, dick, stops. Now I'm left with a sharp, throbbing pain. And the smell of my own burning flesh stuck in my nose.

"Charlie?" I gasp. "Is he ok?"

"He is," John says, wrapping my stump with bandages from the emergency kit Greta found. Gotta remember to thank her for finding that. Saved my shit.

Maybe…

"Will it work?" Stella asks quietly from the front, her eyes finding mine. "Will it keep him from turning?"

"Jace?" Stuart asks. "How do you feel?"

"Really, dude?" I ask. "That's your fucking question?"

"You know what he means, Jace!" Stella shouts. "Tell him how you feel!"

"Right," I say. "Sorry."

We've all watched friends and family turn. Sometimes it's fast, sometimes it's slow. When they die, they come back in just minutes. Bam, they're a Z! But when bitten? It's variable. Some take days, coming down with what seems like just the flu or a bad cold. Then they die and get all bitey. Others have turned in minutes, whatever it is rushing through their systems, killing them and turning them faster than anyone can track.

Regardless of how they turn, every single person has said they feel like their head is swimming, like their mind is being squeezed and then covered in gauze. They say they can't think straight; they can't reason. And all they start to feel is a gnawing hunger in their belly.

I do feel a bit peckish, but that's probably because I haven't eaten in who knows how fucking long. And I need to pee. Like really bad. I look down. Oh, wait, I think I just took care of that.

"I feel shitty," I say honestly. "But I feel like me."

They all watch me as John finishes dressing my stump. Looks like I'm gonna need to swing by Wal-Mart and check out their selection of hooks and prosthetic arms. They do carry prosthetic arms, right? Sure, they'll be cheap, and made by the hands of Vietnamese five year olds, but I don't want to start expensive and find out I'm more of a just let it hang free guy. Try one on, and then invest wisely in an upgrade later.

"Jace!" Slap. "Jace!"

"Don't hit me," I say, swatting at Stuart as he gets ready to smack me again. "I'm sensitive right now." I yawn and lean back, out of his reach. "Just going to take a nap. Wake me when we get to Wal-Mart."

"What the fuck?" Greta says.

"He's going into shock," John says. "We have to keep him awake."

He starts to climb over the seat, but Elsbeth grabs him and pushes him down.

"I'll do it," Elsbeth says. Or I think she does. Is this a dream? What the fuck is that smell?

"Just keep him conscious," John says. "Whatever you have to do, make sure he doesn't fall asleep."

"But Jacey is tired," I moan. "Jacey needs sleepy sleep."

"Jacey is not getting sleepy sleep," Stuart says then sighs. "God, he's got me talking like him."

"Dad, you can't fall asleep," Greta says from the front.

"Hey, sweetie!" I say, waving to her. "You got the front of the rollercoaster. Cool. Be sure to hold your hands up on the first drop. That's the best."

"Is he going to live?" Greta asks, turning to her mother. "Even if he doesn't, you know, turn?"

"I don't know, sweetheart," Stella says. "Maybe."

"He sure knows how to make a fucking mess of himself," Stuart says. "But he also knows how to survive. Don't worry about your dad, he'll make it."

"Yep," I smile. "Right after I take a nap."

My eyes close then shoot right back fucking open, OH MY GOD!

Elsbeth's face is right in mine and she's smiling. Her hand is on my stump and her thumb is right on the end, pressing.

"Long Pork doesn't nap," she says. "Right?"

"Yeah…right…no nap," I pant. She smiles wider. "Fuck, you're enjoying this, aren't you?"

"After this we will be even," she states. No need to comment on that. I'll just let it stand as it is.

She settles in next to me, our backs against the gore/puke/piss covered rear doors of the SUV, and looks at everyone else. "How are we getting out?"

Each person looks from one to the other.

"That's a good question," Stuart says. "Thoughts?"

"What the…fuck…am I doing…down here?" Critter moans from the middle row of seats

"Shit," John says. "I totally forgot about him when it all went crazy."

"Yes, because it's nothing but sanity and order now," I say, pointing at the Zs still trying to get in at us. "Hey, Critter, how's it going?"

Critter peaks his head over the seat, his skin white and clammy looking. "I ain't feelin' too good," he says. He looks down at himself. "Bleedin' like a stuck pig."

John and Stuart look at each other, look at me, and then up at Greta.

"Hey, Greta…?" John asks. "Any more flares in there?"

"No, but there's another small medical kit with some needle and thread," she replies. "Maybe we can sew him closed instead of stinking up the car again?"

"Flares?" Critter asks. "What the fuck y'all talkin' 'bout?"

"Hey there," I say, waving my stump at him. His eyes go wide as I gasp at the pain I cause myself. "Ow. Gotta remember there's no waving until at least twenty minutes after severing one's arm from one's body."

"You still have part of your arm," Elsbeth says, patting my shoulder.

"Thanks, El," I nod. "That's the bright side I was looking for."

"Speaking of bright sides," Stella says, pointing up at the dome light that is starting to dim. "I think we're about to run the battery down."

"Darkness it is then," Stuart says. "Let's try to get some sleep, except for Jace, and we'll figure out a plan when it's daytime. The tunnel will still be dark, but not like now. Light will reflect in here and we'll be able to see what we're up against."

"We stay quiet and maybe a few Zs will wander off," John says.

None of us really believes that.

"Sounds good," I say. Well, moan really. "You sleep. I'll keep watch."

"And I'll watch you," Elsbeth says. "Make sure Jace doesn't sleepy sleep."

"Yes, looking forward to that," I say, turning myself so my stump is further away from her. She just smiles at me. Yikes.

"Okay, so lights out," Stella says. "Rest then plan."

"Rest then plan," Stuart agrees.

"Uh, you guys want to hold on?" John says as he climbs into the seat with Critter. "I'm gonna need that light."

He tears off Critter's shirt and presses it to his wound then takes the kit Greta hands him. I'll give Critter credit, he doesn't make a fucking sound as John stitches him up. And just in time since the dome light is going, going, gone.

"That'll do for now," John says. "But we need to get him back so Dr. McCormick or Reaper can do a real job."

"Damn hack," I snort. "You and your life saving field surgery. Fucking whatever."

"Jace, baby?" Stella says.

"Yes, light of my life?"

"Hush."

"Right."

We all go quiet as we let the darkness wash around us. The sound of the Zs, while always disturbing, is oddly hypnotic and I find myself fighting with all my strength not to fall asleep. Not to worry, though, Elsbeth is there for the assist. Each time I feel her reach over to poke my stump, I slap her hand away. It's like a game! An excruciatingly painful game. That never fucking ends.

I can tell from all the sounds of shifting and shuffling that no one is asleep, except maybe Charlie. That lack of oxygen to the brain thing really wears a person out. Fingers crossed he doesn't have brain damage. And we all know what hand I'm using to cross those fingers.

Slapping Elsbeth's hand away for the umpteenth time, I notice how the tunnel is starting to brighten. Must be dawn out there. Soon we'll be able to see a little more clearly how far up shit creek without even a fucking boat we are.

Huh…that's interesting. It's really getting bright. Like the day is on time lapse and we are speeding past morning and right into noon. No, that's not it, because that's some serious fucking light out there. What the fuck?

"Are those headlights?" Greta asks. "Is someone coming?"

Gunfire makes us all duck down. Just fucking great. People. None of us are in any shape to fucking fight people. We can't even handle the undead, and all they do is shamble and nip at ya. Right? Look at my arm. Just a little nip.

More gunfire and we can hear Zs dropping to the pavement. A couple bullets ping off the SUV, but thank Jeebus for bulletproof glass and armored doors. We wait, our ears straining to hear who's out there as the gunfire dwindles down and then stops.

"Hello!" a voice bellows over a bullhorn. "If you are alive in that vehicle, then it would be appreciated if you stepped on out with your hands up!"

"Well, I'll be dipped in shit," Critter laughs. "Not what I was expectin'."

"What are you talking about?" Stuart asks.

"Don't you recognize that voice?" Critter asks. "That's my nephew, Buzz. Sounds like he's done brung the cavalry."

"So can we get out now?" Greta asks. "Please? I have to pee. Like really bad."

"Yes," Stella laughs, hugging her to her chest. "We can get out now. I have to pee too."

"Let's all go pee!" I shout. It isn't as funny out loud as it was in my head.

"Long Pork," Elsbeth says. "You already went pee. You're crazy."

"Thanks," I say. I don't mention the irony of that coming from her.

The doors open and we see familiar faces just stare at us.

"Holy shit," Buzz says as he pulls open the back doors. "What the hell happened to ya'll?"

"Blanchard Fitzpatrick," Big Daddy's voice snaps. "There is no need for that language. Oh…" He limps up to the SUV, a crutch under one arm and his leg bandaged, sees us and his jaw drops. "Well, I'll be. There might be an exception this one time."

His eyes go to my stump and I smile.

"I didn't fall asleep and die from shock," I say. "So I've got that going for me."

"My goodness, Jason," Big Daddy says. "What happened here?"

"I'll handle the situation report," Stuart says. "But on the drive back." He climbs out of the SUV and looks down the tunnel. "Please tell me you drove. I don't think any of us will be walking back to the Farm."

"We drove," Melissa says as she comes up to us. "Here, let me help." She takes Greta's hand, but my girl dashes off into the tunnel.

"We have to pee," Stella laughs. "Care to bring that rifle and watch over us?"

"You bet," Melissa says. "Anyone else need a potty break?"

Elsbeth already has her belt undone and is unzipping her pants when she looks at us. "What?"

"Maybe not right here, dear," Melissa says. "Come on, I'll take you to the girl's room."

"There's no rooms in a tunnel," Elsbeth says. "That's stupid."

"Right," Melissa says. "Okay."

"Y'all got some water for a dying old man?" Critter asks. "Or some hooch? I could go for a slug of shine right about now."

"Not while you're still bleeding," John says.

"Bleeding?" Big Daddy asks, looking at his brother. "How bad is it?"

"Ain't nothing but a scratch," Critter says.

"Little more than that," John says.

"Hey…," Charlie says from the SUV, "what's going on? Where's President Asshole?"

"He had a meeting with his constituents," I say. "They ate him up."

"God, Dad, that was horrible," Charlie laughs. "You really need…to…"

His eyes find the stump.

"Yeah, you missed a couple things," I say, smiling at him weakly. "It was worth it." I think I smile at him. Not sure. I know I do something weakly. Well, pretty much everything weakly. I'm a weakly son of a bitch right now.

"Where's Mom?" he asks, tears welling in his eyes.

"She's using the facilities," I answer, going to him. "Don't worry, bud. It's all cool. Just a little Z bite, but all taken care of."

The sound of various weapons being raised, locked, loaded, fills the tunnel.

Uh-oh…

"I haven't turned," I say, "you can put the guns down."

"Yet," Buzz says.

"I'm afraid my son is right, Jace," Big Daddy says. "You haven't turned yet. I think everyone here knows that it could be days before you get sick and die."

"I fucking sliced my arm off, BD," I say. "I got to it in time."

"You don't know that," he says. "Nobody knows that."

"As much as I hate to do it, I'll have to be agreeing with my brother," Critter says, eyeing me. "You ain't safe, Long Pork."

"Who isn't safe?" Stella asks as she and Greta walk up to us. I catch Elsbeth's eye and nod, hoping she knows to stay cool. "Jace? What's going on?"

"Your man was bit," Big Daddy says, "and despite the loss of his arm, we can't take any risks."

"Despite the loss of his arm?" Stella snaps, stomping up to Big Daddy. "Despite it? Oh, right, just a little thing, cutting off an arm. But, despite that extreme measure, you can't take any risks?"

She turns about, looking at everyone. And there's a lot of people here. I finally notice that Big Daddy really brought it. He doesn't fuck around when he comes to the rescue. There has to be thirty people here amidst the various vehicles. Some of the people are dressed like PCs and I have to wonder what deal Big Daddy struck with them. Many of the people I don't recognize. Some of Mondello's laborers?

"Does everyone feel this way?" Stella asks. "That despite the fact my husband chopped his own fucking arm off to stop the infection, he's still a risk?"

"We just don't know, Stella," Andy Crespo asks, one of Stuart's defense crew. "No one knows. It may be as simple as an infection or not. All we know is that if you're bitten, you turn."

"He's right," Melissa says, "you gotta listen to reason, girl."

"Fuck reason!" Stella shouts as she grabs me and kisses me hard. "How's that for reason?"

"I liked it," I say, "but they're right."

She looks at me, stunned, like I have slapped her or something.

"Jace..."

"No, listen, please," I say. I'm a little unsteady and I lean on her for support. This small action makes everyone grip their weapons tighter. I look around and see the fear and stress. "See? I scare everyone, Stella. I don't take it personally. I'd be scared too if it was someone else."

"So what then?" Stella asks, looking at me then at everyone else. "What now? You abandon us?"

"No, no," Big Daddy says, "never anything like that. Jason will have to be quarantined. He'll need to be watched until we know for sure he's not going to turn."

"That's fair," I say, "and smart. Which is my expertise, the smart stuff. If I say it's smart then it must be smart."

"God, I think I'm going to puke," Critter says.

"Jeez, I was just kidding," I say.

"No, I'm gonna-" He pukes.

"We need to get the wounded down the mountain," John says, "and I include myself in that."

Big Daddy raises a radio to his mouth. "Gunga? You read me?"

"Read ya, Daddy," Gunga replies. "Everything alright up there?"

"All fine," Big Daddy says, "but we got some folk that are hurt. Has Dr. McCormick arrived?"

"She's here and helping all these people," Gunga says, laughing.

"What's so funny, son?"

"She's ordering Pup and Porky around like they're nurses," Gunga says, "it's pretty funny."

"And the prisoners?" Big Daddy asks. "The ones that decided they didn't want to play ball?"

"Toad and Scoot have them covered," Gunga says. "We got them locked in one of the dining rooms. Ya'll coming back soon?"

"We are, son," Big Daddy says. "Will you let Dr. McCormick know we'll need a quarantine room ready?"

"Quarantine?" Gunga asks. "Do I want to know?"

"You'll get filled in when we get there," Big Daddy says. "See ya soon, son. Out." Big Daddy looks at the radio and nods back at some of the PCs. "Some of the private contractors, as I have learned they like to be called, were not so keen on their previous job. Apparently forcing folks into slave labor wasn't what they signed up for. And they didn't particularly like working for President Mondello."

"Speaking of?" Melissa asks. "Where is the man? He get away?"

"No, he did not," Stuart says. "Jace handled that."

They all look to me, waiting for an answer.

"He was forced out of office," I say. Nailed it!

"Oh, Dad," Greta says. "My dad killed him by shoving him out the back of the SUV. He was ripped apart and eaten. End of story."

Everyone turns their attention to the dead Zs on the pavement.

"Wow, Jace," Buzz says, "you assassinated the President of the United States."

"Well it's not like I voted for him," I shrug, then nearly pass out from the pain. "Ow."

"You can say that again," Stuart says. "Let's get this party moving, okay? I'll ride with Big Daddy and fill him in. Who's got balls enough to drive the Stanfords?"

"I'll do it," Buzz says.

"I'll ride with them," John adds. "I'm honestly not worried about him turning. He took that arm off like a pro."

"There're professional amputaters?" I ask.

"Yeah," John says, "they're called surgeons."

"Oh, yeah, right," I nod. "I knew that."

"Okay, folks!" Big Daddy shouts. "Let's turn it around! We need to get back to the Grove Park and regroup. There's a lot of work to be done before the day is over!" He turns back to me. "I am glad you're alive, Jason. We'll get you all taken care of at the Grove Park. You can rest up there until we know you're safe."

"I'm staying with him," Stella says.

"Me too," Greta adds.

"And me," Charlie says.

"I'm staying," Elsbeth says. "I'm family."

"Damn skippy," I say. "Thanks, guys."

"We'll find you one of them fancy suites, how's that?" Big Daddy asks, smiling at us all. "Not the same as freedom, but you'll be comfortable."

"Is the water running?" Stella asks. "I could so use a bath in one of those bug tubs."

"Whoa, whoa, whoa," Melissa says, "there's big bathtubs? Damn, I may go with them too."

"Just load up, ya'll," Big Daddy says. "We'll talk about baths later."

The group quickly gets back in their vehicles and I follow Buzz over to his big truck. It's a four door diesel, so it fits us all easily. Surprisingly some of the PCs jump into the bed, their rifles to their shoulders, as we leave the tunnel.

"How do you feel about those guys?" I ask Buzz from the backseat. Stella and Greta are up front, with Elsbeth in the back next to me, John next to her, and Charlie on the far side. "You think your father's making a mistake trusting them?"

"Nah," Buzz says. "We had some of them captive at the Farm. Learned a lot about their operation. Once we got to the Grove Park, and they found out what happened to their boss, they signed up with us in a flash."

Foster. The image of her severed head comes into my mind. Wonder where that rolled off to?

"Boss?" Elsbeth asks quietly. "The soldier lady?"

"Yeah, her," Buzz says. "Found her body, and only her body. Looks like she took on the wrong person."

"So did he," Elsbeth says.

"What's that?" Buzz asks, looking in the rearview mirror.

"Nothing," Elsbeth says, hanging her head.

"Do you know who she was, El?" I ask. "Why she was in your dreams?"

She shakes her head and I don't push anymore. She'll tell us in her own time. Maybe.

Ugh, it all makes my head hurt. Which means every part of my body is now officially in agony. Awesome.

"So, if I wanted to take just a little nap, would anybody object?" I ask.

"Yes!" they all say.

"Just a little wee nap?" I beg. "So tired. So very tired."

"You can sleep after Dr. McCormick gives the okay," John says.

Elsbeth places her hand on my stump and smiles. "I'll keep you awake."

"No, no, I'm good, El!" I say. "Seriously. Wide fucking awake. No need to poke the stump. The stump is good too. Happy stump. Right, Stumpy? You're good. Tell the pretty lady how good you are."

All heads are turned and looking at me.

"What?" I ask. "It would be rude of me not to ask him."

"Are you going to call him Stumpy from now on?" Greta asks.

"Yes, yes I am," I say. "Or Fernando. I may call him Fernando. That way I can sing that ABBA song every time someone talks about him. 'You come to me Fernando!' Awesome, right?"

"Mom, tell him he can't name his stump," Greta says.

"Your father just lost most of his arm, baby," Stella says. "We'll wait until he's mostly healed before we gang up on him."

"Until then, I dub thee Fernando!" I say to my stump.

"You are so messed up," Charlie says.

"Crazy," Elsbeth adds.

"Crazy like a stump," I say.

"No, Jace," Stella says. "Just no."

"Fine, fine, I'll give it a rest," I say. "But the bad jokes and humor are what're keeping me awake. And keeping me from being depressed. I did just lose an arm, you know. Maybe this is my version of shock."

"No, it's not," John says. "But it is how you're coping. Trust me. I used to know quite a few amputees."

We all nod at this. Yeah, I bet he did. A horrible thought fills my head and I'm glad I lost an arm and not a leg. How the fuck do

189

you get away from Zs with one leg? Or no legs? God, what happened to those poor guys on Z-Day?

"You okay, hon?" Stella asks, looking back at me. "You went really pale."

"Just bad thoughts," I say. "See, take my jokes away and I instantly go to my dark place."

"You don't have a dark place," Charlie says. "Or if you do, it's well hidden."

"Like this truck's sense of humor!" I laugh. "Zinger!"

"Look out the window and watch the trees go by," Stella says, a smile on her face. "We'll be at the Grove Park soon."

I do as I'm told and watch the trees, their late fall leaves pretty much gone way up here on the Parkway, and try to keep the bad thoughts at bay. It's hard. I may be all jokes and funny stuff on the outside, but inside I don't know. My arm is screaming at me bad. I'm struggling not to breakdown in front of the kids. It's like I can barely breathe the pain is so bad.

But that's life, right? Filled with pain and discomfort.

Or it is now, post-Z. Filled with all kinds of unpleasant shit.

CHAPTER ELEVEN

Two weeks. Two fucking weeks I have to stay quarantined. You'd think after the first week of not showing any signs of turning they'd be all, "Hey, Jace! Looks like you're not a Z after all! Come on out and have some hot cocoa! There's mini-marshmallows!"

But they didn't do that. And not because there aren't really any mini-marshmallows.

No, I had to be cooped up in the Presidential suite (oh, the irony!) for two weeks. Not that it was awful, mind you. I mean, come on, it is the Presidential suite. And Mondello had left plenty of reading material to go through.

The man had file after file on the current government and also on the Consortium. The government? Bare bones and basically nothing. Looks like we lost most of the military, including the National Guard in each state. They were called into all of the major metropolitan areas to establish order and quarantine the cities. That didn't work so well. Turns out a few thousand soldiers can't stop millions of undead. Bad math.

As for the Consortium, I now have a broad picture of what they are trying to accomplish. Atlanta isn't gone; not even close. How they managed to do it, I'm not sure, but according to the documents, they quickly secured the center of the city. They have a wide perimeter of Zs they use as a dead flesh wall that keeps curious travelers and desperate survivors out. It also keeps other groups from making a move.

And there are other groups.

In Kansas City, there's the Combine; Boulder has the Stronghold; Salt Lake City is the Temple; and Portland, OR is the Garden. All thriving and secure. Others were tried, but they couldn't hold up to the Zs, to the weather, the landscape, or the people. The people, man. They are the fucking worst. Seriously, after the past few months, I'll take a starving horde of Zs any day.

It wasn't like I sat there all alone, stuck inside the suite, left with my files. Stella and the kids came and went, but mainly stayed with me. Stuart, Critter, Platt, Big Daddy- they all stopped in. Most of the time, I was in a manic, hyper-focused state, so they'd stick around for a few minutes, laugh at me, and take off. There were never really any sit downs or pow wows.

Most of all, there was no mention of the stump. Mr. Stumpy. Stumpy McStumperson. Lord Stumpercrumpet. Stumply of the Suite. Senor Stumpio Gonzales. And my personal favorite-Stumpageddon, Lord of All Stumps.

Which is why I'm glad to be sitting in the Grove Park lobby now with everyone, stump plainly visible. Tables are pushed together and we sit here snacking on some late apples and cheese from the Farm. Thank you, Big Daddy! Seated are Platt, Stuart, Big Daddy, Critter, Brenda Kelly, and a couple of new faces, Lourdes Torres, the head of the PCs that stuck around, and Edgar Lassiter, the head of the laborers that didn't bolt as soon as they could.

Platt looks at the papers in his hands and then up at me, back to the papers, up to me. Repeat.

"What are we supposed to do with this?" he asks, passing the papers on.

"Not a clue," I say. "But it is good information. Charlottesville is trying to connect these power groups and rebuild a system of government."

"Sounds more like Charlottesville is just trying to stay relevant in a world that don't need them no more," Critter says. "Looks to me like these so-called power groups are doing just fine without them."

"You're probably right," I say. "Which is why Mondello was kissing so much ass and personally overseeing the securing and repair of the Blue Ridge Parkway. I was wondering why the

President, even with a background in construction, was doing it himself. Didn't make sense until I saw these files."

"What does this matter?" Brenda asks, taking a handful of papers and waving them around. "This doesn't grow food or kill Zs. These don't rebuild our homes that Jason Stanford burned to the ground."

"The fire burned them down," I say, "I just watched."

"Don't be flip," Brenda snaps.

"I'm not," I say, "I'm being Jace."

"This is intolerable," Brenda says. "Why is he here? I represent Whispering Pines. He doesn't. I have been duly elected by the residents and members of the HOA to be their sole representative in all matters of importance."

"You see, Brenda," I smile, "that's where you're wrong. You were elected Board Chairperson. That's all. There is still a HOA Board with other members on it. You aren't the dictator of Whispering Pines, no matter how much your fat, little heart wants to be."

"Well! I never!"

"You never what?" I ask. "You never had a useful thought in your life? Never considered the feelings, thoughts, needs of others? Never bathed properly, Madame Stinknuts?"

"Jace," Big Daddy warns, "easy now."

"Easy?" I laugh, waving Stumpageddon about. "Please, BD, let's talk about easy. Easy is now my middle name. Hold a baseball bat? Easy. Shoot a pistol? Easy. Eat with chopsticks? Easy. Tie my shoes? Oh, not so easy. Button my own shirt? Nope, not so easy. Climb a rope? Not so easy. Hug my children? Partially easy."

The table is silent.

"Y'all think because I laugh and joke that I'm not taking everything serious," I continue. "Well, you're all fucking wrong on that." I hold up my hand, cutting off Big Daddy's protest. "You're just going to have to deal with the language, BD. This isn't the Farm. This is real fucking life. Got me?"

We lock eyes and he nods.

"Good. And no disrespect meant. I just want all of you to know just how serious I am now. There are other groups out there. Big groups, groups that have taken over entire cities. It is only a matter of time before they begin chopping this country up into territories. Before they lay claim to what they think is theirs.

"Where do you think the Consortium is going to start first? Here. Right here in Asheville. For all the reasons Mondello gave me and more. Big Daddy has been right from the start, we need to rebuild Asheville and we need to do it fast. We have maybe a year to get things up and going, or at least enough that we won't have to start from scratch every time something goes wrong."

"That's a lot to ask," Stuart says. "Do we have enough resources to begin?"

"We have more than enough resources," I say. "This city is nothing but resources waiting to be collected. Empty houses and buildings, vehicles, and weapons. We're in a temperate climate with a natural defense system of mountains surrounding us. We can grow what food we need, there's wind, solar, hydro, and geothermal energy. Not to mention a natural gas system that seems to be doing fine, despite a set back or two." I look at Lourdes and Edgar. "We have new faces and new numbers to add to us. And who knows what Critter has hidden in his holler."

"And none of y'all will ever know," Critter smiles, "unless ya need to."

"See?" I grin. "Critter's on board in his own way."

"I know I'm new and many of your people don't trust me and my people," Lourdes says, "but we can offer a lot. I have men that did tours in Iraq during the rebuild. They'll get the water and sewer systems fully up and running. Maybe even the electrical grid."

"There you go," I say. "And thank you, Lourdes. I'll be sure that Carl comes and talks with your guys about that. He set up the grid at Whispering Pines."

"This will take a lot of manpower to pull off in the time frame you're talking about," Platt says.

"I believe Edgar has that covered, right?" I say.

"Yes, I think so," Edgar says, clearing his throat. "Those that have stayed say they will do whatever they need to, to earn their keep. No one wants to be sent back out there. It's not safe."

"It's barely safe here," Brenda says, staring right at Stumpageddon.

"Safer than out in the open," Edgar says. "Trust me. I spent over a year running from place to place with my family. We were hunted by Zs as well as people. I have done horrible things to keep us alive. I don't want to do those things anymore; I don't want to be that person. And I can confidently say I speak for everyone else on that. Asheville is way better than being on the road."

"Labor taken care of," I say. "And you have defense, Platt."

"What about Lourdes and her crew?" Critter asks.

"I'm security," Lourdes says, "that's our specialty, not defense. Just like in Iraq and Afghanistan. We make sure everyone gets to their jobs safely and stays safe doing them. I've already drawn up a roster of eight teams. That should be enough to cover the work crews that go out, no matter where they go."

"Which means Platt will lead defense," I say, "making sure any outside element doesn't overtake us."

"Which is fine in theory, Jace," Platt says. "But now we do run into a manpower issue."

"Stuart?" I ask, nodding to him.

"With Edgar covering labor, that frees up everyone that was on my Whispering Pines defense team," Stuart says, "plus, I believe Big Daddy has some candidates."

"I do at that," Big Daddy says, "more than a few. Not everyone is cut out for farming. Some are just good at fighting."

"I can throw in some of my boys," Critter says, "they'll like playing soldier."

"Plus you'll have access to inside information," I smile. "Just saying."

"And I ain't disagreein'," Critter nods.

"This...this...this is not what was voted on," Brenda Kelly says. "I will not have Whispering Pines be a part of this." She stands up, her chair falling over as her ample thighs smack it. "You can say you are rebuilding Asheville all you want, but it won't be official. Not if I have my say."

"Which you won't," I say. "Sit down, Brenda. There's more you need to hear."

"I will not be ordered to do anything by you," she snarls. "You are not-"

"SIT THE FUCK DOWN!" I roar at her. She takes a step back, trips over her chair, and falls on her ass. "Good. That'll work."

I get up and stand over her, making sure she can see Stumpageddon very clearly.

"I have not been idle these past two weeks and neither has my wife," I state. "While you've been busy playing at leadership, Stella has actually been doing the work. And tomorrow it will be made official."

"Wha…wha…what?" Brenda stutters.

"Tomorrow, there will be an HOA vote," I say, "in Whispering Pines, not out at the Farm. Big Daddy, Master Sergeant Platt, and PC Torres will oversee the caravan and make sure it is safe. We will meet in Whispering Pines and have an official vote for a new Board Chairperson. You are welcome to join, but don't feel like you have to." I lean in close; close enough to see the tiny beads of sweat forming in her quite visible moustache. "And no matter how much you sputter and whine, it will be official. Are we clear?"

I hold out my hand to help her up, but she just stares at it.

"I think we are," I say as I turn and sit back down. I smile at everyone and then look from Platt to Lourdes. "We were going to take a tour of the key facilities your people are inspecting, right? Then unless anyone else has more to add, I'd like to get the fuck out of this place and feel some fresh air on my face."

"Wear a jacket," Stuart grins, "it's cold out there."

"Thanks, man," I say. "I'll wear a toga if it means leaving this place."

Everyone gets up and says their goodbyes as they go their separate ways, ready to start their various tasks and duties for the day.

"Jason? Can I have a quick word?" Big Daddy says.

"Sure, what's up?" I ask.

He laughs and pats me on the shoulder. "Quite a bit, young man. Quite a bit. That was some speech."

"I just said what needed to be said."

"No, no, I understand that," Big Daddy says, looking off at Brenda as she hurries out the front door. "But maybe you can tone it down just a hair. That woman is insufferable, but she's also dangerous. You aren't giving her enough credit, Jason. Don't underestimate her."

"I don't, BD," I say, "trust me. I've had to deal with that woman for years."

"True, true, but that was a different time," Big Daddy says. "And even in these few years of this living nightmare, I think you've only scratched the surface. I've been watching her, studying her. Always good to know who you may be up against."

"Tell me about it."

"She's smarter than you know," Big Daddy continues, "and she's sneaky. Like a weasel that keeps stealing eggs from the henhouse no matter how secure you think it is. She still gets in there and ruins things."

"I know," I nod, "Stella has been saying the same thing." I sigh. "Okay, maybe I went a little too far." I wave Stumpageddon about. "But then life has gone a little too far, know what I mean?"

"I do at that," Big Daddy says. "I just wanted you to know where I stand."

"Thank you," I say, shaking his hand. "And please don't hesitate to tell me again. I sometimes need reminding."

"I've noticed that too," Big Daddy laughs.

"Ready, Mr. Stanford?" Lourdes asks, body armor on and her rifle resting in the crook of her elbow.

"It's Jace," I say, "please."

She nods at me then nods towards the front door and starts walking. I follow and Platt catches up.

"Not going for diplomacy these days, are you?" Platt states.

"No time," I say.

"As a career soldier, I would agree," Platt says. "I've seen useless diplomacy waste valuable time. But also as a career soldier, I have to disagree. There is a place for it, Jace. You'd be wise to study where and when that place is."

"You and Big Daddy rehearse this?"

"Could be," Platt says. "What we are about to undertake is complex in the best of times. Now? Post-Z? It's mindboggling."

"We'll tackle it one step at a time," I say. "That's all we can do."

"I agree," Platt says as we get to the Humvee waiting for us, with Lourdes at the wheel. "Let's just hope we don't trip too much while taking those steps."

Platt takes the passenger seat and I hop in the back as we roll out. Just in two weeks, the area around the Grove Park Inn has been secured and the needed repairs have begun. We weave through a system of barricades before getting out to the road. Lourdes nods at the armed guards manning the entrance/exit.

"Quite a system," I say. "You've improved on it."

"We need it," Lourdes says. "We aren't just talking about zeds now. We have people to contend with. The barricades help slow vehicles as well as create choke points for zeds. With the amount of people living in the Grove Park, it is a ripe target for both."

"How many people are living there?" I ask.

"Most of Whispering Pines," Platt says. "That's a few dozen. Edgar gave me a count this morning and we have 150 laborers staying on."

"Count my crew of fifty and that's a lot of warm bodies," Lourdes says. "That kind of concentration will attract zeds."

"And it'll attract those survivors in Asheville that haven't come out of the woodwork yet," I add.

"Precisely," Platt says. "We almost have the Grove Park locked down tight. Then we move on to the water plant and power plant. Which is what we're going to look at today."

"What about Whispering Pines?" I ask.

"We're going to leave that up to your new Board Chairperson," Platt says. "Best to keep some semblance of democracy."

"Yeah, you're right," I say.

We work our way through Asheville, our eyes watching the shadows between buildings, always alert for an attack. I finger the grip of a 9mm Glock that Stuart gave me. He says it has decent stopping power, but won't be too much to handle with only, well, one hand. My only problem is getting used to my left hand as my primary. Dr. McCormick says that I'll adapt quickly.

Zs are here and there, but the numbers aren't huge, even when we hit the center of town. Don't get me wrong, there are plenty of the fuckers shambling around, but not enough to present a problem. We drive around those we can and drive over those we can't. Just no hordes to deal with.

Which is fucking fine by me. I've had my fill of Z hordes for a while. Stumpageddon has too.

"According to city records," Platt says, "Asheville has three water treatment plants, 40 pump stations, and 32 reservoirs."

"Jesus, seriously?" I ask. "That's a lot of infrastructure."

"Yeah, it is," Lourdes says, turning down Hilliard St., "and I'm taking you to my guy to talk about it."

Platt laughs.

"What?" I ask.

"Look at you," he laughs some more. "You don't find it ironic that you killed the President of the United States, and now you're being chauffeured around like you're his successor?"

"Yeah, I totally find it ironic," I smile. "Want me to drive?"

"Not particularly," Platt says. "Not sure you'll have the response skills needed."

"Stella can't tell me to put both hands on the wheel anymore, at least," I say. "So I have that."

"It'll be hard to change music on your iPod while driving too," Lourdes says.

"Good one," I laugh.

"Here we are," she says as we pull up to a guarded chain link gate. Two men roll it back and we drive through, parking next to a beat up looking trailer.

A large black man, not fat, but large, like twenty feet tall and about six feet wide, comes out of the trailer, his hand up in greeting. Okay, he's maybe closer to seven feet, but the fucker is tall.

"Joseph Tennant," the man says, offering his hand as I get out of the Humvee. "Call me Joe T. Everyone else does."

"Jason Stanford," I say. "Call me Jace."

"Will do, Jace," he smiles. It's a warm smile, genuine. But knowing that he's part of Lourdes's crew means I won't ever underestimate him. "Care to see where we're at so far?"

"Please," I say.

He walks around the pump station and points out the various parts. I'll be honest and say most of it goes in one ear and out the other. I should be paying more attention, but there's one problem:

pain. I've been trying not to admit it, but losing an arm hurts. I have some painkillers I can take and they're in my pocket, but I'm saving them for when it's really bad. Dr. McCormick warned me not to get dependent and also that they are scarce, so use them wisely.

We check things out and Joe T explains that he did six private tours in Iraq and specialized in infrastructure security. In order to keep that infrastructure secure, he had to know what was vital and what was not. He basically taught himself hydro-engineering. Nice.

As we come to the end of the unbelievably detailed tour, Lourdes lays out the plan.

"I have three man teams going out to each of the 40 pump stations," Lourdes says. "They have instructions from Joe T on how to make sure they're shut off."

"Shut off? Why?" I ask. "Isn't the point to get the water turned on?"

"It sure is, Jace," Joe T says, "but how many people do you think thought to turn their faucets off as they were escaping zeds? Or how many pipes have busted and toilets started leaking over the years? We turn it all on at once and we'll flood this city and the whole system will collapse."

"Right. Got it," I nod, "one step at a time."

"Exactly, my man," Joe T smiles. "We'll start here, learn quite a few things, then take what we learn and apply it to the rest of the stations. It won't be fast, probably take a couple years to work our way through every single one, but we'll get there."

"So you're here for the long haul?" I ask. "No reason to bail and head back to Charlottesville?"

"My reasons died in Baltimore," Joe T says.

"I'm sorry."

"Me too," he nods. "But now I'm here and a good thing too, because y'all can use me."

"True dat," Lourdes says, slapping Joe T on the back. "We're off to Lake Julian now. Have you heard from Shumway?"

"Yeah," Joe T laughs, "he's been busy."

"Zeds?" she asks.

"Oh, yeah, plenty," Joe T says. "Whatever it is about power plants, they seem to attract zeds like flies on shit."

"They do? You've seen it at other places?" I ask.

"Every place," Lourdes answers. "It's weird."

"Then let's go lend a hand," Platt says, then looks at me. "Sorry."

"What?" I ask then look at my arm. "Oh, don't worry, Stumpageddon doesn't care."

They all stare at me for what seems like a very long time.

"What? What did I say?"

"Dude, did you name your stump?" Joe T asks.

"Yeah," I nod. "He has lots of names, but I settled on Stumpageddon, Lord of All Stumps."

"Dude," Joe T says, shaking his head. "That is fucked up. And awesome. But mostly fucked up."

"White folks," Lourdes laughs.

"Kiss my white ass," Platt says. "Don't lump me in with Long Pork."

"Ah, man," I sigh. "I thought we'd dropped that nickname."

"Not if you're going to call your stump Stumpageddon," Platt says. "And don't expect me or any of my team to address it as such."

"You will all kneel before Stumpageddon!" I announce, raising my truncated arm.

"I like this guy," Joe T says. "I like you."

"Right back atcha, Joe T," I say. "Now, where to next?"

"Lake Julian," Lourdes says. "The power plant."

"Sounds good to me," I say.

We get in the Humvee and Lourdes steers us back to Biltmore Ave. Heading south we see more and more Zs. Close to the train tracks, where Biltmore turns into Hendersonville Rd, we get stuck. A large horde has gathered and decides that surrounding our Humvee is a fun way to spend the day. I close my ears while Lourdes stops and Platt opens a top hatch and unloads on them. Using the mounted .50 caliber, part of the supplies Lourdes and the PCs brought with them, Platt mows down row after row of Zs.

He drops enough that Lourdes can get the Humvee moving again. Undead crunch under the tires as we cross the train racks and get through Biltmore Village. I look to my right and see the entrance to the Biltmore Estate.

"Stop," I say, "stop the Humvee."

"We can't stop right here, Jace," Platt says. "We just got clear. We'll be surrounded in seconds and have to start all over."

"What is it?" Lourdes asks. "What do you see?"

"I don't know," I say as we keep going. "I thought I saw someone by the Biltmore."

"It was a zed," Lourdes says. "Or maybe a stray survivor. We're gonna be stirring them up as we search the city more."

"Yeah, could be," I say. But I don't think so. The way the person looked wasn't like other survivors. He or she, I couldn't quite tell, looked…clean. But it was a ways off. I'm probably not thinking or seeing clearly because of the pain.

It's a long drive down to Lake Julian and the power plant. We have to stop twice to get clear of Zs, and then a third time to refuel. Lourdes already has caches of fuel stashed throughout the city so her teams don't get stranded.

By the time we get to Lake Julian, my arm is on fire. I keep wanting to wring my hands together, but I can't, even though I feel my other hand. That phantom limb syndrome? Yeah, it's real. It wakes me up at night sometimes, the feeling like I have both arms still intact. Pretty much half my day is spent trying to scratch an itch that isn't there. It's infuriating.

"You good?" Platt asks as we get past the power plant security and pull up in front of the main offices. "You're sweating and it's 45 degrees out."

"All good," I smile.

Platt and Lourdes exchange looks.

"Come on guys, I'm fine," I say, "just tired. It's my first day out and about. Cut me some slack."

"Where's it at on the scale?" Lourdes asks.

"What scale?"

"The pain scale," she says. "I know a little something about amputees. You just lost your arm two weeks ago. You should still be in bed resting. Or at the very least chilling out on that giant back porch at the Grove Park. Not out here."

"Now you decide to tell me this?" I laugh.

"I told Platt back at the Inn, but he said it was useless," she replies. "You'd just fight and whine and still come with us."

"I don't know about the whining," I say.

"I do," Platt says, "you would have whined."

"Well, we're here now," I say, "let's have a looksee."

The Lake Julian power plant is a coal-fired power plant, which I knew, but can be converted to natural gas with some work. A lot of work. Okay, I'm not doing it justice. It will take a metric fuck ton of work to convert the power plant. In fact, as I stand and listen to the man Lourdes put in charge of the conversion, it sounds like it could be like building the thing all over again.

His name is Albert Shumway and he's as short as Joe T is tall. This guy borders on being a Little Person. But holy fuck is he cut. It's 45 degrees out and the man is wearing a tank top, showing off muscles that are on top of muscles and bullying the muscles they're on top of. Crazy to look at.

"We have maybe one third of the parts we need to start," Shumway says. I quickly learn he does not like to be called Albert or Al. Shumway or go fuck yourself were his exact words, I believe.

"Only a third?" I ask. "Where do we get the rest?"

"Oh, I don't know," he replies, "at the power plant store? Do you mind popping on down there and picking me up eighteen new couplings for generator three? That would be swell, Mr. Stanford."

"It's Jace," I say, "and I get the point."

"Do you, Mr. Stanford?" Shumway asks. "Gee, great, now my problems are solved. Because you get the point."

"Shumway," Lourdes warns, "stop being a dick."

"Why? Because this guy killed Mondello?" Shumway laughs. "Isn't that called a presidential assassination? Shouldn't he be hanged for that?"

"There were extenuating circumstances," I say. "Like the fucker needed to die. So I fucking killed the fucker with my bare hands." I look at Stumpageddon. "And, oh, look! I lost one in the mother fucking process, you GOD DAM FUCKING OOMPA LOOMPA ON FUCKING STERIODS!"

"Okay, we're done for the day," Platt says, grabbing me by the shoulders as I close on Shumway. The short fuck doesn't even flinch. I'll give him that. "Come on, Jace."

"What? Are we done here?" I ask, glaring at Shumway. "I haven't seen the chocolate river yet! Or the everlasting gobstoppers! Aren't you going to sing me a song with a hidden lesson, you ORANGE FUCK!"

"He's not orange," Platt says, "you're just pissed. And tired. And I'm going to have to deal with your wife when I get you back. She didn't want you to go either."

"She's not the boss of me," I say as I collapse into the backseat of the Humvee, my arm throbbing and throbbing.

"Seriously?" Platt says.

"Okay, she is the boss of me," I say. "But I can go where I want when I want."

"Seriously?" he says again.

"Shut up," I frown. "Take me home, Jeeves. I'll be late for tea."

"You are one crazy fuck," Lourdes says. "No wonder you've survived this long."

I don't really remember much of the ride back. There was some shooting and some yelling and then a bit of speeding through the streets as we dodged around quite a fucking herd of Zs. But then we're at the Grove Park Inn and it takes all of my strength to get from the Humvee and up to the suite.

The next thing I know, Stella is shaking me awake.

"Jace? Baby? Wake up," she says, "we have to go to Whispering Pines."

"Already?" I ask. "But I just got back."

"That was fourteen hours ago," she says. "You slept through everything."

"That explains why my bladder hurts and my belly is growling," I say. "I need a piss and some food."

"They taste the same here," Greta says. "Someone needs to learn how to cook around this place."

"The food is fine," Stella says.

"I could do better than these hacks," Greta replies.

"Then go do better," Stella snaps.

"Really? Can I?" Greta asks.

"You go for it!" I say. "And while you're at your new career, how about you rustle me up some ham and eggs?"

"Dad, I'm not going now," she says.

"Then you are worth nothing to me," I say. "Begone! Stumpageddon commands it!"

"Oh, God, not this again," Greta says and walks out of the room.

"Stumpageddon will not tolerate your insolence!" I shout after her then look at Stella. "Is she coming with us?"

"No," Stella says. "Thank God. She's been a brat all morning."

I get up, get dressed (with some help) and follow Stella downstairs. Quite a few of my fellow Whispering Pines homeowners are waiting for us. Most of them haven't seen me since I've come out of quarantine and I get a few friendly smiles, but mostly just cautious nods as we get loaded up in the caravan and head out.

The way to Whispering Pines has been cleared since I last drove it. I don't know who was in charge, but they did a great job. No cars or debris block the road, and we only have to take out maybe a dozen Zs. Nice. Jace likey.

Julio is waiting for us at the main gate into Whispering Pines and he waves us through, then makes sure the gate is secured before hopping on one of the vehicles for the ride up to the Church of Jesus of the Light.

"Preacher Carrey isn't having a fit over this?" I ask.

"Oh, he is," Stella says, "but Julio and Elsbeth had a chat with him and he calmed down quickly."

"Does he still have all of his fingers and toes?" I laugh.

"It was touch and go, but, yes, he still has all of his fingers and toes," Stella says.

We get inside and walk to the large meeting room we used to use for all of our regular HOA meetings. Preacher Carrey isn't anywhere in sight, which is nice, but Brenda Kelly is front and center, which sucks. She's busy talking to the other members of the Board, but stops when she sees us. In her waddling way, she stomps over to us.

"I just want to go on record and say that this vote is not legal under the covenants of the HOA," Brenda says. "Elect whomever you'd like, but it will not be binding. Once the residents realize their mistake, you can bet I will take my position back immediately."

"What? You think you're going to lose, Brenda?" I smile. "That's not a very positive attitude, now is it?"

"You can go to Hell, Jason Stanford," she snaps, turns, and waddles away.

"You handled that well," Stella says.

"I thought so," I nod. "Shall we take our seats?"

We do and wait as the residents staying at the Farm show up. By the time everyone is settled I have to grit my teeth against the pain. Fucking Stumpageddon! Always turning on me at the most inappropriate times. Bastard.

"I call this meeting to order," Brenda says, "under extreme protest."

"Noted," someone on the Board says. Fuck if I care who. My arm hurts.

"This irregular meeting has been called to elect a new Board Chair," Brenda says. "So I'd rather not drag this out forever. If you'd like to put forth a nomination, then please stand and do so now. You are welcome to nominate yourself, but you will need a second." Her eyes lock on me. I wave Stumpageddon at her. I think she gags a little.

"You ready?" Stella asks me. "Jace, can you do this?"

"I can," I nod. "I'm fine. I'm ready. Let's make this happen."

I stand up and clear my throat. I hurt like a mother fucker, but for this I can push the pain away. I've been looking forward to this for a long time.

"As a resident of Whispering Pines, I'd like to nominate," I say, "my wife, Stella Stanford."

Brenda's eyes go wide. "You…what?"

Yeah, she wasn't expecting that.

"I second," Stuart says.

"Me too," Melissa says.

More voices add to the seconds. I guess they become thirds and fourths and shit?

"Fine," Brenda says, "Stella Stanford has been added to the list of nominees. Is there anyone else?"

The room is quiet.

"Okay," Brenda says, "then I'd like to officially nominate myself. Who will second?"

The room is quiet.

"Excuse me? I am nominating myself. I will need someone to second the nomination. You don't have to vote for me. It's just common courtesy."

The room is quiet.

Brenda loses her shit.

"People! I have served you well for years! If not for me, many of you would be dead! I deserve, I EXPECT, A SECOND! SOMEONE WILL STAND UP RIGHT NOW AND SECOND MY NOMINATION!"

Nope. Not happening.

"So what now?" I ask.

"WHAT NOW?" she screams. NOW...NOW...now...now..."

"Damn," Stuart says, "she's broken."

"Now...," she says as she sits down, "we vote."

"Do we need to?" one of the Board members asks. "There's only one nominee?"

"I know that!" Brenda snaps. "But votes must be recorded. So we vote."

We vote. Stella wins.

Brenda doesn't say a word, just gets up and walks outside. The room cheers.

"I'm so proud of you," I tell Stella. "You're gonna rock this job."

"Well, Whispering Pines has needed a leader that can keep you in line," Stella says. "Brenda sucked at that."

"Hey," I smile. "I'm always in line." I wince and my smile falters. I try to recover, but Stella just purses her lips.

"How bad is it?" she asks.

"Not bad," I say.

"That's a lie," Stella says. "See, I'm already better at the job. I know when Jason Stanford is lying. That skill will come in handy."

"I'm not sure I like where this is going," I say.

"Hey, Jace," Julio says, coming up to us. "Stella, congrats."

"Thanks, Julio," she smiles. "What do you need?"

"I need your man here," Julio says. "We have a surprise for him."

"Surprise?" I ask. "Dude, I don't think I need any surprises today. Not sure I'm up to it."

"Oh, you'll be up for this," Julio smiles. "Come on."

We follow him out of the meeting room and down the hall to a room Stella used to use as a classroom for the kids. Waiting inside are Platt, John, Dr. McCormick, Stuart, Melissa, Reaper, and Elsbeth. They are all standing in front of something with smiles on their face.

"What?" I ask. "What's going on?"

They step aside and my jaw drops.

"What...the...fuck?" I say, stunned by the sight.

On a long table are over a dozen prosthetic arms of various sizes, shapes, uses. Some have regular hands, some have hooks, there's one with this crazy pick axe looking thing. Holy crap.

"Are those for me?" I ask.

"No, sweetie, they're for me," Stella says. "Go look."

I do. I walk right over to them and have a good look. A good, hard look. A good, hard look at the reality of who I am now. I look and look at the plastic and metal before me that is supposed to replace what I've lost. The tears that stream down my cheeks are hot.

"Oh, baby," Stella says as I break down into sobs. "Oh, shit, Jace."

"Dude, we thought you'd dig them," Julio says.

"They'll help," Stuart says.

"Give him some space, people," Dr. McCormick orders, "this is all very traumatic."

"Thanks," I say, wiping at my eyes, my chest hitching. "Really. Thank you. This is great." I take a deep breath and smile through the tears. "Just makes it more real, is all. I'm good. Seriously. This is pretty cool. Especially that one."

"It's used for mountain climbing," Reaper says. "Melissa and her scavengers decided to have a peek inside an orthopedics office. There was a whole shop set up with tons of this shit. Don't like these? We'll be able to build anything you need."

I look at Reaper and smile. "Wait? Anything?"

"Jace, what are you thinking?" Stella asks.

"You know what would make Stumpageddon really happy?" I ask aloud.

"God, I hate that name," Platt says.

"I don't know what it means," Elsbeth says.

"What, dude?" Julio asks.

"Stumpageddon needs his own Bitch," I say. "That's what Stumpageddon needs."

"Dude," Julio smiles. "Great idea. Holy fuck."

"What is he talking about?" Dr. McCormick asks.

"That's what he called his bat," Stuart explains, "The Bitch."

"It was my bat first," Elsbeth says, "then I gave it to him. He lost it. You lost it."

"I did," I say, "but maybe we can build a better one?"

"Wait a minute," Dr. McCormick frowns, "your arm cannot take the stress of that, Jace. Not for a long time."

"Well, that's what physical therapy is for," I say, "we'll start small and work up to it." I look at Reaper and can tell he's way into it; so is Julio. "You'll help, right? Train with me until I am one bad ass mother fucker with Stumpageddon and The Bitch. Ha! It's like a bad seventies porn movie. Stumpageddon and The Bitch!"

"So cool," Julio says, "and you could have other ones with blades and shit! Oh, and maybe we can rig a slingshot to the end!"

"Awesome," I grin, "thanks, guys. This is pretty fucking sweet."

"Good," Stella says, kissing me on the cheek, "you talk about your toys while I go back and talk to the other residents. I know there are going to be a lot of suggestions people have kept bottled up for years because of Brenda. This isn't going to be easy."

"Have fun, baby," I say. "Let me know when you're ready to go."

"We can't stay too long," Platt says. "I want us back at the Grove Park by sundown. Easier for security."

"Works for me," I say as the excitement of it all starts to wear off. And the pain kicks back in.

I thank everyone personally as they leave. Julio, Reaper, Stuart, and Elsbeth, stay behind as I pick up each of the prosthetics.

"This one is sexy," I say, holding a very realistic looking arm. "If ya know what I mean."

"Dude," Julio says, shaking his head.

"What? What is he talking about?" Elsbeth asks.

"I'll tell you later," Julio says.

"You two coming back to the Grove Park tonight?" I ask. "You've been staying here like the whole time."

"We're all staying here," Stuart says.

"What?" I ask. "Winter is almost here, man. You can't stay at Whispering Pines, there aren't any houses yet."

"Preacher Carrey has graciously given his okay for a few of us to bunk here," Stuart says. "Especially when he found out that the alternative was being left alone all winter long."

"We're going to keep working on the fences," Julio says. "It'll be hard as the ground freezes, but that will also slow down the Zs."

"The goal is to have the deck and stairs built before January," Stuart says, "and then we'll rebuild the main gate the right way. As it is now, it can stand up to Zs, but not to people."

"Especially if they have heavy vehicles," Julio says.

"I want to get that dump truck of yours moved down here," Stuart says, "make it part of the system. Nothing like a few tons of metal to deter attackers."

"My dump truck?" I say. "I have no claim to that."

"I know that dump truck," Elsbeth smiles. "It's where I found Long Pork all curled up and crying with those pink pajamas on."

"First, I wasn't crying," I say. "I wasn't! And second, those were yoga clothes, thank you. I'm pretty sure they were Juicy Couture, so no making fun."

We all look at each other for a second then burst out laughing.

"I still hate you for making me wear those," I say to Stuart.

"I didn't put a gun to your head," he says, "you could have just stayed naked."

"Yeah, that wasn't going to happen," I say.

We BS for a few minutes more, but they can tell I'm getting tired and the pain is too much.

"Come on," Stuart says, "let's find your wife. Someone needs to get you back and tuck you into bed."

"I've been in bed for two weeks," I protest, "I don't wanna go back. You can't make me."

"You only have one arm," Stuart smiles, "I can pretty much make you do anything I want."

"Oh, thanks for rubbing that in my face," I say, fake crying. "You're mean."

"That doesn't sound real at all," Elsbeth says, "even I know that."

"Come on," Stuart says, "we'll make sure the prosthetics get packed up and taken back to the Grove Park for you."

"I can play fashion show later for Stella," I say.

"I don't want to know," Stuart says.

We start to leave, but I can see Elsbeth is hanging back.

"What's up?" I ask.

"Can I talk with you?" she asks. The others look from me to her then leave. Julio waits a second, but Elsbeth nods and he goes too.

"What's up?" I ask.

"I, uh, want to make sure you aren't angry," Elsbeth says.

"Angry? Why?"

"Because I am staying here with Julio," she says. "And not at the fancy place with you."

"Really? No, that's totally cool," I say. "You can stay where you want, El. You're a grown woman."

"But you and Stella and the kids are family," she says. "Aren't I supposed to stay with family?"

"Not forever," I laugh. "And you'll still be family. Families spread out all over the place. It's normal."

"But we don't live in normal," she says.

"True," I nod, "but you're only going to be a couple miles away. We'll see you lots. And I'll be coming and going from here with Stella to check on progress. It's all good. You stay here with Julio. Live a little."

"Live a little," she says quietly. "Yes. I will."

"Good," I smile. "Then we're good?"

"We're good," she says. "But not done talking."

"Okey doke, what else is there?"

"Me," she says.

"Yeah...not following you."

"I want to talk about me," Elsbeth says, "about where I come from."

"Oh...that," I say. I had been wondering when the subject would come up, but I didn't want to push.

"The president man said I am special," Elsbeth says. "He said that I was part of something. He didn't know it about me until the Foster lady gave away the secret."

"Secret? What secret?" I ask.

She shrugs. "I don't know," Elsbeth says. "President guy says there was a school here in Asheville. That Foster taught there. She was an instructor? Instructor, yeah."

"A school? What kind of school?"

"I don't know," Elsbeth says. "The president guy wouldn't say anymore. He told me he didn't have details, but had heard rumors because he was big chief of home security."

"Secretary of Homeland Security," I say, "before he was President. Although I don't really consider him that."

"Right," Elsbeth nods. "He said there was a school here and a special program for special girls like me." She shakes her head. "He says that's why I fight so well."

"He said all of that while he was driving? When he escaped with you onto the Parkway?" I ask.

"Yes," she nods, "and when I punched him and tied him up. He said more then. But while he was driving too."

"Did he say where the school was?" She shakes her head. "Did he say how many other girls there were?" Another head shake. "Shit. This is crazy. Maybe Platt knows something about it?"

"Maybe," she shrugs. "Will you ask him?"

"You don't want to?"

"No," she says, "he's mad at me because I quit and didn't want to be on his team. He just yelled too much. My pa yelled a lot too. I don't like it."

"Yeah, no problem," I say. "I'll ask him soon."

I watch her closely and smile.

"It's going to be fine, El," I say. "This isn't a bad thing. It's good. You'll get to find out something about your past."

"I thought I knew my past," Elsbeth replies. "I thought I was Pa's daughter and I was canny and that was it."

"But that's not it," I say, "and thank goodness. You are more than all of that. I'll help you find out what that more is, okay?"

"Okay," she nods. "Thank you, Jace."

I'm a little stunned that she didn't call me Long Pork.

"Uh, yeah, you bet," I smile. "That's what family is for."

"Yes it is," Stella says from the doorway. "I don't know what you're talking about, but I agree."

"I'll fill you in later," I say. "If that's alright with you, El?"

212

"Families share," Elsbeth states.

"Exactly," Stella says. "Now how about we go back to the Inn and share the official news with the kids?"

"Sounds great," I nod.

"You coming, Elsbeth?" Stella asks.

"Naw, she's staying here with Julio," I say.

"No, I'm coming," Elsbeth says, "for tonight. Then I'll come back. I want to see Greta and Charlie."

"And they want to see you too, I'm sure," Stella says. "Then let's get going. Platt is getting fidgety about the time."

I walk out of the Church with Stella on one side and Elsbeth on the other. Even with only one arm, I'm a pretty fucking lucky guy. I have what many in this day don't, I have family. And a future.

And a really cool selection of arms for Stumpageddon.

Sweet.

***

The convoy leaves the Church and splits off as they hit 251. The Grove Park half turns right, while the Farm half turns left. The Farm half travels down Hwy 251, also known as Riverside Dr, and comes to Pierson Bridge. As they slow to turn right onto the bridge, a shadow detaches from the bottom of one of the trucks and rolls to the drainage ditch, staying low and still until the convoy is over the bridge and long gone.

The shadow, a young woman, gets up and brushes herself off, starting on her long walk home. She stays to the side of Riverside, off in the cover of the brush and trees, ever mindful of the night sounds that have descended on the area. She avoids the few Zs she comes across, staying still and silent as they shuffle past, and continues on her way.

A couple hours, and several miles later, she comes to a curve in the road, cut into the landscape by the Swannanoa River. Making sure she is unobserved, even though no one would be out at the early morning hour, the young woman fords the river at a specific point, coming up the other side onto another, smaller road.

This road, the smaller one, meanders through a vast estate, once the home of American royalty then later turned into a destination for tourists and history buffs. She walks for another mile or so and cuts across a wide field that would have been planted with corn, but is now planted with a different crop.

Zs.

The young woman weaves her way through the hundreds of Zs that fill the field. If one didn't know the secret, they would think she is crazy, but she knows exactly where to walk and what turns to take through the mass of Zs. They reach out for her, and she ducks under rotten arms when she gets too close, but she doesn't worry about being pursued. Why? Because this truly is a crop of Zs, planted in place by large, steel stakes. The stakes, two feet long, go through the Zs' feet and deep into the ground, holding them where they are, giving the illusion of a horde of Zs for anyone that makes it onto the estate.

Finally, after crossing the field and making her way through dense woods of pines and oaks, the young woman comes to a grand house, America's largest home: the Biltmore.

"Churned," a woman's voice calls out from the shadows.

"Fresh daily," the young woman responds.

The shadow voice, another young woman of similar build and age, steps forward and hugs the first. "Any trouble?"

"No," the first says, "I saw her clearly this time."

"It's her? She's one of us?"

"Yes, for sure," the first says.

"Good, I'll go tell her."

"No, I want to do it," the first says. "I found her and I found our lost sister. I'll tell her."

"Okay," the second says. "They're in the basement showing off."

The young women go inside the mansion by a side door. Following a winding set of stone steps down, they come to a wide room, made completely of stone, and decorated with old, faded wall paintings of witches on brooms and black cats; princes and princesses and old castles.

More young women, eight of them, are sitting on the floor of the basement room, towels in front of them, blindfolds on, all hurrying to assemble the parts before them on the towels.

"Time!" one of them yells, ripping off her blindfold and holding up the reassembled pistol.

"Two point three," a ninth young woman says from the wall, a stopwatch in her hand. "Not bad." She looks up and sees the two arrivals. "There you are? So?"

"She wants to tell her," the second says.

"I found her, I get to tell," the first says.

"Then tell her," the wall woman smiles. "She's over there watching the games."

The first young woman, the one that rolled away from the caravan and walked all the way to the estate, hurries over to a pedestal in the corner. She gets on her knees and smiles at the thing set upon it.

"I found her," she says, "I found our lost sister. She's with those people from that neighborhood. And the soldiers and others. She must be so lost without us."

"Is she their prisoner?" one of the others asks.

"No, I don't think so," the first answers, never taking her eyes from the pedestal. "Isn't that wonderful? That I found her. We'll be sure to bring her back here, to our new home, so you can see her. You'll like her as much as you like us. And she'll love it here."

"Yeah."

"For sure."

"I know I do!"

The young women all hug and smile, glad for the good news. The first turns back to the pedestal and smiles at the thing.

"Once we are all together again, then we'll do what we're supposed to," she says. "Just like you taught us. We're all so glad I found you, Ms. Foster."

The young woman turns back to the others, happy to be home, happy to be with ones she can trust. The thing on the pedestal just watches, unable to move, unable to do anything but want and need. There is a focus to the thing that it had even during life. And that focus waits; waits for the moment one of the delicious young women will make a mistake and get too close to it.

For the head of Ms. Foster is hungry. So very hungry.

THE END

About The Author:

A professional writer since 2009, Jake Bible has a proven record of innovation, invention and creativity. Novelist, short story writer, independent screenwriter, podcaster, and inventor of the Drabble Novel, Jake is able to switch between or mash-up genres with ease to create new and exciting storyscapes that have captivated and built an audience of thousands. He is the author of the horror/military scifi series the Apex Trilogy (*DEAD MECH, The Americans, Metal and Ash*) available from Severed Press. He is also the author of *Bethany and the Zombie Jesus, Stark- An Illustrated Novella* and the YA horror novel *Little Dead*. Jake Bible lives in Asheville, NC with his family. **Find him at www.jakebible.com**.

30955321R00125

Made in the USA
Lexington, KY
24 March 2014